BURIED IN BOUGAINVILLEA

A HIBISCUS ISLAND MYSTERY BOOK 1

LUCY NORMAN

Mulberry Ink

Buried in Bougainvillea

Book 1 in the *Hibiscus Island Mystery* series

Copyright © 2022 by Lucy Norman
ISBN 978-0-9922664-0-0

This is a work of fiction. Names, characters, places and incidents are either the products of the author's imagination or are used fictitiously.

Cover by DLR Cover Designs
Editing by Florentia Editing

1

Holly stepped out of the door of the tiny plane into the hot, humid air of Hibiscus Island. She took a deep breath and pushed her red-gold hair off her face. Behind her, excited tourists crowded onto the steps, exclaiming at the heat, the bright sunshine, and the turquoise water visible from the plane.

"Ugh! It's like a sauna! Why is the humidity so high?"

Holly cringed as the sadly familiar voice of Amelia Cartell bleated on, "And why are there still no jet bridges?" The voice paused, then continued in a critical tone, "I mean, what happens if it rains? Not very efficient, is it?"

As quickly as she could, Holly descended the steps to head toward the airport, hoping to get inside before...

"Miss Gold!"

Holly briefly considered feigning deafness and making a run for it, but old habits die hard. Hibiscus Islanders were *always* polite and courteous towards visitors, who were, after all, the bread and butter of the island. And Holly, no matter how long she'd been away, was still an islander.

Sighing, she turned around, a weak smile plastered on her face.

A large, blowsy woman with brassy gold hair, wearing a bright pink designer suit that hugged ample curves, bustled up importantly. Amelia Cartell had an unpleasant didactic manner and held strong opinions on just about every topic possible. Holly had been unfortunate enough to be seated next to her on the plane.

"Miss Gold!" Amelia exclaimed again. Her heavily made-up face shone in the afternoon sun as she pursed her lips. "I thought we had established you would assist me through your Customs procedure. After all, I *am* staying at your family inn. And my followers, as you know, are very keen to hear my impressions."

Behind Amelia, her private secretary, Lucy, glanced up from struggling gamely with three large carry-ons to give Holly an apologetic look.

Holly took a deep breath. "Of course, Ms. Cartell," she said politely. "I'll do everything I can to help you."

As Amelia swept past her, Holly gritted her teeth and cast her eyes heavenward. Why, oh why had Amelia Cartell chosen the Hibiscus Inn for her holiday?

MUCH LATER, having silently suffered through Amelia's loud comments on everything the Hibiscus Island airport had to offer—from the welcoming island musicians to the state of the restrooms—Holly reached the front of the Customs line. She dropped her carry-on and fumbled for her declaration form.

"Well, Holly Gold, as I live and breathe! Welcome home! How long are you back for?"

The warm voice of the Customs officer jerked Holly upright.

"Uncle Stanley!" A smile broke over her face. "It's so good to see you!" She reached over the counter to grasp the hand of the elderly official. "What are you doing working here? I thought you'd finally retired."

Stanley Foster's dark brown eyes twinkled at Holly as he held out a hand for the paperwork. "My beloved wife said I was underfoot, overfed, and needed to find something to do with myself." He scanned the declaration form before scribbling a signature on it. "I only work part-time. Couple of days a week. Enough to stop her nagging."

Holly laughed. "How's the family?"

"All good." Uncle Stanley leaned against the counter, tilting back his cap to show graying hair atop his warm, smiling dark brown face. "All good," he said. "Although the youngest grandson says he's taking a break from school. Wants to scuba dive instead." Holly grinned as he shook his head in mock despair before continuing, "Well now, how long are you here for this time?"

"Actually, I'm back for good."

A wide smile split Uncle Stanley's face. "Are you now? Well, that's good to hear! Going to help your mama and Gramps up at the Inn?"

"That's the plan," Holly agreed, hazel eyes smiling. "Should be fun!"

Uncle Stanley's guffaw echoed in the Customs hall. "That it will. That it will. Well, Holly girl, you come by and see us sometime."

"I will," Holly promised. She picked up her carry-on and shoved her passport into her jeans. "Are you entering the flower show this weekend?"

"Of course, child! And you can tell your Gramps I have a

3

real contender this year. Going to knock him off his pedestal for sure! The Bougainvillea Trophy will be mine!"

Holly laughed. "I'll let him know," she told him with a grin, then waved her hand and headed off to get her bags.

～

AMELIA CARTELL SAT bolt upright in the front seat of the Hibiscus Inn airport van, a faint frown on her face as she surveyed the bright blue water visible from the airport parking lot. "Why aren't we leaving? Where is that driver? Lucy, find out what's happening!"

Amelia's secretary began to get to her feet.

"He's just loading the bags," another passenger said, peering out of the window. "We'll be underway in a moment, I'm sure."

Bob Schafer was a mousy little man who had buried himself in a book for most of the flight. Now he fingered his grey moustache and looked eagerly at Amelia. "Is this your first visit to the island? Are you here for the Festival?" Receiving a scathing look in reply, he flushed with embarrassment and lowered his gaze.

Amelia leaned out the window, glaring at the hapless young man who was picking up the final piece of luggage. "How long does it take to put a few suitcases in a van? Do you intend for us to parboil inside this vehicle?"

He glanced up with a smile, slid the bag into the van and stood up, brushing off his hands. "That's us all done, Ms. Cartell. We'll be on our way in seconds!"

"I suppose this is what they mean by 'island time'," Amelia sneered. "Not very efficient!"

Holly caught a glimpse of the driver's face as he came around the van. She grinned involuntarily, knowing that

Sebastian's opinion of Amelia was going to be colorful, to say the least.

"Sure you won't change your mind and ride with us?" Sebastian cast a sideways glance at his front seat passenger, then looked at Holly hopefully. "There's plenty of room!"

"Sorry," Holly replied, trying not to laugh at the pleading expression. "My ride is on his way."

With a grimace, Sebastian tried again. "Matt's always late. You'd get home faster if you rode with me." His face fell when Holly shook her head.

"Nope, sorry," she said, with a commiserating smile. She lowered her voice. "It's only a fifteen-minute ride, Sebastian. You'll survive!"

"Young man! *What* is taking so long?"

Sebastian flinched, then glared wordlessly at Holly before plastering a wide smile on his face and leaping into his seat. "Welcome to Hibiscus Island, folks. Let's get you to the Inn as fast as possible so you can get started on your tropical vacation!"

Holly waved as the van moved away from the curb. Settling down to wait, she pulled out her sunglasses, then tipped her head back, feeling the sun on her face and relishing the quiet. It had been a long flight.

A loud tooting, along with the squeal of rubber on asphalt, interrupted her thoughts.

"Hollleeeee!" Her cousin's face was one wide grin as his little pickup truck careened around the corner and came to a grinding halt in front of her. Matt hopped out, slamming the door behind him as he rushed to gather Holly up in a huge hug. "Welcome home, coz!"

"Hi Matt!" Holly eased out of the hug and smiled up at her younger cousin, who towered over her at six foot four. "How are you doing?"

Matt grinned broadly as he shoved the shock of sun-bleached brown hair off his face. "I'm good. I only got home a few weeks ago myself. Exams were deadly this year, but I passed, so I can relax and enjoy the summer now." He grabbed her suitcases and swung them into the back of the pickup. "Is this all you've got? Not much is it?"

"I travel light," Holly said, climbing into the front of the truck. She fanned her face vigorously. "Please tell me this vehicle has A/C!"

"Nope." Matt grinned at her as he swung into his seat and started the engine. "It's not even the height of summer yet, Holls. What are you going to do when the real heat starts?"

"Haha—aaaah!" Holly grabbed the door as Matt revved the engine, accelerating with a squeal of rubber.

As the little pickup raced along the narrow roads of Hibiscus Island, Holly settled back in her seat. They'd taken the coastal road, lined with its hedges of bright pink oleander and signature hibiscus flowers. The occasional palm tree flew by, and burgeoning patches of pale red signaled the poinciana trees were just coming into bloom.

The poincianas looked like they were going to be spectacular this summer, Holly thought, narrowing her eyes against the glare of the sun on the water. She hoped the bougainvillea was good! The Bougainvillea Festival was just one of many events hosted by the Inn and usually drew a large number of horticultural visitors to the island.

A sudden veer made her grab at the door as the pickup truck swung round a sharp corner and she glared at her cousin. Ignoring her, Matt waved wildly out the window. Two young men in a boat waved back. They held up something and shouted. Matt tooted the horn in answer.

"Fish fry tonight," he said to Holly. "Lionfish! Want to go?"

"Not today." Holly smiled, then squeaked in alarm. "Matt! Pay attention to the road!"

Her cousin just laughed and pressed down on the accelerator.

2

By the time they turned into the narrow, winding driveway that led to the Inn, Holly was hot and frazzled. Next time, she swore silently, she'd take a taxi. Or the Inn van. Even listening to Amelia Cartell would have been better than this... this horror ride with her cousin. Thank heavens, Hibiscus Island still had limitations on the number of vehicles allowed on the roads. At least they hadn't met very many people on their death-defying trip.

Matt glanced over at her with a grin. "You've been on the mainland too long, Holly! You need to get used to Hibiscus Island driving again!" He changed gears loudly as the pickup turned the corner, heading up the final hill to Hibiscus Inn.

The insults on Holly's tongue died away as she saw her family home.

Sitting on top of the hill with a 360-degree view of the ocean, the Hibiscus Inn glowed a warm pink in the afternoon sun. Purple bougainvillea and bright pink coralita flowers climbed on trellises around the white shutters that edged windows overlooking the front drive. Hibiscus bushes, smothered in hot pink and white blooms, nestled along the walls, interspersed with the scarlet of China roses and the rich yellow of daylilies. Juniper trees lined the sides of the circular red-bricked drive and, in the center, a stone fountain burbled amidst a riot of shrubs. Blue plumbago sprawled beside more yellow day lilies and bright red geraniums popped above a carpet of golden lantana. The Inn's white rooftops gleamed in the sunshine above the large cedar front doors which stood open, flanked by dark blue ceramic planters overflowing with geraniums.

It was a grand, sprawling old home and Holly's heart stuttered as she looked at it.

Matt's truck ground to a halt behind the Hibiscus Inn van. In the sudden silence Holly heard the raucous shrieking of the yellow-breasted great kiskadees among the junipers. There was a burst of laughter from the open windows on the ground floor and the clink of china. Holly glanced at her watch. Four o'clock. Afternoon tea.

"Perfect timing," Matt said with a smile as he flicked his hair out of his eyes and swung out of the truck. "Come on, Holly Berry. There are scones today! I'll grab your bags."

Noticing she hadn't moved, Matt peered in the truck window and paused, looking at his cousin. His voice softened. "You okay?"

Holly nodded. "Yeah. I'm fine. I'll be right behind you."

She watched Matt's lanky jean-clad body as he heaved her suitcases up the wide shallow steps, and in her mind's eye saw her cousin, dressed in a black suit, walking up those same steps on a sunny day in October. Matt had looked back at her that day, just as he was doing now.

Holly forced a smile and opened the truck door. For a moment, she stood still. The smell of freshly cut grass mixed with the rich scent of roses, a tinge of salt spray, and the tang of the juniper trees as the wind blew through their branches. The breeze lifted her hair and Holly took a deep breath.

At the sight of a figure appearing in the open door of the Inn, Holly broke into a run.

"Mama!"

"Holly!" Maggie Gold opened her arms wide to catch Holly in a hug, staggering back slightly as the two collided. "You're home!"

Holly clutched her mother tightly. Maggie blinked back a couple of tears as she looked down on her daughter's red-gold head before easing back to take in the sight of the slim figure in front of her. "Let's have a look at you. Hmmm. Not bad, chickadee. You've lost some weight though." She slung an arm around Holly's shoulders. "How was your flight? Would you like some tea?"

Grinning, Holly wrapped an arm around her mother's waist as they entered the Inn. "I weigh the same, the flight was okay, and yes, I want some tea. Matt said you made scones."

"I did indeed. I've had a baking frenzy lately." Maggie's blue eyes sparkled with laughter. "The freezer is stuffed with my recent efforts."

Holly glanced around the foyer of the Inn releasing a sigh of pleasure.

The room was large and spacious, with cream-colored painted walls, and varnished dark wooden floors peeping out beneath red and gold patterned rugs. Two large fans spun lazily from the white wooden beams that stretched across the open ceiling, and brightly colored paintings of island flowers decorated the walls.

Near the front doors, an antique wooden desk served as a check-in table, and at the far end of the room, a plush stuffed sofa and two armchairs snuggled up to a red-bricked fireplace that housed a huge scarlet ceramic bowl filled with roses in lieu of an actual fire. The cedar mantle above the fireplace held a collection of wooden Russian matryoshka dolls, much beloved by younger visitors to the Inn, while an unfinished jigsaw puzzle sprawled across the coffee table. A scattering of potted peace lilies on small tables added living green accents and two overflowing bookcases completed the comfortable setting.

To the right of the front doors, a large staircase swept up to the second floor; on the left a set of double doors led through to the breakfast and tearoom. A smaller door at the far end of the room opened into a narrow hallway.

"Everyone's checked in," Maggie said, linking her arm through Holly's as they walked along the corridor. "We'll have our tea and a snack in the kitchen. If Matt and Sebastian have left us anything, that is."

The two young men lounging at the large center island sat up straight when Holly entered the bright sunny kitchen.

Matt waved a half-eaten scone at her. "Hey, Holly, come and tell me about your friend Amelia!" He smiled widely. "Sebastian says she's a honey!"

"Sebastian!" Maggie scolded. "What have I told you about talking about our guests?" She moved to the white painted cupboards, took out two blue and white bone china mugs, and began to make tea.

The young van driver swallowed a mouthful of scone. "Yeah, yeah, I know. But this one!" He rolled dark brown eyes and gestured expansively. His voice pitched higher. "Young man, does the Inn have a spa? No? Good heavens, how primitive! Young man! Stop driving so fast! There must be a speed limit—even on this rock! Driver! Did you *see* that pedestrian? Are you *trying* to annihilate people? Botanic

Gardens? What are you talking about, Mr. Schafer? No, I'm not interested at all. Driver! What are those young people doing down there? Is that a *gang*? Fishing? For what, may I ask? Young man! *Must* you change gears like that?"

Sebastian was a good mimic and his monologue had Holly and Matt in fits of laughter. He ran a hand through his tightly curled hair, an incredulous look on his handsome dark brown face. "I'm completely exhausted. Worn out." He looked pityingly at Holly. "And you sat beside her on a plane for nearly an hour? Girl, you deserve a medal! That Lucy girl too. Who'd work for someone like that?"

"Here," Matt said, pushing the plate of scones towards Holly with a grin. "The cranberry ones are good. And they're gluten-free. 'Specially for you, Holly Berry."

"What about the lemon drizzle?" Maggie asked, coming over with two steaming mugs. "It's a new recipe. Did you try them?"

"They're good too," Sebastian said. "I had two of them. But back to the Cartell woman. She has a private secretary and a security guy in tow!" Holly blinked in surprise as Sebastian nodded. "Unbelievable, I know, but one of the guys who was in the van is her personal bodyguard! Who on earth is she, Aunt Maggie?"

A smile tugging at her lips, Maggie took a sip of tea. "She's a travel critic."

"Say what?" Sebastian gaped at her. "Why does someone like that need a bodyguard? Or a secretary for that matter?"

"She's pretty well known," Maggie said. "She writes a line of travel books about places she's visited. You've probably read some of her articles in plane magazines. And she has a very popular blog called *Impressions*."

Sebastian stared. "A *blog*? Are you serious? Well, good luck with her, Aunt Maggie. I think she's going to be hard work." He got up and stretched. "I'm going to head home now unless you need me for anything else today."

"We're good," Maggie said. "You'll be here to help set up on Friday, right?"

"Yes, ma'am," Sebastian replied with a snappy salute, then nodded towards Matt. "This one has been drafted as well. See you later, Holly girl." He tousled Holly's head as he strolled towards the door.

Matt jumped to his feet. "Hey, wait for me. I'll give you a ride. I'm heading to the cove to see the guys. Fish fry tonight."

"Oh yeah?" Sebastian asked, interest coloring his tone. "Lionfish? Who caught them?"

Maggie smiled fondly at their retreating backs. "They're good boys. I'll miss them when they go back to college. They're a big help around the place."

Holly watched her mother lift the top of a large crockpot and stir the contents.

"It's split pea soup tonight," Maggie said, taking a small teaspoon to sample it. She added a bit more salt. "I just have to pop the rolls in, and everything will be ready."

The Hibiscus Inn was a bed-and-breakfast, but Maggie always put out a crockpot of soup or a selection of sandwiches in the evenings for guests who didn't want to go out for dinner. At this time of year, there was also usually a cold pasta salad and fruit and, of course, afternoon tea was always served at four o'clock.

Although Maggie was the official owner, the Inn was a family concern. Holly and her friends had worked as summer students, helping to turn rooms and serve breakfast, and family members could always be relied upon to do the odd shift if necessary. The day-to-day running of the Inn, however, was in the hands of Maggie and her best friend, Sarah. The two women were both easy-going and flexible, and divided the early morning and evening shifts as it suited them.

Maggie crossed the kitchen and looked through the door into the front room. "Hmmm. Looks like everyone's left. Maybe I could clear up now." She smiled at Holly. "Why don't you go and get yourself sorted out, then find your Gramps and tell him to come up here for dinner? We can have a little chat about this weekend and what needs to be done. I thought we could just get through the Bougainvillea Festival before we iron out your job and benefits and such. Would that be okay?"

"That's fine," Holly agreed. "Mama..." She stopped as her throat tightened and then tried again. "Mama, I'm sorry it... it took me so long to come back." Her voice choked and Maggie turned in surprise.

"Hey now, what's all this, chickadee?" she asked, crossing rapidly to Holly. She peered into the hazel eyes, now welling with tears, then pulled her daughter into a hug. "Oh Holly. Don't be so silly."

"I left you," Holly said, her voice catching.

Maggie drew back and raised her daughter's chin. "No, you didn't. You went back to a job that you loved. And did I or did I not tell you that it was absolutely fine?" Holly nodded. "Well then, what are the tears for? Believe you me, you'll be making up for that time away when your Gramps gets you into his garden. You may be wishing you were back in your mainland garden center!" She ran a hand down the bright red-gold hair.

Holly gave a watery smile. "Okay. If you're sure..."

"Holly, you helped when it counted the most." Maggie studied her daughter with a serious expression. "You helped when your dad needed you, when I needed you. And I'm glad to have you home again now. But I won't be pleased if I think you've only come home for me and not for yourself. You hear me?"

"I haven't," Holly protested. "I want to be here. Honest!"

Maggie grinned and tousled her hair, just as Sebastian had done. "That's okay, then. Now go get yourself unpacked. Scoot, chickadee."

Holly scooted.

3

The Hibiscus Inn was a large sprawling property surrounded by six acres of grounds. The main house had been expanded several times over the years, each generation adding on rooms or wings as their fancy—and their wallets—allowed. These sometimes-quirky additions meandered haphazardly down the terraced hill, all connected by white roofs. Rooms opened onto tiny balconies or hidden courtyards and small winding pathways snaked their way around the pink buildings and lush plantings. Visitors loved the intricate details, the surprises around every corner and the privacy afforded by the somewhat convoluted architecture.

There were ten suites for guests—all named after island flowers—and a family wing hidden away at the back of the main house. It was to this wing that Holly headed after leaving the kitchen.

She pushed open the arched door leading into the courtyard which separated the main Inn from their private living space, and paused.

The paved courtyard was a sun trap in the height of

summer, so most of the planting was concentrated around the edges under small white wooden pergolas. This summer, the beds were packed with white Michaelmas daisy shrubs and underplanted with purslane. Holly grinned at all the colors—hot pink, bright yellow, red, magenta and yellow stripes. Gramps was obviously using this area as a nursery. It was gaudy, but surprisingly satisfying.

In one corner of the courtyard, an enormous showy, pink James Walker bougainvillea grew against the wall. It was one of the oldest bougainvilleas on the property, with a gnarled, twisting wooden trunk and a dense canopy of blossoms that sprawled over the white pergola and up onto the roof. Holly patted its trunk affectionately as she walked past before stepping into her home.

French doors led to a large open plan living room, kitchen, and dining area with wooden floors and a high beamed ceiling. The kitchen end sported sleek espresso-colored cupboards and granite countertops with a long, curved island in the center surrounded with wooden counter stools. At the other end of the room, triple arched windows looked out over the gardens and the north shore sea.

Deep red overstuffed sofas and two enormous leather armchairs were grouped around a large fireplace, and low bookcases, filled with an eclectic assortment of books, lined the walls. Quilted wall-hangings, the result of one of Maggie's hobbies, hung above the bookshelves, interspersed with groupings of family photos.

It was a haphazard and slightly messy room, well lived in and well loved. Holly smiled as she looked around, noting the unfinished jigsaw puzzle on a table, the scattering of acrylic paints on the kitchen counter, and the dog toys strewn around the floor.

"Truffle!" she called. "Where are you?"

There was a surprised woof, then a thump followed by the pattering of paws. A small black curly cavapoo rounded the corner at full speed and hurled itself on Holly, moaning with excitement.

"Hey, Truff!" Holly crouched down, laughing as the small dog scrabbled furiously at her. "What were you doing?"

Truffle squeaked ecstatically, her tail wagging a mile a minute.

"Really? Is that so? You did?" Holly scooped Truffle up into her arms and nuzzled the little dog's face. "Well, now that I'm home, you'll be able to come to work with me in the gardens. You'll like that, won't you? Come and help me unpack." She put the dog down and Truffle pranced happily beside her down the corridor to Holly's rooms.

Some years earlier, her parents had renovated the area, turning two of the bedrooms into a mini apartment for Holly. She now had her original bedroom plus a private bathroom, a miniscule galley kitchen and a large sitting room that opened out onto a tiny shady courtyard garden.

Turning to her suitcases, which were sitting in the middle of the room, where Matt had dumped them, Holly began to get settled. She unpacked her photos carefully and placed them on the dresser in her bedroom, gently touching the large framed picture of her parents.

Inspector Peter 'Solid' Gold, resplendent in his formal police uniform, smiled down at Maggie, his brown eyes twinkling as he twirled his wife around the dance floor. Maggie's face was alive with laughter, her head tilted back, blue eyes glowing. Holly had taken the photo at one of the

Inn's Christmas parties. Her dad had arrived late and had swept Maggie into a dance, ignoring her protests. He was a terrible dancer, known for trampling toes and tripping over feet, but Holly's snapshot perfectly captured the love that her parents had for each other.

Tears pricked her eyes as she remembered coming into her dad's hospital room one night. The room had been dim, and Maggie had been sitting beside her husband, her hand resting on his.

"You're my best friend, Maggie," Peter had said, his words slurring. "You know that, right? You know I love you, right?"

Her mom had leaned forward to lay her head against his. "I know, Peter," she'd said softly. "I love you too. Why don't you try and sleep now?"

"Okay. Love you, Maggie. Love you."

Holly's dad had died the following week, ending his nearly three-year battle with cancer. He was buried in the old churchyard on the north shore, underneath some juniper trees overlooking the ocean. While Maggie and Holly rarely visited his grave, they'd planted a juniper tree for him at the Inn, and each Christmas Eve since, they had decorated it with red and gold ornaments.

Holly sighed, briefly touching the photo again.

She had just graduated from college and started a job in a plant nursery on the mainland when her dad became ill. Since Peter's illness required treatment that wasn't available on Hibiscus Island, her parents had spent a lot of time on the mainland. Holly had divided her time between her job and helping her mother, until the day the doctors told Maggie there was nothing more to be done.

Holly had gone home with her parents, but after her dad died, she scuttled back to her job, wanting—and needing—

to get away. She'd felt guilty about it every day for the next two years.

Maggie was always cheerful when they'd spoken over video, but she'd been thrilled when Holly had called to say she wanted to come home permanently.

"Of course there's a job at the Inn!" she'd exclaimed when Holly asked. "Gramps will love having your expertise —the job is getting a bit too much for him now, even with help. Don't tell him I said that! And if you need a change of pace at any time, you know there's always work to be done inside." Her face lit up on the screen. "It'll be wonderful to have you home again, Holly Berry!"

So here I am, Holly thought, looking around her room. *Back on Hibiscus Island. Back home.*

It felt good.

"Come on, Truff," she said, swinging the cavapoo into her arms. "Let's go take a walk before supper."

WITH TRUFFLE CAVORTING at her side, Holly rounded the corner of the house onto a narrow walkway that twisted and turned downhill. Much of the property was terraced, land-scaped gardens but at least two acres had been left as natural woodland with trails cut through it.

Juniper and palm trees mingled with allspice and Surinam cherry over an underbrush of snowberry bushes, sword ferns, and wild philodendrons. It was peaceful, with only the sound of birds and Truffle's snuffling to break the silence.

"Blast it!"

Holly grinned involuntarily as more expletives, less child-friendly, echoed along the trail. Truffle raced ahead, barking excitedly and Holly quickened her steps as she heard her grandfather greet the little dog.

"What're you making all that noise for, you little mop? Come here. Stop that leaping and prancing. Behave like a real dog, why don't you? Look at Roxie! Do you see her slobbering all over me? No. She's a proper dog, she is, not a designer special like you."

Holly laughed as she came around the corner and saw her Gramps crouching down, rubbing an ecstatically wriggling Truffle. Beside him, a large dark brindle Boxer sat patiently. Her tail thumped wildly when she saw Holly, but she made no attempt to stand.

Gramps looked up. "Holly girl! So, you're home, are you? Ready to do some real work now?" He got to his feet slowly and smiled at her. "Come give me a hug, child."

"Hi, Gramps," Holly said, as she submitted to his embrace, then looked up in mock indignation. "What do you mean 'real work'? I'll have you know I worked really hard on the mainland."

"Pah!" Gramps retorted. "Greenhouse work. Easy. Landscaping now—that's real work!"

His brown eyes twinkled at her from his sunburnt, wrinkled face. His now-thinning white hair was closely cut and his beard was trimmed short. Gramps wiped his hands on an ancient blue sweater that topped equally ancient shorts. As usual, he was barefoot.

"Where are your shoes, Gramps?" Holly asked. "And what have you done to your leg?"

Gramps looked at the scrape on his calf, welling with blood, and scowled. "Blasted ladder. Gets slippery sometimes."

Holly sighed inwardly. Two ladders leaned against the steep rockface, leading up onto a large outcropping that was in the process of being planted. A tray of ornamental asparagus fern perched on the top, beside Gramps's shoes.

"Does Mama know you've been climbing up there?" she asked.

Gramps's face reddened in outrage. "It's got nothing to do with your mama. I know what I'm doing!"

"Uh-huh." Holly grinned wryly, knowing there was no point in arguing with Gramps. He was a stubborn old islander who had been working in horticulture his entire life. The gardens at Hibiscus Inn were his design and his life's work. Gramps was an artist—and had the temperament to go with it.

"I'll get your shoes for you." She scampered up the ladder before he could stop her.

Gramps huffed indignantly as she handed them to him, and then smiled. "Thanks, child," he said. "Call that fluffball of Maggie's and let's go see what's for dinner. I've worked up a good appetite out here today. Come on, Roxie girl."

The Boxer stretched slowly, then padded over, wagging her tail.

"Roxie looks good, Gramps."

Gramps fondly rubbed the Boxer's ears. Seeming to smile, the dog lifted her grey muzzle and her tail wagged faster. "She's ten and a half now, a good age for a Boxer. Slowed down quite a lot, but she still likes to come to work with me."

They headed slowly back to the Inn, Gramps pointing out all the newest plantings to Holly on the way. "This purple thing here..." He stopped and scowled at it. "Can't remember the name of it, but it's a complete pest. Spreads like wildfire."

"Chinese violet," Holly said, inspecting the purple bell-shaped flowers. "It's pretty. And good for a filler."

Gramps huffed. "Too good. We have to cut it back constantly. Might be better in pots." He continued along the path. "I've got two young guys working with me now. Bit younger than you, I think. They've both done the Botanic Gardens apprenticeship scheme. Not bad workers. Need to study up on their plants a bit more, but not bad."

They rounded the corner, emerging onto a flat lawn edged with shrub beds. A white-pillared gazebo, with a table and four chairs, stood at one end of the lawn, and beyond it a winding set of stone steps meandered up towards the main house. Two large red Ruby bougainvilleas dominated the scene, growing up weathered stone retaining walls and spilling over onto the steps. And in the middle of the profusion of flowers, a stout, bright pink figure wielded clippers.

4

Gramps stopped short and drew in his breath in outrage. "What d'you think you're doing to my bougainvillea, missy?" he bellowed, striding towards her. "Drop those scissors, d'you hear me?"

"Gramps!" Holly darted forward, grabbing at her grandfather's arm. "That's Ms. Cartell!"

"I don't care if she's the queen herself!" Gramps surged into the garden and snatched the offending clippers from Amelia Cartell's hand. "The Bougainvillea Festival is in four days' time and here's this woman chopping my Ruby plants!" Veins popped in his forehead as he glared furiously at Amelia.

"Well!" Amelia exclaimed, putting her hands on her ample hips. "How extraordinarily rude! I am a guest at this facility! Surely it isn't too much to expect common courtesy from the staff!"

"A guest? A guest? You're a bougainvillea saboteur is what you are!" Gramps retorted, pushing past her. He gave a yell of anger as he inspected the plants. "Look at this butchery! My Rubies! Chopped to bits! And look! Look at all these other branches!" Gramps's voice failed him for a moment. "My Bridal Bouquet! Mutilated!" He rounded on Amelia. "This is a... a... wholesale slaughter! You've destroyed my bougainvillea!"

"Gramps! Stop!" Holly squeaked in vain.

A man rounded the corner at a sprint. "What's going on?" he snapped, advancing on Gramps. "Step back, sir."

Gramps's head whipped around. "Is this your mother, young man? Because—"

"Mother? I certainly am not!" Amelia Cartell exclaimed indignantly. "Mr. Hartford is my employee!" Looking in disdain at Gramps, she stepped away from him and brushed down her suit. "And you, sir, are overreacting in a ridiculous way."

"Overreacting?" Gramps voice rose in rage. He brandished chopped branches of flowering bougainvillea, his face beet red. "Half this plant is gone! I'll have you know this was one of the finest specimens on the property!"

"And I'm telling you," Amelia snapped back, "that this Ruby bougainvillea hasn't been hurt in the slightest. I am staying in the Bougainvillea Suite and there appears to have been an oversight in providing me with appropriate floral arrangements."

"Hasn't been hurt? Oversight?" Gramps spluttered. "Woman, did you not hear me? This is the Festival week! We're going to have hundreds of people here to tour my gardens and what are they going to see?" His voice rose again. "Butchered bougainvillea! That's what!"

The bodyguard, for so Holly assumed him to be, made another attempt to speak and was waved summarily aside by both combatants. Rolling his eyes, he moved away, shoved his hands in his pockets, and watched his employer with a morose expression on his face.

Truffle huddled, quaking, behind Holly while Roxie sighed heavily and settled herself on the ground. The old dog was used to hearing Gramps shout.

"Good heavens!" The voice behind Holly was startled and she turned to see Bob Schafer staring at the battle. "Who's the old gentleman? He's real fired up, isn't he? What happened?"

Holly sighed. "That's my grandfather, Stuart Mackin-tosh." She gestured around. "He designed and maintains the gardens so he's a little... uh... proprietary of them."

"Well, his proprietary nature may have just landed you in a whole heap of trouble," Amelia's security detail said curtly. "Ms. Cartell's blog is a big deal in the traveling world and is followed by thousands. A good review from *Impressions* will get you visitors in the hundreds; a bad one could kill your business! Your grandfather would have done better to control his temper!"

Holly stiffened. "Well, let me tell *you*," she retorted hotly, "that the Hibiscus Island Bougainvillea Festival is a pretty big deal too! And my grandfather is known around the *world* in horticultural circles! He has good reason to be upset about this! Ms. Cartell hasn't just cut a few sprigs of bougainvillea! Look at that pile! She didn't need to cut *that* much for her room! And besides—"

The security man blinked, then raised his hands in surrender. "Okay, okay. I get it." He sighed. "I didn't mean to snap. It's been a stressful day." He removed his sunglasses and ran a hand through his short, dark hair. "I'm Pete Hart-ford. Personal security for Ms. Cartell."

Holly flushed suddenly, aghast at her outburst. What a way to speak to a guest! She opened her mouth, but Pete forestalled any apology.

"I'm serious about her reviews," he warned. "Lucy can't

always—" He paused before continuing, "What I mean is, you'll do yourselves a favor if you can calm Ms. Cartell down."

"Well, I must say, I really think it's Mr. Mackintosh who needs to be appeased," Bob Schafer interjected stuffily. "It's his plant that's been destroyed, after all. I can certainly understand why he's upset." He glanced at Holly, ignoring the younger man's narrow-eyed stare. "His gardens are truly spectacular, Holly! I'd love a chance to pick his brain."

"Are you a horticulturist, Mr. Schafer?" Holly asked, grabbing at the distraction, even as she kept an anxious eye on Gramps. The battle had picked up pace and some inventive insults were being hurled by both opponents.

"I have a small slat house," Schafer said eagerly. "We collect heirloom seeds and propagate unusual or unique plants. I saw social media posts of this festival last year and thought I'd like to visit the island. I'd like to see if I can get some cuttings or seeds of some of the plants here."

Another shout from the combat zone refocused Holly's full attention on Gramps. "Mr. Schafer, I'm sorry," she said, "but I really think that I—"

A final enraged bellow from Gramps stopped her short. Amelia shot Gramps one last defiant look before she turned and marched up the steps towards the Inn.

Pete gave a heartfelt groan. "She'll be in a foul mood now. I'd better go. It's not fair to leave Lucy to deal with it all." He replaced his sunglasses, gave Holly a rueful nod, and went after Amelia.

Gramps stormed towards Holly, carrying a pile of bougainvillea branches.

"Oh my," Schafer murmured. "This may not be the best time to introduce myself. I'll arrange a time to meet with Mr. Mackintosh later." He eased away from Holly.

"That woman! That thieving old hag! That—"

"Gramps! Stop!" Holly cried, stepping in front of her grandfather.

Stuart Mackintosh glared at her, choleric with rage. "Look at this!" he snarled, shoving the armful of bougainvillea at his granddaughter. "Look what that old witch did!"

Holly winced. "Is that California Gold as well?"

"Yes, it is!" Gramps yelled. "And look! Look at how much of my Ruby she... she *slaughtered*! I'm telling you, Holly, I'd better not see that woman in my gardens again or I won't be responsible for my actions! Not a single apology, mark you! Not one! Nattering on about who she was and how much she knew about flowers, and how she was going to report me and what she was going to say on her block or some such thing!"

"Her blog," Holly said. "She writes a travel blog."

"Blog, block! Who cares?" Gramps snapped.

"Gramps," Holly sighed. "She's a guest. You know Mama is going to have to deal with this now."

Gramps glared. "Keep her out of my gardens, Holly!" He looked at the pile of branches he was holding. "I'm going to see if I can get cuttings out of these. Salvage what I can. Tell your mama I won't be in for dinner. I'll defrost something. Thieving woman. Saboteur..."

His muttered expletives faded away as he stalked down the hill towards his slat house and cottage, followed by a placid Roxie. Holly choked back an unwilling laugh as a final "bougainvillea bandit" reached her, then she sighed. She'd have to let her mother know what had happened and hope that together they could smooth Amelia Cartell's ruffled feathers.

MUCH LATER, she slumped across the kitchen island and stared at her mother. "We have a doozy this time," she said, holding out her wine glass.

Maggie topped it up. "That's the nature of the hospitality business," she said with a shrug. "I think we calmed her down a bit."

Holly took a gulp of wine. "Sure, with a free night," she said sourly. "What possessed her to go around chopping the bougainvillea? I mean, really, of all the plants to choose! I looked at the California Gold and there's not a flower left on it! Gramps is going to be wild when he sees it." An involuntary laugh escaped her. "Oh, you should have heard him, Mama. He really let himself go."

"So it seems," Maggie said dryly. "Ms. Cartell gave me a thorough account."

"Gramps told me she writes a block," Holly continued. She gurgled with laughter as she picked up a bread roll. "I wonder what her blog is like?"

"It's big," Maggie said, sitting down at the counter. "Including all social media accounts and subscribers, she has close to half a million followers. It's one of the largest travel blogs in the world, actually."

Holly choked. "What?"

"Yep. Not to mention the fact that her travel books are immensely popular. She's very well-known in the industry." Maggie sighed. "And she's already assured me that she'll be reviewing the Inn."

Holly eyed her mother over the top of her wine glass. "Are you worried? What happens if she writes a bad review?"

Maggie shrugged. "She's just one reviewer, albeit an

important one, so she won't put us out of business if that's what you're asking. But she does have a lot of followers and I'd rather get a glowing review from her if possible." She grinned ruefully. "We'll just have to keep her away from Gramps for the rest of her stay!"

Holly nodded and took a sip of her wine, then looked at her mother questioningly as Maggie pushed a piece of paper towards her. "Look, this is the program for the Festival so far. We're hosting the opening dinner on Friday. The weather forecast looks good, so I thought we'd set up on the lower terrace. If you don't have any plans for tomorrow, I wondered if you'd pop downtown and talk to Jamie about the hors d'oeuvres and see what she's come up with. Does she know you're back?"

Holly nodded. "I texted her when I landed. Sure, I'll do that. Anything else you need while I'm there?"

"I'll write you a list."

5

Although Holly woke up early the next day, her mother beat her into the kitchen. Maggie had a cup of tea in front of her and her computer open. She looked up with a smile when Holly came in.

"High of eighty predicted on Saturday but low humidity, praise be."

"There's no such thing as low humidity at this time of year," Holly said, getting out a mug. She looked at it closely. "Hey, this is cute. Where'd you get it?"

"Tiny Treasures," Maggie replied, naming a small shop in town. "They have a new fairytale collection, and I couldn't resist! I have four of them now."

Holly grinned as she turned on the kettle. Her mother claimed that tea tasted better when drunk from bone china and had an eclectic collection of teacups and mugs.

"So, have you got that list for me?"

"Well, actually," Maggie said, sipping her tea, "I thought I'd drive down with you. We can have breakfast at Jamie's if you want and then we can divide the errands and be back for lunch. Have your tea first though."

Holly glanced at her watch. "No, that's okay. I'll wait and have it with breakfast. Give me half an hour and I'll meet you out front."

~

HOLLY TOOK LESS than twenty minutes to shower, pull her still-damp hair back into a ponytail and throw on denim shorts and a green t-shirt. She beat her mother to the car by about thirty seconds.

Maggie rushed out, carrying a huge canvas bag and a straw hat. She wore khaki capri hiking pants and a black t-shirt that said "All I need is tea and books." Her short, dark hair, now showing a few white strands, was tousled over enormous sunglasses. She smiled at Holly as she fumbled for the car keys. "Did you put on sunscreen?"

"Yes, Mama," Holly replied with a grin. "And I have a hat. And extra sunscreen in my bag. Want to check?" She looked at her mother's fair skin, asking pointedly, "Do *you* have sunscreen on?"

Maggie laughed, then waved gaily as the Hibiscus Inn van rounded the corner of the drive. "Have a great day," she called to the passengers.

"Where are they going?" Holly asked as she settled herself in her mother's small blue Kia.

"Bob Schafer is going to the Botanic Gardens. There's a tour booked at nine thirty and then he'll get dropped off in town for some shopping. The rest are going straight into town. They'll do their own things from there." Maggie snapped her seatbelt into place and turned the ignition key.

"What's Ms. Cartell doing, do you know?"

"Oh, she has a comprehensive itinerary. Lucy, her secretary, showed it to me yesterday because she wanted to know how to get to some places." Maggie edged the little car out onto the main road. "Ms. Cartell has certainly done her research on the island. There are places on the list I thought only locals knew about. Lucy said they also want to visit the gardens that are open for the Festival and take photos. I suggested she visit a couple each day."

Holly trailed her hand out of the car window, feeling the warm air rush by, and sighed happily. "It's nice being back."

Maggie beamed. "Oh, I'm so glad to hear you say that! I worried the island might be too small for you after life on the mainland."

"The island's plenty big enough." Holly glanced at her mother. Her voice turning soft, she said, "I really am glad to be home, Mama."

"I'm glad you're back too." Maggie's voice wobbled a little as she patted Holly's leg.

A moment later, her face brightened as she peered ahead. "We're coming into town. Keep your eyes peeled for a parking space."

"Park down at the harbor," Holly suggested. "We can walk from there. How much do you have to get?"

"Well, I've got a book order to collect, a couple of things from the pharmacy, Sarah asked for some tea towels... Not a lot."

"How *many* books?" Holly asked, raising a knowing eyebrow at her mother.

"Not too many. If you help me, we can manage them. I'll park on Harbor Road," Maggie said decisively, flicking on her turn signal. "There's nowhere here anyway."

Holly looked at all the empty parking spots along the street and grinned. Her mother had an almost obsessive hatred of parallel parking.

Maggie steered the little Kia down the hill and into the

carpark at the edge of the waterfront. "I'm absolutely starving and ready for some of Jamie's amazing pancakes. She has a gluten-free menu now, so you'll be in heaven."

"She told me," Holly said, linking her arm through her mother's as they started up the narrow hill to the town center.

Hibiscus Island was part of a small chain of eight islands, the largest of which, Grand Island, known colloquially as the mainland, was just under an hour's flight away, while the smallest, Wreck Rock, was only four square miles in size and visible from the south shore. At fifteen miles long, Hibiscus Island had two small villages that dated back to the early seventeenth century when the first settlers had landed: Castlebay at the east end of the island and Bridgeport in the center. Bridgeport housed both the main harbor and the business center of the island.

For the most part, life on Hibiscus Island was laidback, and Bridgeport reflected this. It was a leisurely, relaxed place full of red-bricked pedestrian zones lined by huge concrete planters overflowing with tropical flowers. Scarlet cordia trees were spaced evenly along the street, shops sported pastel-colored fronts, doors stood open in welcome, and a hodgepodge of accents filled the air as islanders interacted with the strolling sunburnt tourists.

After making their way along Bay Street, Holly and Maggie stopped outside a small café.

"Wow!" Holly gasped. "The Bean has had a facelift! When did Jamie do *this*? She never said anything to me!"

"She wanted it to be a surprise," Maggie said, pushing open the door. "We were all sworn to secrecy."

A divine aroma of baked goods and coffee filled the cool air. Sleek, dark grey tables replaced the old wooden ones that had previously graced the café, and the floor sported new espresso-colored wood planks. The café counter was now a pale birchwood, a shade repeated in modern criss-crossing beams overhead and the legs of the grey cushioned chairs around the tables. The welcoming space was filled with the hum of contented customers and the hiss of coffee machines.

Pale blue walls held the work of local artists, with discreet price tags for customers interested in purchasing. A large birchwood sideboard against one wall housed an eclectic collection of coffee accessories and above it, displayed prominently, there was a huge photograph of a grey and white dog.

Holly stared around in growing approval. "It looks great! I'm glad she kept the local artwork." She wandered over to take a closer look while her mother found a table.

"Heaven help us! I'm blinded!" Holly spun around at the sound of the lilting voice. "Girl! I need sunglasses to look at you! Your legs are *white*! What happened to your tan? You have got to get some sun on you!" Jamie grinned and held out her arms. "Give me a hug, girlfriend."

Holly squeaked and flung herself on her best friend. "Jamie!"

"Holly Berry! It's great to have you back! And about time too! You look good. Well, apart from your extreme pale-ness." Jamie smiled broadly as she held her friend at arm's length and looked her up and down.

Holly laughed. "Yes, well, we can't all be island goddesses like you, can we?"

Jamie tossed back her dark curly hair and batted ridicu-lously long eyelashes. "It's a gift, honey," she drawled, striking a pose. Her bright teal t-shirt enhanced the smooth brown tones of her skin and matched the bright earrings that dangled from her ears. Her dark brown eyes danced. "Oh Holls, it's so good to have you home! Come on, let's sit down. I have time for a chat."

Holly linked an arm through her friend's as they headed toward Maggie's table. "The place looks amazing, Jamie. When did you do all this? And how come you didn't tell me?"

Jamie giggled. "It was spur of the moment—and I wanted you to be surprised. Hi, Aunt Maggie!" She leaned down to give Maggie a resounding kiss on the cheek. "I like your t-shirt."

"It's 'Maggie', not 'Aunt'," Maggie said in a pained voice. "How many times do I have to tell you..."

"...that 'aunt' makes you feel old," Jamie and Holly chanted in a singsong voice, before bursting into laughter.

"You'll never be old, Maggie," Jamie said sliding into a chair across from her and handing a menu to Holly. "Here, have a look. I have a whole gluten-free menu now. Just for you." She grinned and leaned back, shoving her hands into the pockets of her white capris.

Holly studied the front of the menu. The same grey and white dog graced the updated cover. A coffee cup with the Bean's logo on it was at his feet. Holly smiled. It was an appealing image.

Catching the eye of a waitress, Jamie waved her over, then looked at Maggie and Holly. "Have you guys decided? Getting your usual, Maggie?"

Maggie closed the menu. "Yes, please." She smiled at the girl taking the order. "And a latte as well, Angie. Oh, and maybe some blueberries?"

"Sure thing, Mrs. Gold," Angie said with a smile. She looked enquiringly at Holly.

"I'll have the gluten-free pancakes and an orange juice." Holly watched as Angie walked back behind the counter. "Was that Angie Roberts? Good grief. I babysat her!"

"I felt the same when she applied for the job," Jamie said, looking mournfully at Holly. "We're getting old, Holls. We're practically over the hill!"

Maggie snorted. "Old! Ha!"

The girls grinned at each other. After a moment, Holly tapped the menu. "So, who's the dog?"

Jamie's face lit up. "That's Teddy. He's my new honey. I'll take you back for an introduction after you've eaten. He's such a sweetie."

"You, Jamie White, have a dog?" Holly laughed and inspected the photo on the menu more closely. "He's got unusual coloring, hasn't he?"

"He's a parti poodle," Jamie explained, laughing at Holly's expression. "Not that kind of party! That's what that patchy kind of look is called. Someone brought him to the island to breed but his temperament was wrong, so I got him for free."

"He's very cute," Holly agreed, "and I love the new menu cover. But how did you afford all the renovations? I thought you said you wouldn't be remodeling for another couple of years."

"That was the plan," Jamie agreed, "but when my great-auntie Rosie died she left me some money in her will. She always said she would, but I didn't think it would be that much. Anyway, it seems Auntie Rosie had quite a bit stashed away! So, when her probate finally cleared, I got this little windfall." Jamie waved her hand around expansively, beaming. "So, I remodeled."

"It's awesome," Holly said. "It really is, Jamie. And I'm—"

A stern voice cut Holly off.

"When I say I want a soy, decaf latte, that is what I expect to get. This, young woman, is *not* a soy latte!"

"Oh no," Holly groaned, recognizing the voice.

Amelia Cartell sat at a table by the window. Three tables over, her secretary got to her feet, an anxious look on her face. She stopped when Pete Hartford put his hand over hers. He said something and Lucy sat down reluctantly.

"Hang on, let me go sort this out." Jamie strode across the café to join the flustered waitress standing beside Amelia.

"Are you the owner of this establishment?" Amelia asked, looking Jamie up and down.

Jamie smiled pleasantly. "I'm Jamie White, and yes, I own the Bean. How can I help?"

Amelia gestured towards the frothy latte on the table. "This," she said, rather disdainfully, "is not soy milk."

"Oh, I can assure you it is," Jamie said brightly. "We have special cups reserved for the soy drinks. There're a lot of people on the island with dairy allergies so we make sure we keep the cups separate and we always have non-dairy milk on tap, so to speak."

Amelia's eyes narrowed. "This drink has a froth."

Jamie looked puzzled. "Lattes usually do," she pointed out politely.

"It's very difficult to get a good froth on a soy latte." Amelia sat back, her arms folded across her chest.

"It can be," Jamie agreed with a smile, "but we have a great barista. And as I said, lots of allergies on the island. So, we've perfected our non-dairy technique."

"Humph." Amelia returned her attention to her cup. "Perfected? You're very sure of yourself, aren't you? I will form my own opinion of your perfection, young woman and you may read that opinion on my blog, *Impressions*."

Jamie blinked in astonishment, then smiled. "Oh, you write a blog? I'll make sure to look it up."

Amelia looked disdainful and leaned back in her chair. "The trouble with small islands like this," she began, "is that you're all so insular. You really don't know what's happening in the outside world or how you measure up to it." Jamie's eyes narrowed, but Amelia plowed on. "From what I've observed, people who live on islands like this have an exaggerated sense of their own importance and ability."

Her voice was loud, and the café had fallen quiet as she spoke. Now all eyes turned to Jamie. The locals, knowing her hair-trigger temper, held their breaths in anticipation. As Jamie started to open her mouth, however, there was a nervous interruption.

"Ms. Cartell, I'm so sorry, but we have to leave now if we're to see everything on your list today." Lucy shot Jamie an anxious and apologetic glance. "Do you think we could have Ms. Cartell's latte to go?"

Jamie took a deep breath and nodded. Lips compressed, she turned away, her knuckles white as she carried the glass to the counter. As Amelia exited the café, radiating superiority from every tightly encased part of her body, excited conversation broke out amongst the other customers.

"Did she say *Impressions*? That's a travel blog, isn't it? Was that the author? We must look it up."

"My goodness, what an unpleasant woman!"

"You know, she looks very familiar... What did you say, Violet? No, no more coffee for me."

"A *blog*, Harold! She said she writes a blog! Turn your hearing aid on, Harold!"

"Well really, who drinks soy lattes anyway? What's wrong with plain coffee?"

"That was Amelia Cartell. Yes, you know, the one who writes those travel books. Remember we read the one about Scotland? What do you mean, you don't remember? Of course you do. We have a copy of the book at home."

Gradually the café conversation returned to normal.

6

Jamie returned to Holly's table, collapsing onto a chair. "What a nasty, nasty woman!" she exclaimed. "Why is she even visiting Hibiscus Island if that's what she thinks about us? And what a fuss about a latte! Froth indeed! It's not me who has an 'exaggerated sense of my own importance', that's for sure!"

Holly patted her hand. "I am so impressed that you kept your temper! Looks like it's not just the café that's changed!"

"Yes, well, although I know some people find it entertaining"—Jamie grinned across the room at old Mrs. Smith, who was raising her coffee cup in a smiling toast toward her —"I'd rather the café be known for exceptional food and service instead of a fiery owner." She rolled her shoulders and sighed. "Honestly, some people! I feel sorry for whoever that woman is staying with because it won't be easy keeping her happy, that's for sure!" Jamie caught sight of Maggie's face and gasped. "No! She's with you? Oh, you poor things!"

Maggie grinned at Jamie's appalled expression. "We're keeping our fingers crossed that the island will mellow her."

Jamie snorted. "Ha! Good luck with that.".

~

"DELICIOUS!" Holly sat back with a satisfied smile, looking idly around the small café. "Best pancakes I've had in ages. Jamie's done a good job with this place, hasn't she?"

Maggie took a final sip of her latte. "Yep. We're all proud of Jamie, and were so pleased when Rosie left her that little windfall. She didn't just remodel. She hired François Dumont as well. Remember him? He went away to culinary school and was running a home bakery. He and Jamie have become partners of a sort. He's the magic behind those pancakes you inhaled."

Holly peered across the café, trying to see through the small window leading into the kitchen. "François, huh? Jamie had a crush on him in high school."

Maggie laughed, pushing back her chair. "He's married now, to a girl he met in England. She's very nice. François and Jamie are just friends." She picked up her bag. "I'm going to pop into the pharmacy, then go get Sarah's tea towels. I'll meet you at the Book Worm in, say, half an hour or so? Will that work?"

"Perfect," Holly agreed, catching sight of Jamie waving to her to come to the back. "Looks like I'm about to meet Teddy."

Jamie's café was in one of the older buildings downtown which had originally been a home. It was a two story, boxy-shaped house with a traditional white roof topping blue-bird-blue walls. Large windows edged with white shutters let light into the open-plan café, housed in what used to be the living and dining rooms. The old kitchen, in the back of the house, had been upgraded to meet the island's health standards and was now a bustling hub of noise amid stainless steel appliances and industrial-quality ovens. Upstairs, four small rooms housed Jamie's office, two storage areas, and a small staff breakroom.

Holly trotted up the stairs and peeked into the staffroom. "Come in! Come in!"

Jamie was sprawled on a large overstuffed turquoise-patterned sofa with a rather nervous looking big dog. His white fluffy tail drooped when he saw Holly.

"Aww Teddy. Put your tail up," Jamie cajoled, hugging the poodle. "This is Auntie Holly. She's a friend."

"He's beautiful," Holly said, approaching slowly, her hand extended. "Hi Teddy. Aren't you a gorgeous boy?" After a cautious sniff, the poodle wagged his tail hesitantly.

"He'll get used to you eventually," Jamie said.

Holly plopped down in an armchair on the other side of the room and grinned at her friend. "You with a dog. I never thought I'd see the day."

"I know, right?" Jamie laughed. She leaned back, her hand still stroking Teddy's neck. "It's nice bringing him to work. And with the Waterfront Park right outside, it's easy to take him out."

Holly glanced through the large windows. Behind the Bean, the Waterfront Park stretched down to the harbor, an oasis of green in the middle of town. Tables and benches made it a favorite lunch place for those working in town and Holly could see several tourists sipping coffees and poring over the colorful, printed maps of the island provided by the tourism office. She smiled when she saw old man Sanders, hot chocolate in hand, sitting in his usual spot underneath the cassia tree. Some things never changed on the island.

Teddy's ears pricked forward and he turned his head towards the windows overlooking the street before ambling over to peer out.

Bridgeport was laid out like a slightly rambling grid,

with the central part of town all pedestrianized. The Bean was in the middle of Windward Street, flanked on each side by shops—Antiquities on the left and Baby Boutique on the right. The street ran from north to south, with the harbor on the northern end and City Hall at the southern end.

Jamie joined Teddy at the window. "Hey look, Holls, it's your horrible guest. Ms. Frothy Latte herself. Strutting along with her minions. Looking down on the insular islanders." She snorted.

Peering out, Holly saw Lucy and Pete wandering along behind Amelia. Every now and then, Lucy snapped a photo or murmured into her phone.

"Who's the girl?" Jamie said, leaning out a little. "And the guy? He seems grumpy. He must hate his job whatever it is. Can't say I blame him. Imagine working for that woman!"

"That's Lucy and Pete, secretary and security for Ms. Cartell."

"Security?" Jamie asked, turning around. "Is that normal? Good grief. Who knew writing a blog was such a dangerous job! Does she have deranged fans or something?"

Holly laughed. "I have no idea."

"Mind you," Jamie continued darkly, "if she writes like she talks, I can understand the need for a bodyguard! Obnoxious woman. Is she here for the Bougainvillea Festival?"

"I'm not sure. She asked about it on the plane, but I don't think she's really a fan. She'd have known better than to cut branches for her room, if she was."

Jamie's eyes bulged. "She cut Mr. Mack's bougainvillea? Three days before the Festival? No way! Does he know? He does? Oh, he must have been wild!"

Holly giggled. "He called her a saboteur and a bougainvillea bandit."

Jamie rocked with sudden laughter. "I can just hear him."

Holly laughed as well, then sighed. "She's not going to be an easy guest, that's for sure. She's already got a free night out of us because of Gramps's outburst, and she's here for ten days!"

"I don't envy you," Jamie said in a commiserating tone as she headed to the door. "I've got to get back to work, Holls. No, Teddy. You have to stay here. We'll go for walkies later." She nuzzled the big dog's nose and held the door for Holly. "I'll see you later, right?"

"Yeah. Oh, I was supposed to ask you about the hors d'oeuvres for the opening party. Are you good with everything?"

"Yep," Jamie said cheerfully. "We've got a lot of the basic things already prepped and we'll start baking tomorrow. Tell Maggie we'll be up around four o'clock on Friday to set up if that's okay."

Holly grinned. "Will do."

THE BOOK WORM was a block away from Jamie's café, tucked away on Amberjack Lane. Holly held the door politely for the two ladies who were just leaving, and received a beaming smile from Miss Greenley.

"Welcome home, Holly!" she exclaimed breathlessly. "Your aunt Laura *just* told us you were back. How *lovely*. Isn't it wonderful, Carolyn?" She glanced eagerly at her companion, who gave her a curt nod. "You *must* join the Garden Club, Holly dear. It would be *lovely* to have a *real* horticulturist to give us all advice. Do think about it, dear. Oh yes, I'm coming, Carolyn. Goodbye, Holly. *Lovely* to see you!"

Holly, who hadn't been able to get a word in, grinned, waved, and walked into the little bookstore, glancing around for her Aunt Laura.

The sun slanted in the huge glass windowpanes, spotlighting some of the book displays sprawled across antique tables. Bookshelves lined every wall of the small store, which was housed in another of Hibiscus Island's old homes. The vintage wooden floors and beams, coupled with the original fireplace in one of the walls, retained the charm of years past, while comfortable armchairs and small sofas made the Book Worm a favorite place for the island's seniors. The bookstore hosted several different book clubs, including one for teens.

Holly ran her hand along the spines of the latest bestsellers as she walked to the counter. "Hello? Anyone here?"

There was a rustle and Laura Connolly popped out from a tiny office. "Oh Holly, it's you! Come on back. Your mom's here." Laura smiled broadly as Holly squeezed behind the counter. "Give me a hug, favorite niece! It's lovely to see you!"

"I'm your only niece," Holly said, laughing as she submitted to the hug. "You look great, Aunt Laura! Have you lost weight?" She looked her mother's sister up and down.

Laura preened, running a hand through her shoulder-length dark hair and looking down complacently at the jeans and V-necked shirt she wore. "I'm walking miles every day and watching what I eat. Thanks for noticing, honey." She ushered Holly into the little office where Maggie looked up from the computer with a grin.

"Sorry, Holly. We got a little side-tracked."

"What are you guys doing?" Holly asked, going closer. "Oh, is that Ms. Cartell's blog?"

"Yes, it is." Laura drew in a deep breath. "Because she was just in here for ages!"

"Ten minutes." Maggie winked at Holly.

Laura rattled on. "She cross-examined me about my inventory, inspected all the displays, wanted to know how long it took books to get here, as if we're in the middle of nowhere or something, and even *wiped her finger along a shelf*!" Laura's face flushed. "Even Carolyn Sullivan frowned at that, and you know how critical she is!" She took another breath. "However, then the Cartell woman said she'd review me on her blog! I've never heard of this *Impressions* thing, so Maggie just pulled it up for me to see!"

"I told you, Laura, you don't need to worry," Maggie said patiently.

"That's what you say," Laura replied darkly, pushing Maggie's hands away from the keyboard. "Show Holly that one we saw. The restaurant in California. She crucified that guy!" She beckoned Holly closer. "Look, Holls. Look at this!"

"The Western Seaboard," Holly read, hanging over her mother's shoulder. "Vastly overpriced, incompetent employees, substandard fare... Oh! Dishonest and fraudulent owner who cheats customers... Wow. Is she allowed to print things like that? Isn't that libel or something?"

"She destroyed the business, Holly!" Laura exclaimed. "It closed last year!"

Maggie reclaimed the keyboard and scrolled down through more entries. "That type of post is very rare, Laura, and, judging by the comments, there was a lot of push back from the community. In fact, the discussion got so heated, they had to turn the comments off." Maggie looked at her sister. "Most of her reviews are very balanced and fair, although, personally, I like her travel books better. Her descriptive writing is beautiful, and I do like her reflective essays. It's strange that such an unpleasant woman can write so lyrically."

"I wouldn't worry about the Worm," Holly reassured her aunt. "It's the best bookstore on the island."

"It's the *only* bookstore on the island," Laura retorted. "What if she gives me a bad review? What if people stop coming? What if I end up like that restaurant?" She threw her hands up in despair.

Holly grinned at her aunt's theatrics, but Maggie rolled her eyes.

"Oh honestly, Laura! I'll tell you the same thing I told Holly yesterday. It's one travel blog and one reviewer. We're not talking global headlines here. And really, what difference would a bad review make anyway? All the islanders love the Worm! And that's not going to change because someone writes about you on a blog."

Laura looked unconvinced.

"Mama's right," Holly agreed. "I don't think you need to worry at all, Aunt Laura."

"Well... maybe. But what about *you*?" Laura demanded. "The Inn depends on visitors, not locals! After that fiasco yesterday, what sort of a review will she give you?"

Maggie grinned involuntarily. "Dad was still foaming at the mouth this morning. Ms. Cartell really rattled his cage!"

"It's not funny, Maggie. He can't behave to guests like that!" Laura rounded on Holly. "How bad was he, Holly? Did he actually call her a saboteur?"

Holly nodded, stifling a laugh when her aunt gave a dramatic moan. "Ms. Cartell gave as good as she got, I can assure you. And she calmed right down once she got her free night."

"As one does," Maggie said dryly. "Relax, Laura. We'll just keep her away from Dad. It'll be fine. And I made sure she had some bougainvillea in her room today." She grinned at Holly. "I stole it from the one in the courtyard. No one's going to see it and it will make her happy. Well, maybe. I'm not sure anything can actually make that woman happy." She rolled her eyes.

The small bell above the shop door tinkled and the sound of voices was heard.

"Oh, I'd better get back out there," Laura said. "I'll see you on Friday, Maggie. Phil and I will come up early to help set up, okay?"

"Thanks." Maggie smiled at her sister. "We need to get back as well. Where are my books? Come on Holly, grab that pile over there." She picked up her canvas bag, now stuffed with paperbacks, and headed for the storefront.

Holly gathered the remaining two bags of books. "Bye, Aunt Laura," she said, following her mother out. "Tell Uncle Phil I said hi."

Laura waved amiably before turning to help her customers.

7

Over the next two days, Holly found she was in hot demand by just about everyone as the Hibiscus Inn began to prepare for the Bougainvillea Festival.

Thursday flew by in a blur of activity with people coming and going in a continuous flow. Holly pitched in to turn rooms, direct guests away from major traffic areas, arrange transportation for touring visitors, and pinch hit wherever she was needed most.

"Tents?" Maggie exclaimed. "Already? I wasn't expecting them until later. Holly, will you just show them where to set up? Down on the lower terrace. And make sure that they don't skewer any of Gramps's plants like they did last year. They need to set the poles where I've marked the grass, okay? Oh, and the smallest tent goes down nearer the slat house. It's for the Bougainvillea Exhibit. Let the men know, so that they can start to put the display stages in."

With the men directed to the lower terrace, and the assembling of the large dome-shaped white tents underway, Holly returned to the Inn.

"Holly! There you are! Can you give me a hand with

this?" Sarah pushed a trolley laden with afternoon tea goodies out of the kitchen. "If you wouldn't mind setting this up? And could you boil the water? There's a delivery that I need to deal with."

"No problem," Holly agreed, taking charge of the trolley.

The breakfast and tearoom was one of her favorite places at the Inn, overlooking not only the main driveway but also a small, enclosed rose garden. French doors opened onto a little patio, and at the right time of year, with the old roses in full bloom, it was an enchanting place for breakfast or tea. Even now, with the roses fading slightly, the garden was beautiful. Holly glanced out, noticing a few guests, including Amelia, enjoying the sunshine as they sat at the ornate iron tables. Amelia's face was tipped back, her eyes were closed and there was a small smile on her face.

A few tables away, Pete Hartford read a book. He looked up when Amelia waved languidly at him and said a few words. With a curt nod, he stood to head indoors.

"Hi, Pete," Holly said cheerfully as he approached. "Tea will be ready in five minutes." She glanced out at the garden. "Ms. Cartell looks like she's enjoying the sunshine. It's been a beautiful day, hasn't it? Did you get to more of the gardens on the tour today?"

Pete paused and Holly blinked in surprise at the scowl that crossed his face. He erased it quickly, forcing a small smile of his own. "Yeah. We went to one of your national parks first and then visited a couple of gardens at the end of the island. Pretty cool. One of them had a whole pile of seaside plants and some stunning views from the cliffs. Lucy loved it."

"What about you?" Holly asked with a grin.

Pete shrugged. "I'm not that crazy about plants," he admitted. "The guy who owned the seaside place is really into them though. Seems he's one of these survivalist types. Lives off the land, he says." Pete rolled his eyes.

Holly laughed. "Oh, you must have gone to Sea Bright. He's not a survivalist, but Mr. Sullivan is very keen on organic gardening. He does a lot of companion planting from what I remember, and he'll be doing the culinary lecture later in the week. You should go. He's very interesting, and you'll be able to taste test some recipes."

"Uh, no, I don't think so," Pete replied. "The man was talking about nasturtium soup today! Why would anyone want to eat a flower soup?"

Holly grinned. "It's actually pretty good," she said, "but nasturtium's a late-spring, early-summer flower, so you won't be getting that right now. Mr. Sullivan will be showcasing bougainvillea flowers at his talk this week. Seriously, you should all go. He's going to do a whole buffet of plant-based foods. It'll be great."

Pete looked skeptical. "I'll see what Lucy says," he hedged.

"It would make a great blog post." Holly raised an eyebrow.

Pete avoided Holly's gaze. "Uh huh, maybe. Look, sorry, but I've got to get Lucy. See you, Holly."

Holly stared after him as he rushed off, then shrugged and pushed the tea trolley into the room.

ON FRIDAY, pandemonium reigned.

"Holly girl, there you are. The Garden Club is coming in an hour, and they'll be wanting the tables set up by the slat house for their sale. You know I can't abide their chitter-chatter. Will you deal with them? Myrtle will tell you what's needed." Gramps waved his thanks before Holly could even reply and trotted at full speed towards the trail into the woods, desperate to escape before the mostly female brigade of the Garden Club arrived.

"Gramps!" Holly shouted after him. "Get back here!" Her order fell on deaf ears as Gramps disappeared around the corner. Holly groaned in defeat.

Commandeering the services of the two apprentice landscapers, she got the tables set up, then surveyed the contents of the slat house.

"Any idea what he's donating this year?" she asked.

"Yeah. A bunch of roses, sedums, some dwarf bougainvillea... There's a lot. We've got them all labeled and ready to put out. We can take care of it. You'd best go meet Myrtle. She'll be mad as fire that Mr. Mack's gone into hiding."

Holly trudged back up the hill to the Inn just in time to see the arrival of the Garden Club convoy.

The Hibiscus Island Garden Club was a force to be reckoned with. It consisted of a multitude of mostly retired seniors who met twice a month at the Botanic Gardens Horticultural Hall for lectures, films, practical seminars, flower arranging, bonsai classes, growing tomatoes under glass, and similar activities. You name it, the Garden Club did it. Well-fortified with tea and gossip.

The first car swept up and disgorged the supreme commander of the Garden Club, Ms. Myrtle Collier, who immediately leapt into action. Immaculately dressed, as always, in a trim powder-blue suit, the well-preserved septuagenarian directed the unloading of cars and the loading of trolleys by both the Garden Club members and their coopted spouses. Without disturbing one hair on her beautifully coiffed silver head, Myrtle controlled operations with military precision, and within minutes, the driveway was cleared, a dazzling array of plants on its way down the hill to the Garden Club tables.

"Holly, darling girl! It's so lovely to have you home again," Myrtle cried, grabbing Holly's hands and air-kissing her cheeks. "Stuart must be thrilled to have you helping him. Where is he, dear?" She looked around for Gramps.

"Oh, somewhere about," Holly said evasively. "It's nice to see you too, Myrtle!"

Myrtle Collier had made it abundantly clear to the youth of Hibiscus Island she was not to be called "aunt" or "Ms. Collier," as was customary for her age group. Many of the older generation disapproved, but Myrtle had stood her ground. "My first name is good enough for me and for everyone else," she had said.

"Here, let me show you where we've set everything up," Holly continued in an attempt to change the subject. "The guys are down at the slat house and will help with anything else you need."

Myrtle's eyes narrowed. "Stuart's hiding again, isn't he?"

A shout from the lower terrace saved Holly from having to answer.

"Sorry, Myrtle. That's Sebastian yelling for me. I'll come down to the slat house later."

"HEY, HOLLY!" Matt staggered around the corner of the Inn, his arms full of tablecloths. "Where do you want these? Jamie just called and said she's on her way with the goodies."

"Over there." Holly gestured toward the tables already

set up under the tents. She pushed the sweaty hair off her face, groaning as she stretched her back out.

Sebastian swung another table up and into position. "What's the time, Matt?"

"Time to work faster," Matt said. "We need to hurry up with the tables so we can start moving the crockery." He grinned at his friend's disgruntled expression. "You volunteered for this, remember?"

Jamie swept in just after four o'clock. She and François Dumont set up the buffet tables with an efficient alacrity and were stacking plates and glasses when Myrtle reappeared with a posse from the Garden Club.

"Very nice," Myrtle said, her approval evident. "It all looks lovely. We'll get the table decorations done and be out of your way so you can get the food organized on time."

Short, square glass vases were filled with clear glass pebbles. Ferns were added, then sprigs of flowering bougainvillea were popped into each vase.

"Oh, it's so pretty!" a voice said in admiring tones. Amelia's secretary, her hands shoved into jean pockets, stood just under the edge of the tent. The afternoon sunlight glinted on her slightly tousled short blonde hair as she looked around in delight. "I can't wait for the flower show tomorrow! I've heard it's just an amazing sight with all the different varieties on display! May I take some photos?" She whipped out her phone.

Myrtle beamed and nodded. "Are you a bougainvillea fancier, my dear? The Garden Club will be selling some lovely specimens this weekend, if you'd like to visit the slat house later."

Lucy looked regretful. "I wish I could, but I wouldn't be able to take one with me. We're touring several islands this summer. I won't be getting home until the end of August."

"Well, bougainvillea grows all over the tropics," Myrtle said. "I'm sure you could pick one up in your travels. It sounds like you have a lovely holiday planned. What islands are you visiting?"

Lucy shook her head. "Oh, it's not a holiday. It's my job. I work for Amelia Cartell. She writes the big travel blog, *Impress—*"

"*Impressions.* Yes. I've heard of it." Myrtle's voice had cooled, and Holly looked up in surprise from where she was helping Jamie unpack containers of pastries.

Lucy snapped a few close-ups of the table decorations, then stepped back, typing something into her phone. "I'll get some more photos this evening." With one last wistful glance at the flowers, Lucy raised her head to scan the garden. "I was actually looking for Ms. Cartell. She was supposed to be back by now so we could put something together about the gardens we've visited so far. She told me to meet her in the breakfast room, but she's not there."

Myrtle sniffed. "I'm afraid I can't help you with that."

Noticing a number of volunteers had paused to listen, Myrtle frowned, then clapped her hands briskly. "Back to work, ladies!" She produced a small smile for Lucy. "If you'll excuse me, dear, I must get on. We have a lot to do before all our guests start arriving at six."

"Oh yes, of course. I'm sorry." Lucy wandered out of the tent.

Myrtle sniffed again and hustled across the pavilion to regain her command of the decorating corps.

8

By seven thirty that evening, the Hibiscus Inn was buzzing with laughter, conversation, and music. Islanders and Inn guests alike nibbled on finger foods, sipped at their drinks, and talked plants, plants, and more plants.

The Hibiscus Island Garden Club had set up a display board with a map of the island, detailing all the gardens open to visitors in this year's Festival. There were also small glossy programs available for people to take home. Holly picked up one of these and noticed that, although many private gardens were opening their gates to the public, the Garden Club was particularly pleased to have finally convinced Sir James Murray, a retired judge, to re-open his garden. Sir James, Holly remembered, had a magnificent bonsai collection, among which he included several bougainvillea varieties.

Holly noted the usual horticultural lectures about the ornamental shrub, a propagation seminar to demonstrate the art of taking cuttings, and the very popular culinary evening where participants could learn how to use the edible papery flower bracts in drinks and food. The Bougainvillea Festival stretched out over the week, culminating with a Bougainvillea Banquet on the last night.

Closing the brochure, Holly glanced around the party. Behind the buffet table, Jamie, attired in a tall chef's hat and white apron, sparkled with energy as she helped the guests to plates of food. Red glittery earrings swung from her ears, catching the light as she rotated her head this way and that, laughing and talking.

In another corner of the tent, Gramps huddled with Uncle Stanley. The two elderly men looked around furtively and then ambled towards the exit with a false casualness. Holly grinned, knowing that they were heading to Gramps's cottage, to indulge in a glass of Scotch and boast about their anticipated winning entries in the Bougainvillea Exhibit.

Maggie, Aunt Laura, and Uncle Phil were chatting with Mr. and Mrs. Sullivan on the far side of the tent, while next to them, Myrtle gestured at a bowl of bougainvillea and talked animatedly to Lucy Robinson, who was taking notes on her phone.

At another table, Amelia Cartell sipped at a glass of wine and sneered at Bob Schafer. Bob's face flushed. He got to his feet abruptly and walked away. Amelia watched him go, then tossed back the rest of her wine and stood up herself, staggering slightly. Pete, hovering nearby, grasped her arm to steady her, earning himself a snarl as Amelia jerked out of his reach.

"Hey, Holly!" Matt's voice drew Holly's attention away from the travel critic. "Let's grab some food. Myrtle's going to start moving everyone out in about an hour so we can set up for the Flower Show, so let's take a break while we can!"

~

HOURS LATER, Holly looked around the rearranged tent and nodded in approval. The white cloths and decorations had been replaced with utilitarian green table coverings and row upon row of plastic green vases, ready to receive the cut flower entries in the morning.

Along with the rest of the Hibiscus Inn crew and the Hibiscus Island Garden Club, Holly would be up early, processing flower entries, attaching tags, and ensuring everything was ready for the first judging at ten. The Flower Show had begun as a display of bougainvillea only, but had morphed into an "anything goes" floral extravaganza that was very popular with islanders and visitors. There was now a separate Bougainvillea Exhibit for the serious fanciers, which would be judged at twelve noon. Bougainvillea competitors had been hard at work since Thursday, setting up their displays.

"It all looks good, Holly," Maggie said, coming to stand beside her daughter. "Let's call it a day. I'm exhausted." On cue, she yawned.

"Me too," Holly agreed.

Arms linked, the two women left the terrace and headed up the steps towards the Inn.

Voices caught Holly's attention as they passed the swimming pool, and Holly glanced over the low stone wall surrounding the pool patio. Lucy Robinson sat hunched over in a deck chair; Pete Hartford turned away from the young woman, exasperation radiating from him.

"Lucy, we've had this conversation over and over," he said. "Nothing's going to change unless you—" Catching sight of Holly, Pete stopped abruptly before nodding curtly at her.

Holly gave a little wave and followed her mother into the Inn.

~

THE FIRST EXHIBITORS arrived at seven on the dot on Saturday morning. Holly was kept busy tagging and arranging entries until the judges arrived at nine thirty, at which point she moved down to the Bougainvillea Exhibit.

"Stuart!" Myrtle put her hands on her hips. "Leave those flowers alone. I'm sure your expertise could be better used at the slat house." She rounded on Sir James Murray and Uncle Stanley. "And that goes for you two as well. You're like a bunch of old women, fussing with your babies."

Gramps's face reddened, Uncle Stanley looked sheepish, and Sir James gave the Garden Club president a withering glance.

A large lady in a bright red suit with an enormous hat perched on top of her white sausage-shaped curls, peered across the tent from where she was sorting a pile of paper. "You men, get out right now or I'll disqualify all of you."

"You can't do that, Elma," Uncle Stanley protested. "You're not a judge. And I just need to tweak this a tiny bit more..." His voice trailed away as his wife got to her feet and put her hands firmly on her ample hips.

All three men cringed.

"I'll be on my way," Sir James said quickly. The retired judge picked up his lightweight jacket and placed his straw hat on his head. He tipped it politely towards the women. "Myrtle. Elma." Sir James exited with dignity.

Uncle Stanley sighed. "Come on, Stuart. There's nothing more we can do now." He looked sideways at his friend. "At least—not until after the judging when you can congratulate me on my victory."

Gramps's mulish expression faded as he scoffed. "My victory, you mean," he corrected, looking fondly at his small, cascading Blueberry Ice entry. "Look at this beauty! Variegated leaves, gorgeous color. It's stunning. Guaranteed to win the trophy."

"Ha! It doesn't even begin to compare to my Gold Rush," Uncle Stanley began.

"Out, I said! Go talk about your flowers somewhere else!" Interrupting her husband, Elma Foster gestured sternly towards the exit and the two elderly men moved out, still vigorously debating the merits of their respective plants.

"It's the same thing every year," Myrtle said, shaking her head. "They're like children."

Elma caught sight of Holly and her face lit up. "Holly child! Come and give me a hug!" She enveloped Holly in her arms. "How have you been? Have you got a young man yet? Did Uncle Stanley tell you about that grandson of ours? Maybe you can talk to him, Holly. He might listen to someone closer to his age. Taking a year off indeed! I swear I just don't understand young people today!"

Holly wriggled out of Elma's embrace, grinning. "It's lovely to see you again, Auntie Elma."

Elma beamed and stroked Holly's hair. "Come for tea next Sunday," she ordered, before turning back to the table full of paper. "Now, come and help me with these things. You know what will happen if we mix up anything!" She rolled her eyes with an expressive sigh.

There was a small but dedicated Bougainvillea Fanciers club on the island and each of its members, along with other assorted representatives of the community, had entered an exhibit.

Each exhibitor was given a three-sided plywood booth with an area of about twenty-five square feet. Only one variety of bougainvillea was allowed in each exhibit and the plants had to be in pots, but competitors could choose how to arrange their displays. Most of them prepped in advance, and the minute the tent had been set up on Thursday, they had moved in, knowing no one else would be allowed in until the day of the show. Now Holly looked around in admiration.

The results were varied, creative, and fanciful. Mr. Sullivan's *Study in White* featured a tiny paved courtyard, complete with a miniature fountain and stone wall. A stunning White Stripe bougainvillea climbed up the wall from a large square white ceramic pot, while two smaller specimens cascaded out of short, white urns.

Gramps had constructed a ruined gray stone stairway and arranged his dwarf Blueberry Ice bougainvillea on the steps. The pale lilac flowers tumbled down, creating the impression of a turbulent river gorge from a world of fantasy. Holly inspected the display intently and grinned when she finally spotted elven runes carved into the stone. Gramps, an ardent fan of Tolkien, always found a way to incorporate something from Middle Earth into his bougainvillea display. It was an expected tradition now with many visitors enjoying the hunt for the reference.

Holly gasped when she saw Sir James's entry. The retired judge had built a Japanese garden in miniature within his display area. Raked gravel covered the floor, interspersed with large, smooth boulders. A *trompe l'oeil* painting of a Japanese pergola created the perfect background for the two bonsais forming the focal point of the exhibit. The small trees were brilliant with fuchsia blossoms, and the whole effect was magical. The name of the exhibit was so perfect, Holly grinned: *And Zen There Was Bonsai.*

Uncle Stanley had used the name of *his* bougainvillea both as inspiration and the title of his exhibit, and Holly exclaimed with delight at the picturesque effect of the Gold

Rush bougainvillea sprawling over the rock face behind a gold miner's camp.

"It's fantastic! Look at that plant," she marveled as Auntie Elma approached. "I love the pickaxes too! Great touch."

Elma pursed her lips. "It's not bad," she admitted. "Stanley got some of those faux stone panels to create the effect."

"It's really good." Holly took a step back, surveying the tent. "I don't envy the judges this year. It's going to be a tough decision."

"And they'll be here before we know it, so let's get hopping. I'm going to leave you with the write-ups to go on the display boards, Holly. You know all the different varieties and won't get them mixed up! No need to do the *Study in White* display, though. Carolyn Sullivan was fussing about all yesterday afternoon doing that one." Elma shook her head. "That woman! I swear she just can't leave the display alone. Here at all hours. And Sir James has already done his as well, I believe. Myrtle and I will finish the main information board at the front."

Pausing, Elma looked around the tent and shook her head. "All this color and it's not even from the flowers. Visitors are always astonished when they learn that."

"The flowers are sort of insignificant," Holly agreed. "Personally, I'm not a huge fan of bougainvillea, but I have to admit, when you see them all on display like this, I can understand why people get obsessed. They're quite spectacular. I'll get the boards done as quick as I can, Auntie Elma."

At eleven forty-five, the judges arrived and Holly left the tent to wander back up to the Inn. The general public would be allowed in at noon and Holly had promised to help man the refreshment tables that were set up around the pool.

When they arrived, visitors would be able to tour the grounds of the Inn, purchase plants from the Garden Center stalls down at the slat house, and of course, visit the Flower Show and the Bougainvillea Exhibit.

Lucy Robinson was just exiting the flower tent, phone in hand, when Holly passed. "Oh, Holly," she called. "You haven't seen Ms. Cartell, have you?"

"No. But I've been in the Bougainvillea Exhibit since about ten, so I haven't really seen anyone."

Lucy looked worried. "I don't know where she is. We were supposed to meet at ten, but I haven't seen her all morning and no one else has either."

"I'm sure she's somewhere about," Holly soothed, wondering why Lucy was so bothered. "Maybe she just went for a walk along the trails."

"Yes, but I haven't seen her since last—" Lucy stopped short and forced a smile. "Never mind. I'm sure you're right. Oh, there's Pete." Pete veered towards them as she waved.

"No, I haven't found her!" He sounded exasperated. "What's the point in hiring me to protect her if she keeps disappearing. I'm done with this, Lucy! Come on. I want a drink."

He dragged a protesting Lucy up the hill, leaving Holly staring after them in surprise. When they were out of sight, she glanced at her watch and gave a yelp. Twelve o'clock. Holly took off at a run.

The first wave of visitors surged into the gardens five minutes later. Excitedly, they headed for the flower tent and spread out into the grounds, exclaiming over the perennial borders and snapping photos of themselves and various plants they particularly admired.

At twelve thirty-five, screams rang out.

9

Holly peered over the stone balustrade and gave a huff of frustration. "When do you think they'll get to us?"

Taking a sip of her drink, Jamie shrugged. Truffle snuggled on her lap and Jamie stroked the little cavapoo gently. "No idea. Who's left?"

"It looks like it's just a few of the Garden Club people now. Everyone else has been sent home." Holly sat down with a thump beside her friend. "I can't believe this has happened!"

"You've said that before," Jamie reminded her.

"Yes, I know! But we've never had anything like this at the Inn! Never!"

Jamie took another sip of her drink and then opened her mouth.

Holly glared at her. "Don't say it again," she warned.

"I have to," Jamie retorted. "If I say it enough times, maybe you'll actually listen to me!"

Holly eyed her friend in exasperation and slumped back on her chair, knowing what was coming.

"Look Holls, the Cartell woman travels—traveled—with

a security guy! There has to be a reason for that. She must have had enemies! She probably enraged people wherever she went!" Jamie widened her eyes at Holly. "Maybe she *didn't* fall! Maybe Amelia Cartell was murdered!"

Holly rolled her eyes. "She was not!" She looked at the eager face in front of her and groaned. "You just want to play detective and I'm telling you right now, Jamie, that I am not getting involved!"

"Oh, come on, Holls. Don't be so stuffy! Didn't you notice anything when you saw the body?"

Holly stared at her in silence for a moment and then heaved an enormous sigh. "I just know I'm going to regret this," she muttered, before taking a deep breath. "I didn't see the body, Jamie. Miss Greenley was moaning and screeching all over the place; Mrs. Sullivan was just standing there staring; Myrtle was poking around under the tree; and then Lucy appeared and had hysterics. Gramps came rushing up and Myrtle took over completely."

"Of course she did!" Jamie rolled her eyes.

"And I brought Lucy and the other women back up here, so I wasn't there when the police arrived."

"Well, we can always ask Mr. Mack what happened when they got there," Jamie said, her eyes gleaming.

"And also," Holly paused, reluctance in her tone, "the body was completely—"

A new voice intervened before Holly could finish her sentence.

"Good afternoon. Thank you for waiting so patiently, ladies and gentlemen. We'll just get your statements and then you'll be free to leave this area." The speaker looked at Holly's mother with a smile. "Maggie, could I start with you? Perhaps inside the breakfast room, if you don't mind?"

"Yes of course." Maggie gave him a small smile and walked inside.

Holly gaped after them. "Who was that?"

Jamie waggled her eyebrows. "That was Rob Tucker, the new Inspector on Hibiscus Island! Pretty good-looking, isn't he?"

"Inspector?" Holly asked. "But what happened to Sergeant Hollis? I thought he was supposed to take over after Dad—" She stopped.

"Hollis didn't want the promotion. He subbed in while they were interviewing candidates, but Rob Tucker's been here for about four months now. Your mom didn't tell you?"

"No."

All hint of theatrics abandoned, Jamie looked at her friend with a serious expression. "Someone had to do the job, Holly. And Rob's a decent enough guy."

"I know. I know. It's just—" Holly took a deep breath. "It feels weird."

"That's because you haven't been here for quite a while." Jamie held up her hands. "I'm not criticizing! I get why you needed some time away." She sighed at the look on her friend's face. "Look, Holly, we all miss your dad. Uncle Solid was awesome, but he's been gone for two years now, and Sergeant Hollis didn't want the job. Just give Rob a chance, will you?"

"Of course I'll give him a chance," Holly said, still frowning. "Why would you think I wouldn't?"

Jamie raised an eyebrow. "Well," she drawled, "partly because of the look on your face right now. You're already blaming the poor man for taking your dad's job!"

"I am not!" Holly protested. Jamie just looked at her and Holly flushed. "I'm not! I know it's not his fault. I'm not unfair, Jamie."

"No, just sort of... protective of Uncle Solid. And you don't need to be."

Sudden tears pricked Holly's eyes. After a moment of silence, she sighed heavily and muttered, "I hate it when you do your psychic thing."

Jamie grinned even as she gave Holly a sympathetic pat. "My witchy powers know no bounds." She leaned back in her recliner, cuddling Truffle to her. After a moment, she changed the subject. "Why do you think he's taking statements anyway? Is that normal procedure? For someone who 'fell' over a wall?"

Holly shrugged.

"Don't be huffy, Holls," Jamie chided, grinning at the glare her friend sent her way. She pondered for a moment more and then her eyes lit up. "Maybe they *did* find something suspicious at the scene!"

"Why don't you ask Myrtle?" Holly suggested, a touch of malice edging her voice.

"Good idea!" Jamie exclaimed, then laughed outright at the expression on Holly's face. "Come on, Holls. Snap out of it! You know you're curious too! Just admit it."

Holly looked at her friend's twinkling eyes, heaved a huge sigh, and produced a tiny smile. "She's over there," she said, directing Jamie's attention to the far end of the pool, where Myrtle had Gramps corralled. His face was slowly reddening as she waved her finger at him.

Jamie grinned as she put Truffle on the ground and stood up. "Mr. Mack looks like he need rescuing. Come on."

As the young women approached, Myrtle's voice rose in irritation.

"Stuart! Stop arguing with me. I'm telling you there was California Gold on top of the woman. Do you think I don't know my plants? Me? The president of the Garden Club?"

She held up a warning finger as Gramps opened his mouth. "Don't say it again. I know what I saw!"

"What's California Gold?" Jamie asked, dropping down on a deck chair beside Myrtle. "And why's it important?"

Holly frowned. "It's a bougainvillea variety," she said slowly. "Are you sure, Myrtle? I assumed those branches had broken off when Ms. Cartell fell."

Myrtle shook her head. "No, Holly, they didn't. There was no damage to that tree at all. And there were pieces of Ruby and Bridal Bouquet on the scene as well." She glared at Gramps. "Besides, as I was saying to Stuart, that wall is only fifteen feet high, and if she'd fallen, the bougainvillea would have slowed her fall. She might have broken a bone, but she wouldn't have died!"

Jamie latched onto Myrtle's statement and sat up in excitement. "*If* she'd fallen! So, you don't think it was an accident either!"

Myrtle nodded with self-importance. "I certainly do not. It was obviously murder!"

"Absolute rubbish!" The words exploded out of Gramps's mouth. "You've been watching too many of those murder mystery television shows, Myrtle. The woman fell over the wall, landed wrong, and broke her neck."

"Oh honestly, Stuart!" Myrtle looked disgusted. "You saw how she was lying. Did that look like a fall to you?"

"What do you mean?" Jamie asked eagerly. "Was there something suspicious about the way she landed?"

"Very suspicious! She was flat on her back, like she was lying in bed. Nobody lands like that in a fall! But more importantly, she was completely covered in branches. Every part of her. The body was placed there. Someone was trying to hide her!"

Jamie's mouth dropped open and she turned towards Holly. "She was *hidden*?"

"I was about to tell you," Holly protested.

Myrtle carried on. "It was definitely murder. And not really surprising, all things considered."

"Oh, come now, Myrtle," Gramps began, only to be cut off.

"Don't 'come now' me, Stuart! I remember that woman very well, thank you. I knew her as soon as I set eyes on her this week. And she knew me too, I can tell you that. As unpleasant as she ever was! The wonder is that no one murdered her long before this!"

"Wait! What?" Jamie exclaimed in surprise.

Holly gaped at Myrtle. "You knew her? You knew Amelia Cartell? But how? I thought this was her first visit to the island!"

Myrtle snorted. "It certainly was not! She worked on the island for five years as Emily Carter. Ridiculous name change, but that's Emily for you. She left, oh, about ten years ago now." She looked at Gramps. "Isn't that right, Stuart? You recognized her as well, didn't you?"

Gramps nodded reluctantly. "Not immediately. She's changed."

"She's put on weight," Myrtle said, "and dyed her hair, and I'm sure she's had work done on her face. But she was the same nasty, insinuating Emily!"

Weak with shock, Holly sat down. "But I sat beside her on the plane from the mainland, and I swear, she never once suggested that she'd been here before! She asked endless questions about the island. Why would she do that?"

"I don't remember her at all." Jamie eyed Myrtle with fascination. "Was she really that awful?"

"Well, you two would have been in your teens when she

left," the older woman said. "Totally wrapped up in yourselves and your own lives. It's hardly surprising you don't remember. And yes, she was a very unpleasant woman. Always interfering in everyone else's business."

Holly's lips twitched and she looked away hastily.

"Regardless," Myrtle continued, "the woman lied about being on Hibiscus Island before. She was found dead at the bottom of a wall, hidden under bougainvillea branches which didn't belong to the one she supposedly fell through—"

"And she had a personal bodyguard—which suggests she needed protection from something!" Jamie interrupted.

"Yes. So, as I said," Myrtle continued, frowning at Jamie, "it's clearly murder, and—"

"Totally!" Jamie exclaimed. "I mean, it's disturbing and all that but it's kind of exciting too! Now, Holly and I will—"

"Oh no!" Holly cut her off as Myrtle stiffened indignantly. "Don't even go there! We're not doing anything! If it is a suspicious death, then this is a matter for the police. All we have to do is tell the police everything we know and stay out of their way. It's not our job to solve crimes!"

Jamie's mouth dropped open. "Who are you? And what have you done with the real Holly Gold?" She stared at Holly pleadingly. "Oh, come on, Holls, we're good at this sort of thing! Remember when we caught Jenny Parkinson stealing from the lockers at school? And the time we figured out who took the birdbath from old man Sanders' lawn, and the time when we—"

"We were kids, Jamie!" Holly interrupted in exasperation. "And those were just small things. This is totally different. We can't interfere in a police investigation."

"I think—" Myrtle began, before she was cut off by an indignant Jamie.

"Well, I wouldn't exactly call it interference. More like... helping!"

Gramps guffawed. "Is that what you call it? Thinking of resurrecting your detective club, eh, Jamie? What did you two call yourselves again?"

Jamie grinned at him. "The Hibiscus Island Detective Club, Mr. Mack. Not very original, I know. We'd just discovered Trixie Belden and wanted to be like her." She turned to Holly again. "Remember, Holls?"

Holly rolled her eyes, even as a small smile crossed her face. "We were ten," she reminded her friend.

"As *I* was saying!" Myrtle put her hands on her hips and glared at the young women.

Oblivious, Jamie carried on. "And remember when Aunt Laura did that golden age mystery book club? With a crime to solve? We solved the mystery first! Remember?"

Seeing Jamie's beam, Holly grinned despite herself. "Yes, but what's happened here is different, Jamie, and you know it."

Her friend's face fell.

"Well! If *I* may speak now," Myrtle said with a huff. Both girls looked at her in surprise.

"Ms. Collier!" A voice rang out from near the Inn.

"Oh, what now?" Myrtle exclaimed. "Who's that?"

"It's Sergeant Hollis," Jamie said. "It must be your turn to see the inspector, Myrtle."

"Ms. Collier! Could you come please?"

"Oh honestly. How many times have I told that man to call me 'Myrtle'! Yes, Derek, I see you. I'm coming." She brushed down her purple suit and patted her hair into place before turning her attention back to the young women. "Now Holly, you've been away on the mainland for a while so it's understandable that you may have forgotten how it works here." She ignored Holly's look of indignation. "Inspector Tucker—Rob—is very new to our island and he's going to need all the assistance he can get. It is no more than our duty as concerned citizens to help him." Gramps snorted and Myrtle leveled a glare at him. "I'll explain this to Rob, and then we'll sit down and compare notes."

Holly gaped in disbelief at the older woman's retreating back. "What did she just say?"

Gramps snorted again as he got to his feet. "Been like this for fifty years. No changing her now. Nosy. That's what Myrtle is." With an abrupt nod, he strode off.

Holly looked wildly at Jamie.

Jamie choked. "Oh Holls," she chortled. "Your face!" She went off into peals of laughter.

10

"Ah, Miss Gold. Come in." The young man sitting at one of the breakfast room tables stood up and held out his hand, giving Holly a warm smile. "Rob Tucker. I just need a quick statement from you about this incident."

As he busied himself with a piece of paper, Holly looked at him curiously. Inspector Rob Tucker was six feet tall or so and solidly muscled. He had short dark hair, dark brown skin, was casually dressed in khaki trousers and a blue golf shirt, and, judging by his accent, had spent some time in England. A golf cap rested on the table beside him, leading Holly to wonder if he'd been on the golf course when he got the call about the accident.

Inspector Tucker looked up and caught her looking at the cap. "I was on the fourteenth green," he offered with a grin. "Normally I'd be dressed a little more formally for an occasion like this but... Well, as a policeman's daughter, you know how it is, I'm sure." He smiled at Holly's surprised expression. "I've heard a lot about Solid Gold since I arrived. He sounds like he was a great guy."

"He was," Holly said with a smile of her own. "So, what

do you want to know, Inspector? I'm not sure I'll be much use. I didn't see Ms. Cartell at all today, until I heard the screams and went to find out what had happened."

"When's the last time you did see her?" Rob asked.

Holly thought back. "It must have been last night. At the opening dinner. I saw her sitting with Mr. Schafer at one point and then she left."

Rob made a note. "Did you see her leave the tent?"

"No. I remember thinking she might have had a little too much to drink, though. She was a bit wobbly on her feet, but I think Pete would have helped her if she needed it. He's her security guy." She narrowed her eyes at the inspector. "Are you thinking it wasn't an accident? Is that why you're taking statements?"

"We take statements at accidents all the time," Rob replied without looking up from his notes.

Holly frowned. "Witness statements," she pointed out. "I didn't witness anything."

"You said you heard screams," Rob began, ignoring her comment. "What time was that?... Twelve thirty-five? Thank you. And you ran to where they were coming from. How did you know where to go? Where were you at that time?"

"I was up at the top, helping with the refreshments. You can see quite a lot of the garden from there. When I heard the screaming, I looked over the wall—that one,"—Holly gestured out the window—"and I could see two people down on the fifth level staring at something. I couldn't see what it was, so I went down."

"And you got there at...? Twelve thirty-nine? That's very precise."

"I looked at my watch," Holly said shortly.

"And can you tell me what you saw when you arrived at the scene?" Rob leaned back in his chair and gazed at her.

"Miss Greenley and Mrs. Sullivan were standing near the wall..."

"You know them?"

"Oh yes. I've known them for years. Miss Greenley owns Tiny Treasures, a store downtown, and Mrs. Sullivan used to work in the bank. Anyway, Mrs. Sullivan seemed shocked, and Miss Greenley was having complete hysterics." Holly took a breath. "Ms. Cartell was lying underneath the bougainvillea tree with branches covering her. Gramps and Myrtle were there too. Myrtle used to be a nurse before she retired so she had gone to check for a pulse, I guess. I was just about to go over when Lucy arrived and was... upset... so Myrtle told me she would wait for the EMTs. Gramps had called them, so he stayed with Myrtle while I took the other women back up to the Inn."

"Very concise," Rob said, scribbling furiously. "Tell me something—how did you know it was Amelia Cartell?"

"What do you mean, how did I know?" Holly asked, frowning.

"The body was entirely covered in vegetation. When we arrived, her face was visible, but that was because Ms. Collier had uncovered it. You said you didn't go near the body, so how did you know who it was?"

Holly blinked and thought back. She hadn't seen Amelia's face at the time, she realized. "Well, someone said it, I think. I don't remember who... Oh—and I recognized the shoe. She had these very glittery, high-heeled sandals that went with the gold suit she was wearing. One was visible." Holly blinked again in startled realization. "That was what she was wearing at the opening dinner! But... but that must mean she died last night!"

Rob leaned back and fiddled with his pen. "I've been

told you're a horticulturist, Miss Gold, so I'm guessing you know something about bougainvillea."

Holly nodded. "Some. My Gramps is the expert though."

"What variety is planted on the wall where Ms. Cartell was found?"

"It's a pink James Walker," Holly replied. "It's about twenty years old and has been trained as a tree so that the canopy reaches the top of the wall. It's really meant to be viewed from above."

"James Walker, huh?" Rob consulted his notes. "Ms. Collier tells me most of the vegetation on the victim's body was of a bougainvillea variety called California Gold. Is that correct?"

"There is a variety called that, but I didn't notice whether those were the branches on top of Ms. Cartell. I didn't look closely enough."

"Ms. Collier also mentioned two other varieties—Bridal Bouquet and Ruby. Would you say she is an expert on bougainvillea?"

Holly nodded again. "She's the president of the Garden Club. She knows her plants very well."

"Where do these plants grow on the property?"

"The California Gold is up on the first level, by the Inn. There are a couple of Bridal bushes up at the top as well, but the Rubies are mostly on the middle levels. Why?"

"Were they recently pruned?" Rob asked.

"Yes," Holly said warily. "We had to, because Ms. Cartell cut some the first day she got here. She wanted flowers for her room. Unfortunately, she helped herself to all the flowering branches at the worst possible time. We had to tidy the bushes after she hacked them, and the branches went to the slat house. We were going to take cuttings."

"Ah yes," Rob said, flipping back through his notes. "I

heard there was a fight about that. Mr. Stuart Mackintosh accused Ms. Cartell of 'butchering his bougainvillea' and called her a 'saboteur.' I understand it was quite a heated argument and that Mr. Mackintosh threatened violence if he saw Ms. Cartell in his gardens again."

Holly stiffened in outrage, glaring at Rob. "Who told you that? There was a bit of an altercation, but it wasn't a fight, and he didn't threaten violence!" Her voice rose. "My Gramps had *nothing* to do with her death! He's very proud of his gardens and it was infuriating to have bougainvillea chopped to pieces three days before the Festival—but Gramps would never hurt anyone! Never! You can ask anyone on the island, and they'll tell you the same thing!"

Rob raised an eyebrow and met her angry look calmly. "Your opinion is duly noted. Who had access to the slat house?"

"Practically anyone," Holly snapped. "Half of the island has been at the Inn this week and we don't lock the place."

"I thought Mr. Mackintosh had quite a valuable collection of plants. He doesn't secure them?"

Holly scoffed. "No one would steal them. We've never locked the slat house. This is Hibiscus Island. It's perfectly safe."

"Not that safe, it appears," Rob murmured. "Well, Miss Gold, I think we're about done. One more question and I'll let you go. Can you think of anyone else who might have had a reason to dislike Ms. Cartell?"

"Anyone *else*?" Holly scowled furiously at Rob. "Look, I didn't know the woman but since she had a bodyguard, I'd be willing to bet there were plenty of people who didn't like her! With far more reason than my Gramps, let me tell you!"

"But you don't know of anyone personally," Rob interrupted. He stood up. "Anything else you want to tell me, Miss Gold? No? Then, thank you for your time."

He returned Holly's fulminating glare with a neutral expression and raised eyebrow. Muttering under her breath, she left the room.

Jamie's eyes widened as Holly stormed towards her. "What happened?"

"What happened," Holly snapped, "is that our new inspector has Gramps as his prime suspect! I take back everything I said, Jamie. We have to figure out what happened to Amelia Cartell!"

"OH BOY, oh boy, oh boy! This is going to be so much fun!" Jamie rubbed her hands together with glee as she trotted into Holly's apartment. "Where shall we set up?"

"Set up what?" Holly asked, stalking past her and flicking the kettle on. Fuming, she slammed the mugs onto the counter with more force than she'd intended. "I can't believe that guy! The nerve! Thinking that Gramps killed someone!"

"Did Rob actually say that Mr. Mack was a suspect?" Jamie asked, flopping into an armchair. "I'm kind of surprised. He's such a 'by the book' type of guy. I didn't think he'd share information. He certainly didn't tell me anything!"

"He didn't need to spell it out!" Holly snapped. "He said he'd heard Gramps threatened violence and then he asked a ton of questions about those bougainvillea branches. It's obvious what he's thinking! Smug, obnoxious man!"

Jamie's eyebrows shot up, but she didn't say anything.

Holly turned around. "Gramps put those chopped

branches in the slat house, Jamie. I saw them there. He had the California Gold, the Bridal Bouquet and the Ruby all in buckets." She shook her head. "He had to go and properly prune them after Amelia hacked them, so there was a huge pile! Someone had to have taken them out and deliberately put them on top of the body. But *why*? Why try to hide the body?"

Accepting a cup of tea from her friend, Jamie pointed to the armchair opposite her. "Sit," she ordered. "Drink. Relax. We'll figure it out. We need one of those whiteboard or flipchart things. You know, so that we can pin everything up on it."

Holly rolled her eyes. "Seriously?"

"Of course," Jamie retorted. "We have to do this right!" She grinned at Holly and wiggled a finger at her mug. "Do you have any cookies to go with this? Sugar helps me think."

MUCH LATER, Holly sat back with a huge sigh, despondently surveying the pile of paper on the table in front of her. "You're right. We need a whiteboard. This is a mess."

Jamie grinned as she popped another piece of short-bread into her mouth. "I have one at the café. Up in Teddy's room. I can bring it here if you want." She leaned forward and started shuffling papers. "What have we got? Victim—everything we know about her already and what we have to find out. We definitely need to find out about her past life on the island. Maybe she had enemies from ages ago. Myrtle didn't like her, that's for sure. Timeline—well, we need to fill this in more, so that means we have to find out what Amelia was doing yesterday and where our suspects were between last night and twelve thirty today. Suspects—" She held up the blank piece of paper and looked at Holly questioningly.

Holly shrugged. "We don't know when she died, and we can't do a list until we know that. There were so many people here last night, it could be anyone!"

"True," Jamie mused. "We'll need to find out a time of death somehow. Hmmm. I wonder who would tell us that..."

"This could all be a waste of time anyway," Holly said with a sigh, leaning back in her chair. She stared at the mess of paper and groaned. "What on earth are we doing? We don't even know if she really was murdered! Maybe I just overreacted."

"Oh, she was totally murdered," Jamie responded immediately. "Rob asked way too many questions for it to be just an accident. And there's those suspicious bougainvillea branches covering her. As much as it pains me to admit this... we're going to need to talk to Myrtle. She always comes into the Bean for Sunday coffee so we can see her tomorrow."

Holly raised an eyebrow and Jamie groaned. "I know, I know. It's going to kill me, but you know what she's like. She's probably cross-examining people even as we speak. I'll bet she's already got inside information!" Jamie scowled at the thought. "She really thinks she's Miss Marple!"

Holly grinned despite herself. "And what about us? Who are we? Trixie Belden and Nancy Drew?"

Jamie looked at her in mock amazement. "Oh please. We don't need to be fictional characters! We're the Hibiscus Island Detective Club, of course!" She grinned. "And we'll call this case 'The Bougainvillea Incident'."

11

The Hibiscus Island Detective Club stood just outside the yellow caution tape, surveying the crime scene.

"Huh," Jamie said. "I see what Myrtle meant. It's really not a high fall at all, is it? And if you look at the tree, it's not even damaged! How come you didn't notice that, Holls?"

"That would be because I had two hysterical women to deal with. Lucy and Miss Greenley went to pieces! I was a bit distracted!"

Jamie prowled around outside the tape. "So, the body was right back under the tree? Parallel to the wall? And all you could see was a shoe when you arrived?" Jamie fingered her lip and looked around. "Why would someone think this was a good place to hide a body, when they knew there'd be visitors all over the place? Why would they choose this spot?"

Holly considered the question. "Well, this isn't a showy part of the garden. It's really a cart path to the slat house, so it's not marked on the garden tour program that we give out for the Festival. The slat house is just around that corner,"— she gestured down the hill—"and the path continues past it to the compost heap. It's quite a good place actually because no one would really be coming this way on the tour."

She paused, then frowned. "*My* question is, why was she down here at night?" Holly put her hands on her hips and glared at the scene. "And why hide the body at all? Why didn't the killer—if she *was* killed—just leave her where she died?"

Jamie considered this. "Good points. Could she have been poking around the Garden Club tables?"

"I don't know why she'd be down here if that was the case. Remember, the whole property is terraced. This is the fifth level, but the slat house sort of straddles this one and the next terrace up. We have the misting units and cuttings on this level, and keep all the potted plants on the fourth level. The slat house is really two slat houses, one on top of the other. The Garden Club tables are set up outside the top slat house. Up there." She pointed.

"Yeah, but she could have been moved here."

"That's just bizarre, Jamie! Why would anyone move a body?"

"No, hear me out. Maybe the murderer panicked," Jamie suggested. "He killed Amelia and then realized that where she died would draw attention to him."

"Why would her dying near the slat house draw attention to—" Holly's eyes narrowed. "Hey, hang on. You're not suggesting Gramps had anything to do with this, are you?"

"What? No, of course not!" Jamie replied indignantly. "Mr. Mack wouldn't hurt a fly! I just said that Amelia could have been moved here from anywhere. Like... like the Bougainvillea Exhibit, for instance."

"Why would she have been in there?"

"I don't know that she was," Jamie sighed. "I'm just making suggestions."

Holly rolled her eyes.

"Anyway," Jamie continued, "we can't do much else until we know *how* Amelia died. What are you doing tomorrow, Holls? Shall we meet at the café in the morning and see what Myrtle's found out? In a subtle way of course!"

～

THE NEXT MORNING, Holly took her bicycle out of storage and pedaled the two miles into Bridgeport. She pulled up outside the Bean, flushed and out of breath.

"What on earth are you doing?" Jamie exclaimed. "Are you crazy? Cycling at this time of the year? You'll pass out from heat stroke! Here, sit down. I'll get you a drink." Shaking her head at Holly's foolishness, Jamie went behind the counter and started to put together a smoothie.

Holly fanned herself vigorously with a menu, looking around the café. Myrtle hadn't arrived yet, she noted. She smiled at old man Sanders, sitting at a corner table, and waved to François through the serving hatch.

Sliding into the seat across from Holly, Jamie pushed a glass towards her. "Try it. It's mango, peach, banana, and ginger."

Holly took a grateful sip just as Myrtle trotted into the café. She spied the two girls and made a beeline for their table.

"Oh good. You're both here. I've found out some very interesting information," she said, plopping down heavily in the chair beside Holly. She adjusted her fuchsia pink suit jacket, then looked at Jamie. "I'll have a latte instead of coffee this morning, Jamie. And a muffin. I've been to early church and haven't had breakfast yet. Hurry back with it so we can begin." She eyed Holly's smoothie askance. "What *is* that concoction, Holly? And was that your bicycle I saw outside? My dear, surely you know better than to cycle in this heat!"

Jamie rolled her eyes behind Myrtle's back but went to put the order in before returning in a rush, cutting off Holly's feeble attempts to explain her bicycle. "What have you found out, Myrtle? Do you know how she died? Do they really think it was murder?"

So much for subtlety, Holly thought with a grin, watching Myrtle preen.

After a quick glance around, the older woman leaned forward and beckoned the girls closer. Holly smothered an involuntary choke of laughter as Myrtle swept the café with another suspicious look, before whispering, "She was poisoned."

"Poisoned?" Jamie squawked and was vigorously hushed by Myrtle. "With what? How? When? And how'd you find out?"

"My source told me," Myrtle replied, looking very pleased with herself.

"Your *source*? You have a source? Who is it?" Jamie was agog with curiosity.

"Well really, Jamie, naturally I can't divulge any names," Myrtle replied in shocked tones. "I was given the information in confidence."

"Okay, fine. What did you find out?" Jamie rolled her eyes dramatically.

Myrtle frowned, sending a pointed glance at the counter of the café. "I think my order's ready."

Jamie huffed in annoyance but stood up to collect the latte and three blueberry muffins. Depositing them briskly on the table, she pointed out the gluten-free muffin to Holly and sat down again, turning to Myrtle. "Well? What did your source say?"

Myrtle took a slow sip of her latte before relenting. "Emily Carter, aka Amelia Cartell, died of scopolamine poisoning." She sat back triumphantly.

"Scopo-what? What on earth's that?" Jamie asked, scowling slightly as she fumbled for her phone. "I've never heard of it. Let me check."

"It's a prescription medicine, isn't it?" Holly asked. "I think dad used it once for nausea."

Myrtle looked discomposed for a moment, but recovered quickly. "Yes, that's right, Holly. It comes in a patch—"

"—or can be given intravenously," Jamie interrupted, scrolling on her phone. "It says here it's used to treat nausea caused by motion sickness, anesthesia or chemotherapy. It's also used for depression, asthma, and to help people stop smoking. It says there's very little data on what constitutes a lethal dose. What a weird thing to poison someone with. I mean, seriously, what's wrong with plain old arsenic or strychnine?"

Myrtle looked at Jamie's phone with dislike. "According to my human source," she said with emphasis, "there was no patch on the victim. Scopolamine is available in tablet form for some conditions, but there was no evidence of a prescription among the woman's belongings. My source told me the police are treating this as murder."

Rolling her eyes at the continued use of the word 'source', Jamie tucked her phone away. "Did you get a time of death, Myrtle?"

"I did," Myrtle replied, cutting her muffin in two.

Jamie sucked in her breath in exasperation. "Well? What was it?"

"How'd you find out?" Holly asked at the same time. "Surely that's confidential."

Myrtle smirked. "Holly dear, I worked in the medical profession for years. I still have some connections you know!" She took a bite of her muffin, swallowed daintily, and leaned forward. "Emily Carter—Amelia Cartell—is believed to have died between ten at night and one in the morning, which means—"

"—she was poisoned last night at the Inn!" Jamie exclaimed.

"Not necessarily," Holly protested. "We don't know how the scopolamine was given to her, or how long it takes to have an effect."

Myrtle nodded. "That's very true, Holly. However, I happen to know the answers to those points as well." She sipped her drink. "The scopolamine was ingested. Emily—Amelia—what *shall* we call the wretched woman?... Amelia?... Oh, very well. Amelia took the poison by mouth and Doctor—I mean, my source believes, judging by the amount in her system, it took no more than four or five hours to take effect, which means she could have ingested the poison any time between five and ten." Myrtle looked sympathetic. "And that means..."

Holly sighed. "And that means Jamie's right. It's quite likely the murderer was someone at the opening event last night. That's a horrible thought!"

"But at least we have a concrete list of suspects now." Jamie looked at Myrtle. "People had to RSVP to the Garden Club, didn't they?"

Myrtle nodded. "They did. And I have the list here. I thought we could divide it up and each take a section." Head down, she rummaged through her large carry-all, missing the horrified look that Jamie shot towards Holly. "I can question the Garden Club members—" She looked up and her blue eyes narrowed. Her voice saccharine, she asked, "Is there a problem, Jamie?"

Holly tried not to grin as Jamie stopped mouthing frantic silent commands and jerked her head around to look at Myrtle.

"What?"

Myrtle tapped her fingers on the table to emphasize each word. "Is. There. A. Problem?"

"Uh... well... no," Jamie began. "It's just that... well, Holly and I were going to..." She took a deep breath, then started again more forcefully. "I just think it would be better if—"

"Stop stuttering, Jamie! Better if what?" Myrtle demanded. "I know all the Garden Club members, so it makes sense for me to question them as to their whereabouts; Holly is ideally situated to talk to her guests and anyone who was working on site at the Inn; and since most of the rest of the list, barring a few exceptions, frequent your café, it should be quite easy for you to find out information without having to take time off work. In my opinion, this is a sensible and efficient way to divide the labor. I suggest that we work on our lists over the next couple of days and rendezvous again with the information we have amassed. Say on Tuesday or Wednesday." She raised perfectly plucked eyebrows. "I thought you wanted to solve this crime. Was I mistaken?"

In desperation, Jamie looked at Holly, who gave an infinitesimal shrug of her shoulders while trying not to laugh.

"Oh, fine," Jamie muttered. She slumped down and held out a hand. "Where's my list?"

12

Holly moved her bike closer to the hibiscus hedge on the side of the hill to get out of the way of the vehicle coming up behind her.

"Holly Gold! What *are* you doing, child?"

As the small red van stopped alongside her, Holly pushed the hair off her face and looked up into Auntie Elma's appalled stare. The purple Sunday hat on her head bobbed vigorously above white corkscrew curls as Elma launched into speech.

"You get off that bicycle right now, do you hear? Have you no sense? Stanley, get the child's bicycle and put it in the back."

Uncle Stanley, also dressed in his Sunday finery, tutted at Holly, ignored her protestations and slung her bike into the back of the little red van.

Elma twisted around as Holly climbed into the crowded back seat. "Look at you! You're the color of a tomato!"

"It *is* pretty hot," Holly admitted, fanning her face. "The mainland is so much cooler."

"Higher elevation," Uncle Stanley grunted. "Didn't you live near Windgap?"

Holly nodded. "Yes, and you're right. It's about two thousand feet there. We got a fairly constant breeze. I guess I still have to acclimatize to Hibiscus a bit." She smiled at him.

"Get yourself an electric bike," Uncle Stanley suggested. "That way you don't have to work so hard on the hills."

"Or one of those little buggies," Elma added. "Or borrow your mama's car! Either way, don't let me see you cycling in this heat again, you hear me?"

Holly grinned. "Yes, Auntie Elma. And thanks for the ride. Are you on your way to the Inn?"

"Yes." Elma made a tsking sound. "The judges hadn't quite finished with the bougainvillea displays yesterday when all that trouble started, so we arranged for them to return this morning. They should have decided by now and your uncle Stanley is on tenterhooks. Your mama has kindly invited us for lunch." She smiled at Holly.

Uncle Stanley parked his van behind the Inn, next to Maggie's little car and jumped out. "You okay, Elma?"

She flapped a large hand at him. "Yes, yes! Go along, Stanley. Find out who won. Just make sure you bring Stuart up with you when you come back!" Heaving herself out of the van, Elma smoothed down her purple and white dress and adjusted her hat. "There's a dish of potato salad in the back seat, Holly."

"I've got it," Holly said, picking up the large green bowl. "Gosh. There's enough here for an army, Auntie Elma!"

"Your mama has invited your aunt Laura and uncle Phil," Elma said. She smiled, her teeth white against her dark skin. "And Matt."

Holly laughed. "That explains it." She pushed the van door closed and led the way through a small garden to the back door of the family quarters. Animated voices floated out.

The island in Maggie's kitchen was already groaning with food. Holly smiled with pleasure at the sight of all the old Hibiscus Island favorites. She made space for the potato salad between a huge pan of peas 'n rice and an equally large pan of macaroni and cheese.

Elma immediately bustled over to a sofa at the end of the long family room and was soon deep in conversation with Laura Connolly. Holly's Uncle Phil reclined in one of the large armchairs, fruit punch in hand and feet up on a small footstool. Matt perched beside him, laughing at something he'd said.

"Want some help, Mama?" Holly asked her mother, who was dropping corn cobs into a pot of boiling water.

"There's just the salad to put out," Maggie said. "If you do that, we'll be ready to eat as soon as your Gramps and Uncle Stanley get back."

"Who won the Trophy? Do you know the results?" Holly asked, as she opened the fridge and pulled out the huge wooden salad bowl.

"I don't. We were in two minds whether or not to even go ahead with the judging after yesterday, but Rob Tucker said it wouldn't impact his investigation and Myrtle polled the Garden Club and everyone agreed it would be a shame not to have a winner this year." Turning away from the stove, Maggie looked at Holly with a sober expression. "Rob was up here this morning interviewing Lucy Robinson. He's asked her and Pete to remain on the island for a while. Holly, he said that Amelia Cartell was murdered."

"I know, Mama. Myrtle told us she was poisoned."

Maggie's mouth dropped open. "Myrtle told you...?" A

look of intense exasperation crossed her face. "How *does* that woman know everything?"

"Oh, don't let it bother you, Maggie," Uncle Phil remarked, coming over for a refill of his fruit punch. "Half the island knows by now. I heard the news myself this morning when I was down at the dock. Someone heard it from someone who heard it from someone. You know how the island grapevine works!"

Phil Connolly operated a charter fishing boat out of Castlebay Harbor. He was a tall, sunburnt man who wore his dark hair in a military crewcut and liked nothing better than to be out on the water. "I was told it was some kind of anti-nausea drug," he said. "Sounds strange to me."

"I heard it was scopolamine," Holly interjected, "but Myrtle said they hadn't found anything to suggest Amelia had a prescription for it."

"And she would know! Never knew anyone for nosing things out like Myrtle." Phil patted Maggie on the shoulder, his dark brown eyes kind as he looked at his sister-in-law "Take that look off your face, Mags. None of this was your fault. Rob Tucker's a good man. He'll figure it out."

Drawing in a deep breath, Maggie produced a weak smile. Before she could speak, the door flew open and two very disgruntled elderly gentlemen stalked in.

"Yikes," Uncle Phil muttered. "I'm guessing neither of them won the Trophy this year. Hello Stuart. Stanley. How are you?"

Uncle Stanley shook his head. "Could be better, Phil. Could be better." He trailed dispiritedly over to the sofa where his wife was holding court and slumped down beside her.

Matt caught Holly's eye and flashed her a wicked grin. "Hi Gramps. Where's the Trophy?"

Gramps swung around, his face reddening in annoyance. "The judges must have been blind," he exclaimed. "Can you believe it? Sullivan won! Sullivan! With that pale, anemic specimen of White Stripe." His eyebrows beetled with irritation.

Uncle Stanley roused himself. "Oh, now be fair, Stuart. It was a good display. A bit boring, of course. No real personality, but his specimens were good. Can't deny that."

"Pfffttt!" Gramps snorted. "They weren't a patch on my Blueberry Ice." He poured drinks for himself and Stanley. Catching sight of a stern look and raised eyebrow as he lowered himself onto the couch, he said, "Don't worry, Elma. It's non-alcoholic. We'll drown our sorrows in fruit punch today. Cheers, Stanley. Here's to next year!"

"To next year," Uncle Stanley repeated.

Gramps poked his friend. "And to our victory over James Murray. At least we beat him!"

"That we did," Uncle Stanley said, cheering up slightly. "That we did! Silver and bronze, that's us."

Their glasses clinked.

"Lunch is ready," Maggie called.

As HOLLY LEANED back in her chair and surreptitiously loosened the button on her shorts, Matt, on his second full plate of food, grinned at her. "You have no stamina. You know there's still dessert to come, right?"

Holly groaned. "I can't eat another mouthful."

Opposite her, Aunt Laura nodded in agreement as she pushed her empty plate away. "Me neither, Holly. That was wonderful, Maggie. And Elma, your potato salad was magnificent, as always.'

Elma smiled. She wiped her mouth with a napkin and sat back with a contented sigh. "Nothing like a good Sunday lunch."

At the far end of the table, Gramps and Uncle Stanley continued to dissect the judges' decision about the Bougainvillea Trophy. The two dogs, Truffle and Roxie, sat right next to Gramps, their eyes steady on his face, knowing he was the weak link at the table and guaranteed to send tidbits their way. Holly grinned as she saw a small piece of chicken carefully dropped for each dog and returned her attention to her end of the table.

"Auntie Elma," she said, "did you know Amelia Cartell?"

Elma looked puzzled. "The woman who was murdered? How would I have known her, Holly?"

"Myrtle said she used to be called Emily Carter and that she worked here for quite some time," Holly explained. "I just wondered if you knew—"

"*Emily Carter?*" Elma and Laura spoke simultaneously. They gaped at Holly.

Laura found her voice first. "Amelia Cartell was Emily Carter? Are you sure? I didn't recognize her at all when she came in the store! My, she's changed!"

"Who's Emily Carter?" Matt asked, pausing with a forkful of potato salad.

"Stanley!" Elma signaled her husband imperiously. "Holly says that this murdered woman was Emily Carter!"

Stanley blinked. "I believe she was. Didn't you tell me that, Stuart?"

Gramps's nod was brusque.

Elma folded her arms in exasperation. "Well for good-ness' sake! Why wouldn't you tell me, Stanley?"

"Why would I?" Stanley asked, puzzled.

"Stanley! You can't possibly have forgotten Emily Carter! After all that trouble she caused." When Stanley just gazed at her mildly, Elma huffed in annoyance. "Men!" she muttered before turning towards Maggie. "Did you know, Maggie?"

"No," Maggie replied. She frowned. "I'm not sure I really remember her either—"

"Oh of course you do," Laura interjected. "She was the one at the center of that big court case. When was it? Ten years ago? Eleven? Old man Sanders sued the newspaper for libel or whatever it was. You must remember! Sir James Murray was the presiding judge."

"She was an Awful Woman!" Elma pronounced and Holly suppressed a grin at the obvious capital letters. "Carleton Sanders' boy's career was ruined as a result of her unethical and malicious behavior."

"Are you talking about Ryan Sanders?" Matt asked. "I've heard of him. The soccer player, right? There was some big scandal, and he was dropped from the team." He quailed at the look he received from Elma.

"Ryan Sanders," she said with emphasis, "was not involved in any scandal! Emily Carter made up a pack of lies and printed them. Unfortunately, as we all know, dirt sticks, and the nasty rumormongering and talk that resulted cost Ryan a place on an international team. He was twenty-five at the time and he took it very badly."

"Poor guy," Holly said. "How do you know the story wasn't true, Auntie Elma? What did Amelia write about him?"

"Steroids, wasn't it?" Matt piped up again. "He was head-hunted by one of the big England clubs, but they dropped him like a hot potato when the headlines hit."

"He never took them!" Elma snapped. "It was all a

vicious lie! Henry Sullivan should have been ashamed of himself for publishing rubbish like that!"

"Henry Sullivan was a fool," Uncle Phil agreed. "He should never have run those articles without fact checking them in the first place. The Sanders got a huge settlement from the paper, and rightly so, but by then it was too late for Ryan."

"So, Amelia wrote for *The Island Gazette*?" Holly asked. "For how long?"

"About four, five years maybe? She wrote fluff pieces when she first arrived," Aunt Laura said, "and then she did that advice column."

Auntie Elma snorted. "Advice! Sheer nastiness is what it was!"

"Oh! Was she *Dear Priscilla*? She was? Wow. I remember that column. It was all the rage at school. We used to read it every day in eighth grade, trying to figure out who was asking for advice. She was pretty mean at times." Holly shook her head at the memory.

"At times?" Laura exclaimed. "She was horrible. Vindictive, patronizing, sneering... And to think that she was going to review my store on her blog!" Her voice rose in indignation.

"Dodged a bullet there, mom," Matt said with a grin.

Laura ignored him. "The thing is, everyone read that column. It was print only—nothing online—so hard copy sales went through the roof for a while."

"Which is why Sullivan allowed her to do some so-called investigative articles," Uncle Phil added. "It was a huge mistake. Emily Carter didn't seem to have any understanding of journalistic professionalism or the principle of limitation of harm."

"The principle of what?" Matt asked. "Pass the potato salad, would you, Dad?"

Uncle Phil grinned and handed over the huge bowl. "Journalists are supposed to have a responsibility to make sure that other people aren't harmed as a result of their reporting," he explained. "Emily Carter was sadly lacking in this ability. From what I remember, the Sanders case wasn't the only example of unethical reporting, but it was the one that made Sullivan come to his senses."

"Sir James ruled in favor of the Sanders. Sullivan paid out a ton of money and Emily Carter was fired," Laura added. "She left the island, swearing she'd never return. And good riddance."

Uncle Phil frowned. "But she came back—as Amelia Cartell. I wonder why?"

Holly wondered too.

13

"Lucy, are you okay?"

After a morning spent helping Gramps in the slat house, Holly had spied Lucy alone in the small rose garden and detoured immediately, hoping to ask her some questions, but now she looked at her guest in some concern.

Lucy's face was pale, there were dark shadows under her eyes and her hair was tousled. Her hand trembled as she toyed with her teacup, which was still half full.

"Shall I freshen that cup for you?" Holly asked. "Or would you like something cold? Have you had lunch? Would you like something?"

Lucy straightened up with an effort. "No, it's okay. I'm not really hungry. I can't believe this has happened..." Her voice trailed off as she looked piteously at Holly. Tears threatening to overflow, she continued in a whisper, "The police chief said that Amelia was poisoned."

Holly pulled out the chair next to Lucy and sat down. Behind her, bees buzzed soporifically over the orange cape honeysuckle while a couple of Monarch butterflies flitted around the milkweed plants that grew up and around the old China roses. The sun beat down on the yellow umbrella covering them, and Holly adjusted her chair slightly so that it was more in the shade.

"I heard." She patted Lucy's hand in sympathy, then asked hesitantly, "Lucy... did *you* know that Amelia lived on the island about ten years ago?"

"I didn't when we first arrived. She never said anything about being here before—in fact, she pretended she knew nothing about the island—but I found out yesterday that she'd lied to me. I found an old blog open on her computer when I went to her room." She looked helplessly at Holly. "I didn't even know it existed."

"An old blog? She had another blog? Before she started *Impressions*?" Holly asked.

"Yes," Lucy said. "It was written during her time on Hibiscus Island. Everything's anonymous and she used the name Emily Carter, but I recognize some of the places she's described. It's definitely Hibiscus Island, and honestly, it's not very nice reading! It was a private blog—no followers." Lucy paused. "It was more like a diary actually. A pretty vindictive diary."

Holly stared at her. "Vindictive how? I mean, I don't want to upset you, but her current blog has some fairly nasty posts as well—"

"Oh, I know," Lucy cut her off, a despairing note in her voice. "I try so hard, but sometimes she just gets to the blog and undermines everything I've done, and before I can delete the post, there's a million comments, all complaining and threatening. That's why she hired Pete! We've actually had anonymous letters, you know. For a travel blog! It's awful! And then, when she's hired him to protect her, she keeps going off by herself and he doesn't know where she is and—"

"Wait!" Holly stemmed the flood of information. "Undermines everything *you've* done? I don't understand."

Lucy blinked. "Oh... well... I mean..." She stopped and heaved a huge sigh before leaning back and playing with her teacup. "Well, I don't suppose it matters much anymore, does it? The thing is, I'm not just Amelia's secretary. I'm her ghostwriter. Or I was."

"Ghostwriter? You write the blog posts?" Holly's mouth dropped open.

Lucy nodded morosely. "I didn't always. When I first started working for Amelia, I was just her secretary. Her blog was growing, and she was getting a name for herself. I handled emails and comments and stuff like that. Her posts were decent, and she really did try to be fair with reviews."

"She was involved in a lawsuit here. Perhaps that made her more careful," Holly said.

"Well, then her blog became popular. People started recognizing her when she traveled. She loved that! But every now and then she would, I don't know, have a bad day or something and write a really nasty post. And then she'd lose followers, which meant she'd lose revenue and that would upset her." With a sigh, Lucy paused, then looked up at Holly. "You do know how a blog works, right?"

"Sort of," Holly replied. "I know some people make quite a lot of money from them. Ads and stuff."

"That's right," Lucy agreed. "Amelia started with click ads, but as she got more and more followers, she started getting requests for sponsorship. As soon as people knew her next travel destination, she'd be inundated with requests for reviews or sponsored posts, where she'd do an entire post on a particular restaurant or hotel. It was very lucrative, but she couldn't keep up, so she expanded my job description. I wrote the sponsored posts and managed the subscription membership side of the blog—where people pay to have access to members-only content. It takes a lot of time because you have to make sure they get premium content. I liked it at first. I got to travel, and I like writing. But eventually, I found I was doing more and more of the writing and Amelia was still getting the credit. To be fair, she raised my salary substantially, but it started getting to me a bit, you know?"

Lucy sighed again and pushed her teacup away from her. "And then Open Skies Publishing contacted her with a proposal to write travel books, based on the blog posts. They wanted the descriptive pieces and reflective essays—all of which were mine." She made a face. "I was stupid."

"Don't tell me," Holly said. "You wrote the travel books and Amelia got the credit."

"I signed a five-year contract without reading the fine print. So stupid!" Lucy's face darkened. "I wrote everything, but her name was on it. And it locked me into a non-disclosure agreement as well. So even if I quit, I couldn't tell anyone that I wrote the books or the blog. I should have quit anyway but I guess I'm just weak. I told myself that the money was good, and I was traveling on someone else's dime—and then Pete came along." A slight blush rose in her cheeks.

Holly's thoughts were whirling. Did Lucy really not realize she'd just given herself a motive for murdering her boss? "When does your contract end?"

"It has—had—another year to run. This book—*Hidden Gems: Small Islands*—was to be the last Open Skies publication." Lucy looked pensive. "I don't know what will happen now."

～

"GOOD GRIEF! She doesn't seem to be very bright, does she?" Jamie listened, flabbergasted, to Holly's summary of her conversation with Lucy and shook her head in disgust. "I know she has a motive, but honestly, do you think she's intelligent enough to murder Amelia and get away with it? Oh, go ahead, put her down as a suspect, but really, I can't believe anyone that clueless could manage to kill a cockroach, much less a human being! What else did she burble away to you as she broke her non-disclosure agreement left, right and center?!"

Holly grinned as she listened to Jamie continue to expostulate. Her friend had never tolerated fools gladly. Holly added Lucy's name to the suspect column and stood back to admire her 'murder board'. Behind her there was a pause in the monologue as Jamie also inspected it.

"Very nice," she said approvingly. "Wasn't it good that I got a photo of Amelia at the opening dinner? It makes all the difference. More professional, you know."

"More organized anyway," Holly said, "although I'm not sure it helps much."

She sat down on the sofa, idly stroking Teddy's head. Jamie had brought the big poodle with her and after some initial distrust, he had accepted a few dog biscuits and become Holly's new best friend. Truffle sulked at Holly's feet, annoyed that her place on the sofa had been usurped by a stranger.

Holly stared at the board, then sighed. "I think we're out

of our depth here, Jamie. It always looks so easy on television, but it's harder in real life, isn't it?"

"Yeah," Jamie admitted, shoving her hands into the pockets of her bright yellow cargo shorts. Her dark hair was piled haphazardly on top of her head and skewered into place with a glittering butterfly pin that complemented the multi-colored butterflies on her off-the-shoulder top. Long gold earrings swayed mesmerizingly as Jamie rocked back and forth on her heels in front of the board.

She turned around and grinned. "But it's still early days. And we've made a good start. Look! Two suspects so far! Lucy Robinson and Henry Sullivan. Good job on finding out about Mr. Sullivan, by the way. He must have been really mad at having to pay out all that money because of Amelia!" She picked up the marker and advanced toward the whiteboard. "We'll add old man Sanders as well. I mean, it was Amelia who cost his grandson the spot on that professional team. And what about Ryan as a suspect? After all, it's his career that Amelia ruined."

"He wasn't at the dinner. In fact, he's not even on the island anymore. Auntie Elma said he left after the court case and went to Canada. He hasn't been back for years." Holly shook her head sadly. "Auntie Elma said that old man Sanders was devastated when he left. He raised Ryan after his parents died, you know. I don't think you can add old Mr. Sanders either."

Jamie turned around. "Why not?"

"Because he wasn't at the dinner. He was invited as a member of the Garden Club, but he didn't RSVP. I checked the list. You haven't even looked at yours, have you?" Holly grinned at Jamie, who waved a dismissive hand.

"I don't need Myrtle's list. I know who I need to talk to."

"Big words," Holly laughed. "How come you didn't tell *her* that?"

Her friend had the grace to blush. "Oh, come on, Holls. You know what Myrtle's like. It's easier just to go along with her. Anyway, back to old man Sanders,"—she glared at Holly—"he *was* at the dinner. I saw him. He had a plate of shrimps! Two plates actually. He likes our shrimp. Maybe he just forgot to RSVP, because he was definitely there."

"Oh? Well, I didn't notice him. Go ahead and put him down then." She grinned at Jamie's expression and watched her continue to write. "Who's that you're adding? Pete?"

"Of course. It's obvious," Jamie said. "He and Lucy are clearly romantically attached. Yes, they are, Holls. I know these things."

"I'm not arguing," Holly protested. "In fact, I agree with you. Lucy blushes every time she says his name."

"So, Pete knows Lucy's writing the blog and the books and thinks she should get the credit. He bumps off Amelia and, boom, Lucy gets what she deserves." Jamie finished with a flourish. "Four suspects! Anyone else?"

Holly scowled. "Well, the inspector interviewed Gramps again today. He wanted to know where he went when he left the dinner, who he was with, had he seen Amelia, had he spoken to her, and so on." Holly looked indignantly at Jamie. "Why isn't he investigating other people? We've found other suspects! Why is he picking on Gramps?"

Jamie sat down beside her. "Rob's just doing his job, Holls. I'm sure he has other suspects and is just questioning Mr. Mack for more details. You said you were going to be fair to him, remember?"

"You're very defensive of our new inspector," Holly said, suspicion edging her voice. "How come?"

Jamie evaded the question and stared at Holly thoughtfully. "Did Mr. Mack leave the dinner? I didn't notice."

"He snuck out around seven thirty or so. Uncle Stanley was with him. They went for their annual pre-Festival Trophy drink. You know, the one where they boast about their entry and say why they're going to win."

"Hmmm. We should find out what time Uncle Stanley left Mr. Mack's cottage. He might have seen something as he left." Jamie stared at the board again. "And Holls, we really need to see Amelia's old blog!"

14

Lucy was quite willing to show Holly and Jamie the old blog the following afternoon. "I suppose you might recognize some of the people and places," she said as she led the way into her suite. "Everyone seems to know everyone on this island."

"It's a small place," Holly told her.

"The size of a large village, really," Jamie added. "Which has its good points and bad points. You know everyone but everyone also knows you."

Lucy had been given the Frangipani Suite, next door to the Bougainvillea Suite where Amelia had stayed. It was a large, airy one-bedroom suite with a small sitting room and a tiny enclosed courtyard outside. A frangipani tree, covered in yellow and white blooms, shaded the courtyard and provided the color scheme for the suite. The bedroom overlooked the north shore waters, while from the small sitting room, guests could see the terraced gardens of the Inn stretching out below.

"I've always loved this room," Jamie said. "We used to find huge caterpillars on that tree. Big red, yellow, white, and black striped ones. They turned into giant sphinx moths." She wandered over to the window and peered out while Lucy was booting up Amelia's computer. "And it's such a nice view. You overlook all the prettiest gardens. In fact, you can see all the way down to the slat house from here. Look, Holls, they're taking down the main tent. What are they doing about the Bougainvillea Exhibit? Is it going to stay up for the week as usual?"

Holly nodded. "The police said that the Inn's garden could still be on the tour, but they've roped off the bottom level. The Bougainvillea Exhibit tent will stay up until Friday."

Lucy, who had been looking pensive, showed some animation for the first time. "Those displays are amazing! I took a ton of photos of them! I even started drafting a post and making notes for the book before everything happened. I never even heard which one was the winner. Did the judges make a decision?"

Holly nodded. "Mr. Sullivan won. He did the *Study in White* display. He'll receive the Trophy at the Banquet on Saturday night."

"I liked the bonsai one the best, but they were all wonderful. It's such an amazing festival. We've seen a lot of the gardens on the tour already and I booked tickets for the rest. I really want to do the culinary evening." Lucy looked at Holly. "Pete said you'd told him about it. I had no idea bougainvillea was edible! I want to do a double page spread about the Festival in the travel guide. If there is a travel book, that is. I don't know what's going to happen with that…" Lucy's voice trailed off. For a moment, she was silent as she looked down at the computer screen, then she turned the laptop toward the other young women. "Here's the blog. Oh! I told Pete I'd meet him for tea. We need to arrange a meeting with Amelia's executors and things like that. I don't know if I should let you—" She bit her lip.

"How about we come with you?" Jamie said instantly. "We'll sit where you can see us. That way the computer is always in your sight."

"Oh okay, that'll work," Lucy said with relief.

~

"GOOD GRIEF! This woman had a vicious pen! Good thing she never went public; she'd have been sued for libel a million times over!" Jamie scowled at the laptop screen, then jumped to her feet. "I need sustenance to deal with this amount of vitriol. Tea must be nearly ready. I'll go see what Maggie's got and bring you something."

Without waiting for a reply, Jamie trotted off toward the Inn's large kitchen. Holly glanced across the room, saw that Lucy and Pete were still talking outside in the rose garden, and wiggled herself more comfortably into the wide stuffed armchair in the corner of the breakfast room. Less squashed with Jamie gone, and minus the non-stop fidgeting and expostulating of her friend, she settled the computer on her lap and continued scrolling.

Amelia's writing was an eye-opener, shining a veiled— and malicious—light on the Hibiscus Island of the past. Holly became more and more intrigued as she tried to match the anonymous slander to real places and people.

References to a 'snooty, nosy, candy-striper' for instance, could only refer to Myrtle, who had been working as practice nurse for Doctor Eastham at that time. Amelia had clearly run afoul of her and been firmly put in her place. Holly could almost sympathize. Myrtle had ruled the office with a fist of iron, and many a patient had quailed when she had leveled her 'look' at them. Whether it was dispensing medication, prepping a patient or collecting payments, Myrtle tolerated no excuses or drama.

And yet, Holly thought, scrolling to a new post, whenever there was an emergency, it was Myrtle that any true Hibiscus Islander wanted on the scene. It was Myrtle who had saved the life of Russell Briggs when his fishing knife slipped and severed an artery; Myrtle who had doctored any number of jellyfish and Portuguese man-of-war stings incurred by unsuspecting tourists; Myrtle who once lay on the floor of the local high school for two hours, calmly talking to young Sarah Montrose, who had got trapped between floors in the school elevator and was hysterical. Most islanders, when Myrtle was at her most annoying, remembered those times, took a deep breath, and moved on.

Holly paused as a line in an entry caught her eye. '... a bourgeois attempt to emulate the famous Chelsea Flower Show...' The date was June. This was clearly a Bougainvillea Festival from yesteryear. Holly read on, fascinated despite the sneering tones of the writer.

Amelia, assigned to cover the Festival for the newspaper, had visited the Flower Show and the inaugural Bougainvillea Exhibit, toured all the gardens and attended a seminar on how to propagate the shrub. Her writing oozed with sarcastic and belittling comments, and Holly felt her blood pressure rising as Amelia described the amateur gardener, who had won the Trophy with a 'decidedly substandard specimen displayed in a mawkish and poorly constructed tribute to a depressing world populated by repulsive orcs and effete elves.'

"Wow," Holly murmured. "I wonder how her account for

the newspaper compares with this. I can't imagine they'd publish anything this derogatory!"

She made a mental note to visit the Bridgeport Library and check out the archives, knowing *The Island Gazette* had only gone digital five years ago.

Amelia's scathing commentary continued with a description of the 'poorly designed' gardens she had visited. She had included photos and Holly peered at them with interest. On a tropical island that was frequently beset with hurricanes and had no winter season, gardens could—and did—change frequently. It was hard to recognize individual places from the angles of Amelia's photos but, after squinting at several, Holly thought she could identify parts of the Inn's terraced gardens as well as Uncle Stanley's quarry garden.

One small but very spectacular bougainvillea specimen caught her eye. It was unusual, sporting pale pink bracts with white hearts, and Holly studied it curiously. She hadn't seen one like that before. Amelia was particularly scathing about the garden it grew in, but Holly was unable to glean any information about its location from the cryptic references. She would have to ask Gramps if he knew of such a flower. Perhaps the bush had died off.

Some photos featured people, and Holly, studiously ignoring the accompanying libelous captions, was delighted to recognize younger versions of Auntie Elma, Mrs. Sullivan, and Myrtle. In one photo, all three of them, plus two more women, stood grouped around the mystery plant, smiling broadly.

Engrossed in the photos, Holly failed to notice the person entering the breakfast room and jumped a mile high when a deep voice spoke disapprovingly beside her.

"Miss Gold, may I ask what you're doing?"

As Rob Tucker frowned down at Holly, Jamie came charging into the room with a plate full of scones. "Holly! Myrtle's outside and—" She stopped short. "Oh. Hi, Rob. Want a scone?"

The inspector blinked—and then a heartfelt sigh escaped him. "I might have known," he muttered. "It's not like I wasn't warned, after all."

"Warned about what? And by whom, may I ask?" Jamie's eyes narrowed. "Hey! What's François been saying to you?"

Holly looked back and forth between the two in surprise. Jamie hadn't told her she was on such easy terms with the police inspector. Her friend, catching the narrow-eyed stare, looked sheepish.

"Rob and François play golf together," she explained in a deprecating tone, "and François is married to Rob's sister. That's how he knew about the job here. I was going to suggest we meet up with Becky next weekend. You'll like her, Holls! She's really into mysteries as well."

Rob interrupted her. "And that's what I was warned about. Exactly that!" He leveled a stern look at Jamie and then Holly. "Now look, ladies, contrary to what most mystery books imply, the police are not incompetent fools." He held up a hand to stop Jamie from bursting into speech. "This is not a game! And I don't need—or want—amateurs stumbling around in my investigation." He met Jamie's outraged look with a calm one of his own.

"We don't think you're a fool!" Jamie exclaimed. "But this is Hibiscus Island, and we've lived here our entire lives. We have insights; we know people; we can help. You have to admit, Rob, that you haven't been here very long. You need us!"

"Exactly what I told the inspector, Jamie," Myrtle said, coming up behind Rob.

The inspector closed his eyes briefly and Holly's mouth twitched in an involuntary smile. She leaned back in her chair and watched with interest as the now-beleaguered police chief tried to fight a battle on two fronts. Her grin widened.

"I'm willing to listen to anything you can tell me about the island that might help, yes, but I'm not actually here to ask questions right now." Ignoring Jamie's scowl and Myrtle's folded arms, Rob turned to Holly. "Ms. Robinson told me that she found a blog that Ms. Cartell wrote when she lived on the island before. Is this it?"

"A blog?" Myrtle exclaimed. "The Cartell woman wrote a blog about us?" She bustled over to Holly and peered over the younger woman's shoulder.

Rob looked at Myrtle in exasperation. "Ms. Collier," he began, flinching when she glared at him before returning her attention to the photo on the screen. "Myrtle," he tried again, only to be interrupted.

"Good heavens! I remember this."

Holly suppressed yet another grin at the look on the inspector's face. He folded his arms and leveled a forbidding stare at Myrtle, who ignored him completely.

"This was an early Bougainvillea Festival. That's Elma Foster, Carolyn Sullivan, me, Sonja Eastham, and Clare Murray." A look of sadness crossed Myrtle's face. "That must have been Clare's last Festival."

Holly and Jamie looked at the picture again in curiosity, noting the pretty summer dress, wide hat, and sunglasses worn by the late Lady Murray. In contrast, Myrtle, smiling widely beside her, was attired in a bright magenta suit, her immaculate hair sporting a tiny black hat.

Jamie grinned as she inspected the long, flowery dresses of the three other women. "It was a lot more formal back then, wasn't it? Everyone dressed up, crystal glasses and china plates on the table—like an English tea party!"

"What do you mean, 'back then'?" Myrtle snapped. "It wasn't that long ago! A mere eleven or twelve years! And we still dress up for the garden tours and use proper china! It's supposed to be an experience!" She peered closer and gasped in outrage. "Just look at what that horrible woman wrote! Well, I never! She knew full well that we only served fruit cordial at that garden! What an insulting thing to suggest!"

"It was a private blog, Myrtle," Holly said in a conciliatory tone. "No one else saw it."

"That's beside the point, Holly!" Myrtle said, swelling ominously. "What a vulgar, vulgar woman she was! It's no wonder she was murdered!"

Just then Maggie pushed the tea trolley into the room. "Hello Rob," she said in surprise, a shadow of anxiety crossing her features. "I didn't know you were coming here today. Have you found out something?"

Rob wiped the exasperation off his face. "We're making progress, Maggie. Don't worry. We'll get there." He smiled down at her as he took over the heavy trolley. "Where do you want this thing?"

"By the window, please," Maggie said, returning the smile. She glanced around. "What are you all doing?"

"We're giving Rob some Hibiscus Island insights," Jamie said with an important air.

"Is that so?" Maggie said dryly. "Well, I assume you know what you're doing. In the meantime, however, I have guests due to check in shortly, so would you mind taking this through to the family part of the Inn? Murder's not exactly good for business." With that, she left the room.

Rob glared at Jamie, who responded with an unrepentant grin. "Seriously," she said, "we can help."

The inspector sighed and pinched the bridge of his nose. "It does appear that your local knowledge might be useful," he admitted, after a pause. "Perhaps, Miss Gold, we could do as Maggie suggested and take this discussion somewhere else?"

"Well, I don't have a lot of time at my disposal because I mustn't be late for the Garden Club seminar tonight," Myrtle said in a pretentious tone, "but it is a citizen's duty to help the police."

"The only assistance I'd like right now," Rob retorted, "is to know what you could tell me about some of these photos."

He spoke to the air as Myrtle bustled out of the room, followed closely by a grinning Jamie. Rob closed his eyes and gave a pained sigh. "After you, Miss Gold," he said.

15

S itting beside the inspector at the kitchen island, Myrtle glanced at her watch. "I really can't stay long. The Garden Club is hosting the propagation seminar tonight and I have to be at the Horticultural Hall to make sure that everything is set up properly. Sir James and Stuart will be demonstrating how to take cuttings, and Sir James has also very kindly agreed to explain his hybridization technique to us tonight." She looked at Holly. "You're coming, of course?"

"Yes. I'm helping Gramps get the bougainvillea there." Holly looked at Rob and said pointedly, "We had to cut more branches for the seminar because the police impounded the ones on the body!" The kettle whistled behind her. "Tea, anyone? Or something cold?"

Rob looked up from the computer screen. "Cold for me, if you don't mind, Miss Gold." His tone was a bit distracted and Holly couldn't tell if he was ignoring her earlier comment or hadn't noticed it. "It's warm outside today. Myrtle, what can you tell me about this photo?"

"It'll be hotter in August," Jamie predicted. "You haven't felt heat till you've had a Hibiscus Island summer, Rob. And what's with all this 'Miss Gold' stuff? Her name's Holly. I'd rather have fruit punch as well, Holls. I've drunk enough coffee today to sink a ship!" She peered over Rob's shoulder. "Who's that?"

Myrtle looked as well. "That's Sonja Eastham and Clare Murray again, at one of the gardens in the Bougainvillea Festival that year."

"Which garden?" Rob asked.

Myrtle squinted at the picture. "I'm not sure. There are no real distinguishing features." She tapped the screen. "But this bougainvillea is quite rare. Only a few people have it in their gardens."

Holly set a tray of punch-filled glasses on the island. "I noticed that one before. What's it called? I don't think I've ever seen it."

"White Heart," Myrtle replied. "It's a unique hybrid. Clare Murray grew it originally, but she gave cuttings to many of us in the Garden Club. Unfortunately, it's not very hardy so few specimens survived. I still have one." She smirked.

Rob scrolled further down the blog, stopping periodically to ask questions about the island, the people in the photos and any comments that caught his eye. Myrtle sat beside him, alternating between indignant exclamations at the slanderous writing and nostalgic reminiscences about the Hibiscus Island Garden Club of the past.

Bored by one particularly long anecdote, Jamie interrupted, "What about the Garden Club of today? Have you questioned them all yet, Myrtle?"

The inspector stiffened. "Questioned the Garden Club?"

"I got statements from everyone, of course," Myrtle said with a smug smile. "Those that were at the dinner, that is.

Some people couldn't attend for various reasons, so I've crossed them off the suspect list."

Rob's face grew thunderous. "Suspect list? What—"

"Who have you got on it?" Jamie persisted. "We have four people so far—Sullivan, Sanders, Lucy and—"

"Hold it! Hold it right there!" Rob's voice was grim as he frowned at Jamie, before glowering in turn at Myrtle and Holly. "Let me make this quite clear. I don't know how things have been done in the past, but *I* will not have members of the public interfering in an investigation."

"Hey," Holly burst out, her scowl matching the inspector's, "are you implying that my dad—"

"I'm not implying anything," Rob snapped. "I'm telling all of you, in no uncertain terms, that you are not to poke around in things that don't concern you. This isn't a stolen rabbit or a missing library book! Amelia Cartell was murdered—and her killer is someone on the island, someone you might know! Someone who might not hesitate to kill again!"

"But that's the point, Rob!" Jamie exclaimed. "We do know everyone! And it does concern us! It concerns all of us. The murderer has to be someone who was at the dinner on the weekend!"

Rob's eyes narrowed. "And it is the police's job to find that person." He stood up and closed the computer. "This was a mistake. From now on, if I have any questions, they will be handled in an official manner. Sergeant Hollis will be in touch. In the meantime, please refrain from any interference or I will charge all of you with obstruction of justice." He nodded at Holly. "Miss Gold. Thank you for your hospitality. I will let Ms. Robinson know that I'm impounding her computer."

The inspector stalked out, leaving a stunned and outraged silence behind him.

And then the women erupted.

"I can't believe he just said that about my dad!"

"Gosh! I didn't think Rob was like that!"

"Well, I never!"

All three spoke at once, loudly and with indignation.

"I am very surprised at that young man's attitude," Myrtle continued with disapproval. "He has a lot to learn about Hibiscus Island!"

"Yes, he does," Jamie agreed, her eyes narrowing. "He certainly does!"

HOLLY WANDERED over to the refreshment table at the Horticultural Hall that evening. "Need some help?" she asked Jamie. "I have nothing else to do now but wait to take Gramps home."

Jamie shook her head. "Not now, but I could use it when they take their break. We'll probably be swamped." She looked around the packed hall. "Good turnout, isn't it?"

"I'm glad," Holly said. "I think Myrtle was really worried the murder would put people off."

Jamie snorted. "Not likely! It's all people are talking about these days. Everyone's got opinions—you should hear the Bean regulars when they get going! Half the people here tonight probably don't know the difference between a hibiscus and a daisy! Poky, that's what they are."

"We're pretty nosy ourselves, according to our new inspector," Holly reminded her friend.

Jamie scowled. "I'm still mad at him! Who knew he was

such a... a... a stick-in-the-mud?" As Holly's lips quirked at the old-fashioned expression, her friend continued her tirade. "His sister's so nice too—and François said Rob's a great guy, lots of fun and easygoing. Ha! What does he know? And to think I actually thought you two would make a cute couple!"

"You *what*?" Holly squawked. "Now look, Jamie, don't start trying to set me up with anyone! Least of all him! I'm serious!" She glared at her friend.

Jamie flapped a hand at her. "Shhh, Holls. Sir James is about to start."

After sending Jamie another scathing look, Holly turned her attention to Sir James Murray who was beginning his lecture. Before she knew it, she was engrossed.

Sir James started with the history of the bougainvillea, explaining that the plant had first been discovered in the 1760s in Brazil.

The story of the French herbalist, Jeanne Baret, who disguised herself as a man and sailed with botanist Philibert Commerson on board the flagship of Admiral Louis Antoine de Bougainville, the first Frenchman to circumnavigate the globe, was an exciting one.

Jeanne Baret was a peasant woman but very knowledgeable about plants. In fact, she knew more than Commerson, whose assistant she was, and he persuaded her to go on the voyage. At a time when a French royal ordinance forbade women being on French navy ships, she took an enormous risk in going on the expedition.

"And she was indeed unmasked during the voyage," Sir James said. "Some accounts say they were in Tahiti when she was discovered while others claim it was Papua New Guinea. The story goes that Philibert Commerson, who was Jeanne's lover, promised the Admiral that if Jeanne received protection from the sailors, he would ensure that the name of de Bougainville would live forever."

"And did he protect her?" someone asked breathlessly from the audience.

Sir James shrugged. "Accounts vary. The Admiral claims he upheld his part of the bargain; some sailors' journals state otherwise. She was the only woman on an expedition of more than three hundred men, and the reality is life expectancy was short for any female on the high seas in the eighteenth century." He shrugged again. "Jeanne's life on board the flagship, *Étoile*, would likely have been grim."

"Gosh, that's an understatement, isn't it?" Jamie whispered. "Grim? It must have been horrendous!"

Sir James seemed to realize the atmosphere had become a little disapproving and hurried to continue his story with a smile. "However, you'll be glad to know that Jeanne Baret *did* return safely to France to live out her life and she holds the distinction of being the first woman to circumnavigate the globe."

"Which no one's ever heard about," Jamie muttered. "At least I hadn't. Had you?"

Holly shook her head. "Shhh," she whispered.

"Jeanne Baret discovered the showy, ornamental bougainvillea vine we all love so much in the hills around Rio de Janeiro," Sir James went on. "Philibert Commerson kept his word, and the plant was named after the ship's commander and was called *Bougainvillea brasiliensis*. We now more commonly call it *Bougainvillea spectabilis*."

"Typical," Jamie said, disgust coloring her tone. "A woman finds it and a man gets all the credit. Absolutely typical."

From the front of the hall, Sir James directed a withering look at her and picked up the pace of his story.

"There are approximately fourteen different species of bougainvillea, all from South America, and thanks to the determined efforts of breeders, we can find flowers in many colors, sizes and forms. Bougainvillea can be grown from seed or from cuttings. My distinguished colleague will now show you how to take a cutting." He finished with a final glare at an unperturbed Jamie, then gestured towards Gramps.

Gramps strode up to the tables at the front. Bougainvillea branches were strewn across the tables, and everyone watched intently as Gramps demonstrated how to cut the bougainvillea into small lengths at the right angle, dip the slips into a rooting hormone, and insert them into small pots of soil.

There was frequent laughter as he told anecdote after anecdote as he deftly snipped and potted, and then invited members of the audience up to try their hand. When he finished, there was a huge round of applause before Myrtle announced a small break.

Jamie and Holly were run off their feet for fifteen minutes before the crowd eased as people slipped outside for some fresh air or returned to their seats to await the next half of the seminar. Holly smiled at Bob Schafer, who had just come to the table.

"Hi, Mr. Schafer. Are you enjoying the lecture?"

"It's wonderful!" Bob replied with enthusiasm. "I've never heard the story of Jeanne Baret before. Fascinating! Just fascinating! I looked her up online just now. Did you know that over six thousand species of plants were collected on that expedition? Commerson named more than seventy after himself, a handful after the Admiral and a few other officers. He only named one plant after Jeanne! One!"

"What was it?" Holly asked in curiosity. Her education in

horticulture had not focused much on the history of the plants and this information was new to her.

"A scraggly thing endemic to Madagascar," Bob replied, scrolling through his phone. "And guess what? It's been renamed now! Reclassified as *Turraea*! All those plants she discovered and not one has her name!"

"We should start a petition," Jamie said, leaning over with a grin. "The Hibiscus Island Baretia Festival! In honor of Jeanne. Think people would support it?"

"No." Gramps had wandered over in time to hear the last part of the conversation. "Stop being an agitator, Jamie." He grinned at her. Gramps liked Jamie and her constant remarks during Sir James's lecture had tickled his fancy. "Bougainvillea is here to stay but Jeanne Baret does have a plant named after her. A new *Solanum* species was discovered in 2012. It's endemic to southern Ecuador and northern Peru and was named *Solanum baretiae* as a tribute to Baret." He smiled at Bob.

"Really? How fascinating!" Bob Schafer was agog.

"What the heck is a solanum?" Jamie asked Holly, as Gramps and Bob continued to talk. "Should I know it?"

Holly grinned. "Tomato, potato, eggplant, deadly nightshade to name a few. Shall I go on? There are about fifteen hundred species of *Solanum*."

Jamie grimaced. "No thanks. That's fine. Well, it's nice that she has something named after her, I suppose."

Holly waved her quiet. Her ears had pricked at something Bob Schafer had just said.

Gramps seemed puzzled. "I wasn't in the Exhibit tent on the night of the dinner."

"I thought for sure it was you. I was going to see if I could arrange a time to talk to you about perhaps supplying me with some cuttings—for my business, you know—but when I saw Ms. Cartell go into the tent, I thought I'd better wait till morning." Bob looked a bit embarrassed.

"You saw Amelia Cartell go into the Bougainvillea Exhibit? On Friday night?" Holly exclaimed.

"Yes, but when I heard raised voices, I just assumed it was Mr. Mackintosh..." Bob's voice trailed away sheepishly.

Gramps looked grim. "Ah yes. You heard my earlier altercation with that woman, didn't you? Well, I can assure you I was not having a clandestine meeting with Amelia Cartell in the Bougainvillea Exhibit!" He glared at the hapless Bob. "I was nowhere near the tent all evening!"

Bob groaned as Gramps stalked away in a huff. "Oh dear."

"Mr. Schafer," Holly said urgently. "What time did you see Amelia go into the tent?"

"I don't know," Bob said, gazing after Gramps in desperation. "Eight? Eight thirty? I didn't look at my watch. Holly, can you speak to your grandfather for me? I really want to talk to him about supplying me with—"

"Did you notice anything else? About Amelia?"

"What? Oh. Well, she'd had too much to drink that's for sure," Bob said. His face darkened. "That woman! Such a malicious tongue. I spoke to her briefly at the dinner about a possible sponsored post for my business and she was unbelievably rude! Said she had bigger fish to fry! Something about a scoop and she didn't have time to deal with penny ante stuff! Honestly, it astonishes me her blog was so popular if that was the way she treated people!" He grimaced. "However, I will be charitable and assume it was the wine speaking. When I saw her later, she was weaving badly and squinting at the lights."

"You saw her later?" Jamie asked. "You mean when she went into the Exhibit?"

"No," Bob said, flushing with embarrassment. "After that. She was going toward the slat house. I didn't want another encounter with her so I... well, I'm afraid I hid behind a bush when she went by. Not my finest hour."

"Was anyone with her?"

"Hmmm? With her? No, I don't think so. I passed someone else on my way back to the main tent, but I couldn't tell you who it was. It was dark." He looked around. "Oh! It looks like the second part is about to start."

Bob Schafer rushed back to his seat, leaving Holly and Jamie staring at each other.

"Gosh, I was right!" Jamie exclaimed. "Amelia *was* in the Bougainvillea Exhibit before she was killed. And you thought I was being ridiculous! Ha!"

"A scoop," Holly mused, ignoring Jamie's expostulations. "I wonder what she meant."

"Yeah," Jamie added. "And if it had any connection to her looking through that old blog!"

16

"Quite an interesting talk, wasn't it?" Jamie said, as she and Holly helped the members of the Garden Club put the hall back in order at the end of the evening. "I've always thought Sir James Murray was a bit of a cold fish, but he was passionate about those hybridized plants."

Holly nodded. Sir James's second talk had been engaging.

He had provided a brief history of the cultivation of bougainvillea in horticultural circles, starting with the first ever cultivar, Scarlet Queen, developed in 1920 by renowned horticulturist Percy Lancaster, and then had described some other notable cultivars such as Mrs. Butt, Mrs. McClean and the famous bicolored Mary Palmer. His slide show presentation was a homage not only to the diversity of the flower, but also to horticulturists around the world who had labored over generations to produce the many varieties of bougainvillea available in modern times.

On the practical front, Sir James had also brought bougainvillea plants to the seminar. In front of a rapt audience, he demonstrated how to extract pollen from a male parent and transfer it to the female parent, as part of the process of developing a new hybrid.

"Once the plant has been pollinated," he had said, delicately touching the pollen-coated swab to the pistil of the waiting plant, "I mark the flower and wait for the fruit to develop."

He showed the audience the half-inch long fruit that had matured at the end of a flower in a different pot. "When the fruit dries completely, I'll collect the seeds and plant them. I use four-inch pots with a soil-less mix, put them in indirect light in my slat house and keep them moist. It can take up to thirty days for them to germinate."

Sir James had willingly answered all questions about the process of hybridizing bougainvilleas, but had sidestepped anything to do with his own research.

"He was quite secretive though, wasn't he?" Holly said thoughtfully while sweeping up a pile of bougainvillea cuttings on the floor. "He didn't tell us anything about his own hybrids. I'd have liked to have seen some of them."

Myrtle overheard and snorted. "Oh, James Murray has always been like that. He's never joined the Garden Club, you know. Clare was a member—and very generous with cuttings and seeds—but James has always hoarded his plants. His slat houses are one of the biggest secrets on Hibiscus Island!" She looked at the two girls. "Have you visited his garden yet? Oh, you must! It's absolutely stunning and it's the first time he's opened it in ten years. When Clare died, James became a virtual hermit. He shut himself away in the house and buried himself in his work. His bonsais are spectacular of course, but he's also hybridized hibiscus and other plants besides the bougainvillea. Unfortunately, he's always refused to open his slat houses to the public!" She huffed.

Holly leaned on her broom. "I only vaguely remember Lady Murray. She was in a lot of the photos on Amelia's blog though. You said she'd hybridized that White Heart bougainvillea."

"Yes, she had quite a green thumb," Myrtle agreed. "If you go to the Murrays' garden, you'll see a unique collection of plants. Make sure you find the Japanese wisteria! It's quite magnificent. I remember when Clare got her cuttings and how she babied those plants along. She'd be very proud of it now!"

Myrtle bustled off and Holly glanced at Jamie, who was wiping down a table. "You know, we should really visit all the gardens that were open for that particular Bougainvillea Festival. Amelia must have had a reason for looking at the photos."

"Like what? And how do you know she was looking at those posts anyway?" Jamie asked reasonably. "She kept her diary the whole time she was on the island. She could have been checking out anything she wrote over five years."

Holly shook her head. "I asked Lucy earlier. Amelia hadn't logged out of her computer and when Lucy opened it up, the blog was open at those entries."

"Mmmm. She still could have been looking through the entire blog though," Jamie pointed out. "I don't think we should focus too much on just those entries."

Holly's face dropped. "I guess. But I still think something happened when she was touring the island that reminded her of the blog. Why else would she have pulled it up? There has to be a connection."

"I'm not disagreeing," Jamie said. "I just don't know how we'll figure out what it is now that we don't have access to

Amelia's computer anymore." She scowled at the thought. "Do we know where she went the first couple of days she was here?"

"That's why I'm saying we should check out the gardens," Holly said, looking at her friend in mild irritation. "I know she visited some because Mama advised Lucy to go before the official opening as they wouldn't be so crowded, and she'd get better photos."

"Oh. Well, let's ask Lucy where they went and if she noticed Amelia acting strangely—"

Holly snapped her fingers. "Oh! That reminds me! Amelia did do something strange! She went off somewhere by herself on Friday. Lucy told me she disappeared around ten in the morning and was late back. They were supposed to meet at four o'clock and Amelia didn't show up! We definitely need to find out where she went."

"You mean, she just disappeared by herself on the day she was murdered? What about needing a security guy for protection? And when did you hear all this?"

"Lucy told me at breakfast this morning." Holly looked at Jamie in contrition. "Sorry. I meant to tell you earlier."

"Doesn't matter. Lucy doesn't know where she went? When did Amelia get back?"

"Lucy didn't know. Apparently, Amelia just said she'd be back soon and took off. Lucy said Pete was livid. They ended up hanging around the inn all day because they didn't know when she'd return."

"Okay, but when did she get back?" Jamie asked insistently. "This is important, Holls! Maybe Amelia wasn't poisoned at the dinner after all!"

Holly stared at her. "What?"

"Time of death, Holls, remember? Myrtle said her source thinks Amelia was poisoned between five and ten, right? Well, if Amelia got back to the Inn after five, then she could have been poisoned somewhere else!"

"Oh!" Holly exclaimed. She looked excited. "And that would mean Gramps..."

"...wouldn't be a suspect," Jamie finished.

Both girls beamed at each other.

HOLLY WAS busy the next day. The Inn had suddenly become the most popular destination on the tour, and as she escorted back-to-back groups of visitors around the Inn's gardens, Holly became heartily sick of telling them that no, they couldn't see where the body was found; that yes, it was all cordoned off; and yes, there was still a policeman on site.

"Is it true the body was actually hidden under bougainvillea branches?" One of the Jones twins peered over the wall, trying to see the crime scene below.

"And is it true that it was Emily Carter? The Emily Carter who worked at Henry Sullivan's newspaper?" the other sister chimed in.

The Jones twins' noses twitched in excitement. Faded blue eyes were bright under identical snow-white crowns of hair as they leveled gimlet gazes on Holly.

"You know, dear," one said, "she really wasn't a nice woman!"

"No," her sister agreed immediately. She looked at Holly and lowered her voice to a whisper. "She wrote that dreadful advice column in the paper!"

Holly nodded. "I remember." She tried to steer the elderly twins away. "Have you seen the Bougainvillea Exhibit yet?"

There was a disapproving sniff. "Henry Sullivan should

have been ashamed. Publishing people's personal business for the whole island to see!"

"But people wrote in themselves," Holly protested, shepherding the elderly ladies down some steps. "They must have wanted advice. I know her answers weren't always very kind but—"

"They were very unkind, dear," one of the sisters countered, "but it was worse than that. When Emily Carter answered those letters, she gave away a lot of information. We nearly always knew who had asked for the advice!"

"And some of that column was suspect," the other twin added darkly. "I know for a fact Ellen Johnstone did *not* write to *Dear Priscilla*, and yet there was a letter that appeared to be from her. She swore she didn't write it and I believed her. Somehow that Emily Carter creature found out about Ellen's business, wrote a fake letter and then answered it. Oh yes," she said in response to Holly's disbelieving look, "it's absolutely true. Ellen Johnstone would never have told tales on anyone, no matter what was going on in the family, and least of all to a newspaper columnist!"

"And Ellen would never have written an anonymous letter. That's not the Hibiscus way!"

"No. The Carter woman faked it."

"She *really* wasn't a nice woman."

There was a disapproving shake of two heads of white curls.

By the time Holly saw the two ladies off the property, she was exhausted and headed straight for the kitchen in search of a restorative cup of tea. Maggie, accompanied by a prancing Truffle, found her slumped across the table.

"The Jones twins?" Maggie patted Holly's shoulder in commiseration. "I saw you coming out of the Bougainvillea Exhibit with them. They looked like they were in fine form."

"Oh, they were," Holly agreed in heartfelt accents as she bent down to pick up Truffle. The little cavapoo wiggled happily before settling in her lap. "They know everything about everybody! I heard more gossip today than I've heard in years!"

Grinning, Maggie poured herself a cup of tea and sat down beside Holly. "They've lived here their entire lives, but they've never even gone to the mainland. I think the furthest they've traveled is to Coral Island on the ferry and they were terrified the entire trip."

Coral Island was only a short hop away by plane but took about three hours by boat. It was a mountainous island and a popular destination for tourists who wanted to hike as well as enjoy fantastic scuba diving in crystal-clear water. Holly couldn't imagine the Jones' twins doing either of those activities.

"They went for a relative's wedding," Maggie said in response to Holly's raised eyebrow. "The elder Miss Jones told me they'd never go again."

Holly grinned and continued to stroke Truffle's curly fur. "They talked a lot about Amelia Cartell. That's all anyone's talked about, actually!" She looked curiously at her mother. "You really don't remember her, Mama?"

Maggie frowned. "I've been trying to think back. Your dad was off the island for about a year during that period. He was getting ready for his police inspector exams so was sent to the mainland for more experience, remember? He came home every two weeks for a couple of days."

"I remember. I was in eighth grade the year he was away. That was the year Amelia wrote the advice column. You don't remember it?"

Maggie shook her head. "I had the Inn to run, and you to look after. I have a vague memory of the column and an even vaguer one of the Sanders lawsuit. I expect I met Emily Carter at some point, but I honestly can't say she made an impression on me."

"You're in the minority, Mama. She seems to have made a pretty bad impression on a lot of people!"

"So I've heard. Well, the gossip will die down once the police solve the case." She looked quizzically at Holly. "Now, what have I said to cause you to make that face?"

"What face? I didn't make any face!" Holly protested. Maggie raised an eyebrow and Holly flushed. "I didn't mean to make a face. I just don't like the inspector very much. He suspects Gramps!" She turned crimson with indignation.

Maggie sighed. "Holly, Rob Tucker's a good man. He's just making sure he has all the information he needs. Just because he questions someone doesn't mean he suspects them of murder!"

"Sure." Holly rolled her eyes.

Maggie frowned. "Be fair. Inspector Tucker has his own way of doing things. It might not be what you're used to, but it doesn't mean he's incompetent."

Holly looked away from her mother's serious gaze. "I know that," she muttered. "I never said I thought he was incompetent. He's just... annoying."

"I like him. He reminds me of your dad a bit."

Holly gaped at her. "He's nothing like Dad! He's smug and he doesn't listen and..." Her voice trailed away at her mother's look.

"What you really mean is he refused to let himself be railroaded by Jamie, Myrtle, and, I presume, yourself. Right? Dare I hope that you all actually listened?" She groaned at the inadvertent flush on Holly's face. "You didn't. Well, I hope you know what you're doing, Holly. I don't want to have to post bail for anyone."

"He wouldn't arrest us just for asking questions."

Maggie cast her eyes heavenward as if praying for patience, then spoke more brightly. "So, tell me—what are your plans for the afternoon? More tours?"

Relieved at the change of topic, Holly said, "No, I'm off duty now, thank goodness. Two of the Garden Club members are taking over for me, and Gramps said he's going fishing so there's nothing to do in the slat house. He's tired of all these tourists interrupting his work, he says. I thought I'd go check out some of the other gardens and see the competition." She paused. "Now what? What's wrong with visiting the gardens?"

"The gardens you were looking at on the computer yesterday?" Maggie asked, one eyebrow raised.

Holly felt herself blushing again. Her mother knew her too well. "I haven't gone on the Bougainvillea Garden Tour for years," she protested. "I just want to see what they all look like. That's all."

"Uh huh." Maggie's skepticism was clear as she eyed her daughter. After a moment, she sighed. "Holly... Just don't start any trouble with the inspector, okay?"

"Start trouble? *Moi*?" Holly batted her eyelashes in exaggerated innocence at her mother. "Remember what dad used to say? 'I didn't start trouble; it was there when I got there.'"

"I remember," Maggie said dryly. "And do you remember what I used to say?"

Holly grinned. "Yep. 'It's easier to stay out of trouble now than it is to get out of it later.'" She gave her mother a hug. "Don't worry, Mama. I promise you, trouble is not in my vocabulary today."

"Mmmm. I wish I could believe that," Maggie said, as she returned the hug.

17

Since the cavapoo wouldn't be welcome in the gardens she planned to visit, Holly returned Truffle to the family part of the Inn. She started Truffle's special music playlist, laughed when the little dog jumped into her bed and rolled over for a nap, and headed for her mother's car.

Holly hummed with the radio as she drove along the south shore of Hibiscus Island. A light south-westerly wind played upon the turquoise water, sending tiny waves up onto the white sand beaches, and Holly sighed with pleasure as she looked out over the open ocean. On this beautiful, clear day, she could see Wreck Rock on the horizon.

A single volcanic peak surrounded by reefs, Wreck Rock was named for the two ships that had foundered and sunk just off the island. It was uninhabited but a great place for hiking, birdwatching and scuba-diving. Visitors to Hibiscus Island frequently took a day trip to the smaller islet since it was only a forty-minute ride by boat.

Holly glanced at the shiny brochure on the passenger seat and headed to the first garden on the list Lucy said she and Amelia had visited—Uncle Stanley Foster's renowned quarry garden. A sign at the bottom of Spice Hill directed her to the Quarry Garden and Holly turned carefully into the narrow lane. Allspice trees, with their silvery white trunks, crowded the road on either side, their aromatic leaves forming a tunnel of sweet-smelling green over the car as Holly drove up the hill. She tooted her horn at every bend, hoping not to meet another car coming down; if so, someone would have to reverse and it would likely be her.

With a sigh of relief, she emerged into a clearing halfway up the hill and drove the last hundred yards into Uncle Stanley's driveway. There was only one other car there, besides the Fosters' little red pickup and Holly pulled in beside it.

Over one hundred years old, Quarry Cottage retained many of the traditional Hibiscus Island architectural features. It was a low, square stone building painted white, with a stepped roof designed to collect rainwater, which was stored in the above ground limestone water tank alongside the house. Flared stone steps, known locally as 'welcoming arms' stairs, led up to a covered porch and hence to the front door. Dark green shutters hung at every sparkling window and a tiny stone buttery with its distinctive conical roof perched at one end of the building.

Built into the side of Spice Hill, the Fosters' family home, as its name implied, was near an old, abandoned stone quarry. Over the years, Uncle Stanley had annexed it as part of his garden and turned it into an enchanting and mysterious grotto. Along with the Foster grandchildren, Holly and Matt had spent many a childhood Sunday afternoon, playing in what was, according to childish whim, a faraway jungle, a fairy kingdom or a magical forest, while their parents and grandparents dozed after a big Sunday lunch.

A gangly young man waved to Holly from the porch. "Heya, Holly. You here for a tour?"

Holly climbed the stairs. "Are you the guide today, Simon? I heard you were cruising around on a glass-bottom boat this summer, scuba diving and generally taking life easy."

The youngest Foster grandson rolled his eyes. "Nana's been talking to you, has she? I keep telling her it's just a gap year. I'll go to college—I just want some time for me, you know, to think about what I want to do. I'm not sure about going into law anymore."

Holly raised her eyebrows in surprise. The Fosters ran a very successful law firm with branches on three other islands as well as Hibiscus. "What do your parents think about that?"

"Oh, they're fine with it. It's just Nana who's freaking out." Simon waved his hand in a dismissive motion. "So, Holly, what's up with this murder? Do you think the new guy will figure it out?" His dark brown eyes sparkled with excitement as he looked at Holly.

She shrugged. "I've only met him a couple of times. What does your brother think?" Simon's older brother was in the police service and Holly was curious about his impressions of the new inspector.

Simon made a face. "Oh, he just says he's cool but doesn't tell me anything. Sergeant Hollis likes him though. Says he's made from the same cloth as Uncle Solid and we're lucky to have him." Holly frowned at yet another glowing recommendation of Inspector Tucker, and Simon flinched. "Sorry, Holls. I know it's probably still hard to hear about Uncle Solid..."

"What? Oh no, that's okay." Holly hurried to reassure

him with a smile. "Really. It's nice that everyone still talks about Dad. It means he isn't forgotten."

Simon looked relieved. "You don't need me to go 'round the garden, do you? Because Pops is working at the airport today, and I have to go pick him up in..." Simon glanced at his watch and jumped up. "Oh, right now, actually. Can you show yourself around? Or are you here to see Nana? She's in the kitchen."

"Whose car is that?" Holly asked curiously, pointing to the white vehicle in the drive. "They didn't want a tour?"

Simon shook his head. "Nah. That's Doc Eastham. Mrs. Eastham is in talking to Nana and the doc is taking Becky Dumont around. You know, François's new wife. They're down in the quarry." He shouted through the door and waited till he heard an indistinct reply. "See you, Holls." Simon charged down the steps, leapt into the red pickup and roared down the hill at a speed that made Holly cringe.

Holly hesitated at the door for a moment, then decided that she'd pop in to see Auntie Elma after touring the garden. It was hot on the hillside and the quarry garden would be cool. Opening the gate in the wall, Holly walked through.

A weathered gray stone path meandered alongside a bed of old China roses so lovely Holly stopped a couple of times to smell the fragrant blossoms. Uncle Stanley loved his roses and had amassed a formidable collection which formed the bulk of the gardens around the house. He had underplanted with a range of sprawling plants including a few dwarf bougainvilleas and a very pretty variegated lily grass. Gradually the path started to slope downwards and ended at the gate that opened into the quarry garden.

The quarry was straight-sided and deep but had originally been carved out in sections, creating natural terraces that circled it. Uncle Stanley had planted these terraces, linking them together with steep stone steps now covered in moss. Holly kept a light hand on the wooden railing and looked about in delight.

The top of the garden received some sunlight and bougainvillea flourished on the walls alongside blue plumbago and cape honeysuckle. An Angel's Trumpet tree, also known as moonflower for its highly scented night-blooming blossoms, shaded the steps, its stunning apricot-colored flowers swaying gently in the breeze. Holly surveyed it thoughtfully, wondering if Uncle Stanley would give her a small cutting. There was a perfect place on her tiny patio for an Angel's Trumpet.

Deeper down, a row of coffee trees, difficult to grow on Hibiscus Island, drew Holly's attention, and she exclaimed at the sight of the small fruits starting to form. The jungle effect Holly remembered from her childhood was still present in the form of ferns and wild philodendron growing alongside snowberry, asparagus fern, and the huge fountain shaped leaves of the giant bird of paradise plant.

Movement below caught Holly's eye. She grinned as she recognized Doctor Eastham's iconic white canvas hat bobbing through the shrubbery, followed by a slightly larger straw hat. As the hats stopped, voices floated up to Holly.

"And this is a particularly fine specimen of *Monstera deliciosa*. We call it 'locust and wild honey' on the island, but it's also known as 'hurricane plant' and 'swiss cheese plant'. It has an edible fruit that looks a bit like a cucumber covered in small tiles." There was a murmured question followed by a laugh. "What does it taste like? Oh, a mix of mango, pineapple, banana and vanilla ice cream in a custard texture! It's quite delicious, hence its botanical name."

As Holly descended the last few steps to the ground

floor of the quarry, she saw Doc Eastham, after determined rummaging, pick a fruit and present it to the slim, petite young woman who was with him. "You mustn't eat it until the tiles fall off," he cautioned. "It's quite toxic until it ripens fully. Just pop it in a brown paper bag and wait for it. François will know when it's ripe." He pushed the green fruit into her hands.

His companion smiled. "I look forward to it."

Doc Eastham straightened up as Holly approached. "Why, Holly Gold!" he exclaimed with pleasure. "How nice to see you! I heard you were back on the island. How's your grandfather? I haven't seen him for ages. You tell him he needs to come and see me for his annual checkup!"

"I'll tell him," Holly replied with a grin, "but I doubt he'll listen."

"I'll have to do a house call." The doctor's eyes twinkled at Holly. "Set in their ways, some of our old-timers! Have you two met yet? Becky, this is Holly Gold, partner in crime to that miscreant, Jamie. She's a horticulturist like her Gramps. Holly, this is Becky Dumont, our new librarian in Bridgeport. She'll be taking over from my spouse next month. Yes," he said, in answer to Holly's surprised look, "my dear wife is actually going to retire after forty years of service!"

"Has Mrs. Eastham been there that long?" Holly exclaimed. "Wow! I hope the town is throwing a big retirement bash!"

"She deserves it," Becky interjected warmly. "The library is amazing and I'm so impressed with the number of book clubs on the island. All the reading rooms have been fully booked all summer. It's fabulous! And I love that there's a summer student intern program as well."

Doc Eastham beamed at this praise of his wife. "Come

along, Holly. You can join us. You probably know all the secrets of this garden. Holly's an island girl," he said to Becky. "Born and bred. I delivered her, you know. She was a squaller."

Holly flushed. "Doc!"

Becky laughed. "You said the same thing about François. Are all island babies squallers?"

"Every one of them!" Doc Eastham agreed, his eyes twinkling. He peered at a dangling flower in front of him. "This is a very nice shell ginger, isn't it, Holly?"

As they wandered around the garden, Holly kept an eye open for anything that resembled a photo scene from Amelia's blog. So far nothing looked familiar. After a moment, she asked Becky, "How long have you been on the island?"

Becky smiled. "Not long. I met François when he was doing a culinary course in London three years ago. We hit it off; I visited a couple of times and then he proposed." A slight blush stained her cheeks. "We got married at the end of last year and I moved to the island. There was a bit of an adjustment period—it's a very small place, isn't it? — but I love it here! It's been fun touring the Festival gardens. Our own garden is very tiny, but I'm getting some ideas."

"Becky is our new inspector's sister," Doc Eastham said, stopping to inspect a bright yellow shrimp plant. "This is quite a nice little shrub, isn't it, Holly? I like how it's been scattered around. Very effective." He eyed Holly with kind concern. "How are you all coping with this incident up at the Inn? Is Maggie managing all right? Tell her to give me a call if it all gets to be too much for her. It's an unpleasant thing, murder, but I'm sure Rob will solve the case quickly. He's a good man. Very like your dad, Holly. Once our new inspector gets used to our little island ways, I'm sure he'll settle right in!"

Before a flustered Holly could respond, an annoyed voice floated down from the top of the quarry. "Colin!"

"Oh dear," Doc Eastham muttered, patting around his body. "I must have left my pager behind again. We'll have to wrap this visit up, I'm afraid."

The three visitors climbed the quarry steps quickly, the doctor opening the top gate for the young women.

"Colin! There's been a call for you! You left your phone up here!" Mrs. Eastham's voice was exasperated as she stood, hands on her hips, beside Auntie Elma in the middle of the garden. "And where's your pager? The hospital called. We're going to have to rush. It's Mrs. Wainwright. She's gone into labor."

Doc Eastham nodded placidly. "I thought she might start early. Well, Elma, I'll have to come by another time to see Stanley. Give him my regards, won't you?" He ambled towards their car, in no noticeable hurry.

Mrs. Eastham looked apologetic. "I'm so sorry, Becky, but we'll have to cancel the rest of the garden visits this afternoon."

"Oh, that's okay," Becky said. "I don't mind at all. Honest."

Auntie Elma looked at Holly. "What are you doing this afternoon? You can take Becky to some of the gardens, can't you? It would be a shame to waste her afternoon off, and you can drop her back in Bridgeport in time for opening."

The Bridgeport Library was closed on Wednesday afternoons but opened again from six till nine in the evening. Library nights were popular with many of the island's teens, who enjoyed the varied activities sponsored by different organizations.

Holly smiled, remembering some of the events she had attended as a high school student. "Sure. I need to pop into the library anyway so that'll work fine." She turned to Becky. "I was going to go see Wreck Point and Blue Horizons today. Have you been there yet?"

Mrs. Eastham smiled with relief, waved a hasty good-bye and hustled her husband towards the car. "Come on, Colin," she scolded. "Babies wait for no man!"

18

Becky Dumont leaned back in the front seat of Holly's car. "You know," she said conversationally, "not having a car of my own has been one of the biggest adjustments to living here. I have a little electric buggy, but it's really more like a golf cart. Okay for town but not the best vehicle for the hills."

Holly grinned. "I know. This is my mama's car. Sometimes the one-car-per-household rule is a pain, but it keeps traffic down and the island really is too small for a lot of vehicles. Besides, given the way some people drive—like my cousin Matt, for instance—it's probably a good idea to keep the numbers down."

"Yes, I know Matt," Becky said with a laugh. "And Sebastian Flynn picked me up once in the Inn van. That was a hair-raising experience—although at least you drive on the same side of the road as we do in England. The island's an interesting cultural mix, isn't it?"

"In what way?" Holly asked.

"Well, the road signs are in kilometers, but everyone uses miles when they talk about distances, for instance. The legal system follows English common law, from originally being a British territory I imagine, but the schools use a North American curriculum and I've noticed a lot of people flipflop between American and British spelling and use of words. I've helped students with homework, and they just use the different spelling interchangeably in essays and don't even notice."

"I'll bet their teachers do," Holly said, speaking from experience.

Becky continued, "And I've met people from around the world here, not just visitors but residents. Islanders love to talk, and it's fascinating to hear where everyone's from." She looked at Holly. "What about you? I know you were born here, but where are your parents from?"

"They were both born here too," Holly said. Then she grinned. "But, to your point, my dad's mother was from Portugal—the Azores islands, actually—and his father was from Ireland. My Gramps was born here, too, but his parents were Scottish, and my late grandmother was from England."

"See? My husband's family have French and Polish roots. And Aunt Elma has French, Spanish, and West African ancestors, although her family's been on the island since the eighteenth century. Uncle Stanley was born here but his father came from Guyana. It's fascinating, isn't it!"

Becky's dark brown eyes sparkled with interest in a tanned face. Her brown hair was cut short, and she looked like an animated pixie in her spring-green t-shirt and denim shorts.

Holly grinned. "I see you've already started using the island vernacular," she teased. "Uncle Stanley and Aunt Elma, huh?"

"They told me to call them that," Becky protested. "I like it. It's very friendly and informal. Not like where I'm from."

"You grew up in England, right?" Holly asked.

"Yes, but my dad's parents were from Nigeria. Our mom is a good Yorkshire lass through and through, although Rob and I grew up down south." Becky looked at Holly, her eyes twinkling. "I hear you've had a run-in with my policeman brother."

Holly jerked in shock, causing the car to swerve. She squeaked and regained control of the wheel. "What—"

"Oh, don't worry, he didn't tell me. I got it from Jamie— and Myrtle was also quite informative when she was in the library yesterday." Becky eyed Holly in speculation. "I also heard you're visiting the Festival gardens looking for something that might shed light on why Amelia Cartell was killed. Is that right?"

"Good grief!" The car swerved again, slowed, then resumed course. "Are they blabbing to the whole island?"

Becky laughed out loud. "Just to me. It was providential meeting you like this, Holly, because I've been headhunted as the fourth Musketeer."

"The fourth—" Holly slowed the car down even more and looked sideways at Becky. "What on earth have they been saying to you?"

Becky's eyes sparkled with laughter. "Well, Jamie told me all about the Hibiscus Island Detective Club and how many cases you've solved—"

"Cases we've solved? We were children!" Holly spluttered.

"—and Myrtle filled me in on everything she's learned from her sources about the poisoning. They both cross-examined me about Rob. Poor guy, he really did put his foot in it with all of you, didn't he? I'm afraid my brother can be a little, shall we say, stiff, at times."

Holly groaned. "I am so sorry," she began, but Becky cut her off.

"Oh, don't be sorry. Rob can be stuffy, as Jamie says. I know that. He's a good cop though. Anyway, according to Myrtle, I'll be an asset to the team due to my superlative research skills. Of course, she also wants me to find out information from Rob, but I've said that's highly unlikely. My brother is very official when he has his detective hat on. Which is why I don't intend to tell him about any of this. At least, not yet." Becky leaned back in her seat and smiled widely. "So, Holly, fill me in. What are we trying to find in these gardens?"

A SHORT WHILE LATER, the two girls stood at the very edge of the garden at Wreck Point, home to a well-respected member of the Garden Club. The house had been built on the top of a cliff and had stunning views over the south shore, with Wreck Rock prominent on the horizon. As well as some phenomenal specimens of bougainvillea—including the elusive White Heart hybrid that Holly had been delighted to see for the first time—Wreck Point offered the visitor the chance to see a comprehensive collection of wind- and salt-tolerant plants in a natural setting.

"Well, I don't see anything even remotely helpful," Holly said in disappointment. "I remember this view from one of the photos on the blog, but I can't see anything suspicious about it. Can you?"

Holly and Becky had left the tour guide and the other visitors sipping on glasses of iced tea in the walled ornamental garden and headed out to the cliffs, where burnt orange and red gaillardia grew amongst silver buttonwood and the bright yellow flowers of the sea oxeye plant.

Now Becky exclaimed over the pink feathery flowers of the ice-plant that tumbled down the cliff to the small beach below. Crouching to take a photo, she answered Holly's question. "Suspicious? No. Why? Did Lucy say anything about this particular garden?" She zoomed in carefully with her camera.

"No," Holly admitted with a sigh. "According to Lucy, Amelia was in a foul mood on Thursday and found fault with just about everything. All she remembers was Amelia went quiet at some point in the afternoon, and she was so relieved to have some peace that she didn't question it." Holly stared out at the sea, noticing clouds gathering offshore. "And when I asked Pete, all he could talk about was how annoying Amelia was and what was the point of hiring personal security if she didn't listen to a word he said. Apparently, he lost her when they stopped somewhere. She disappeared into the woods, and he couldn't find her for about thirty minutes."

When Becky looked puzzled, Holly hastened to explain. "Amelia was getting anonymous threatening letters. That's why Pete was hired. To protect her." She grinned at the expression on Becky's face.

"For a travel blog? It seems a bit far-fetched," the English girl said skeptically, "but then again, someone did kill her, so I guess she was justified. Did Pete say where they were when she disappeared?"

"Yeah, Spanish Cliffs, but there's no mention of them in the old blog—only the gardens—and since that's what we think Amelia was reading when she got back..." Holly shrugged.

"It might be worth a look anyway," Becky suggested. She glanced at her watch. "Do we have time to go there before going back to the library?"

Holly shook her head. "No. They're at the other end of the island. I might be able to get out there tomorrow." She grinned at her new friend. "Anyway, I want to read through some old newspapers, so I'm coming to the library as well. Jamie's meeting me when she finishes work. We thought we'd check out the column Amelia used to write. Maybe there'll be some clues in that. You can join us."

THE BRIDGEPORT LIBRARY was across the street from City Hall, with pedestrian entrances off Compass Avenue and Spinnaker Road. A two-storied building, it was light and airy, with a welcoming lobby complete with circulation desk and information center.

The Children's Library was upstairs. With its brightly painted walls, whimsical murals, and low bookcases, it was a vibrant and popular space for the youngest patrons.

The Teen Library was located downstairs in the west wing of the building. It featured diner-style seating and study spaces, as well as an extensive collection of young adult books. The island's teenagers had access to library laptops, computers, and the very popular media lounge, which could be booked for entertainment and movie nights.

The east wing of the library housed the main book collection, a large lecture hall, three boardrooms that could be booked for meetings, several small study rooms, and a large media technology room containing a number of computers along with printers and copiers.

Although the library was currently in the middle of a

comprehensive digitization project to preserve materials and existing resources, the basement still held an archive of past newspapers, magazines, old photographs, and documents pertaining to island history. The 'stacks' were beloved by some of the island's seniors, and several volunteered their services on a regular basis to scan documents, reminiscing about the past as they worked.

Holly entered the well-lit archives and smiled at the sight of Mr. Graham, in his familiar brightly colored Hawaiian shirt and white gloves, bending carefully over the scanner. Mr. Graham was a longtime member of the Hibiscus Island Historical Society who had devoted his life to researching and preserving the history of the island. He was an avid scuba diver, passionate about the environment, and had a special interest in the ocean and its many mysteries.

Right now, he was studying an old map, and Holly waited patiently until he'd finished.

"Hi, Mr. Graham."

Mr. Graham squinted across the room and then beamed. "Holly Gold! How nice to see you? It's been a while. Are you keeping up with your diving?"

"I haven't done much lately," Holly admitted. "Work kept me busy. But I'm back on the island for good now, so I'm sure I'll get back in the water soon. I'd like to try my hand at lionfish hunting!"

Mr. Graham nodded in approval. "Good, good. They're a scourge on our reefs." He beckoned her over. "Look at this. It's an old map from the seventeenth century! Fascinating, isn't it?"

Holly nodded. "And beautiful too. Are you scanning all these?" She looked at the pile of documents in front of them.

"I'm preparing for a lecture at the end of the summer. The treasure ships of the islands. You'll have to come." Mr. Graham smoothed the map lovingly with a white-tipped finger, then looked at Holly. "What brings you to the archives, Holly?"

"Well, I saw this old blog recently." Holly hesitated. "It was written by Amelia Cartell—she used to be called Emily Carter."

Mr. Graham nodded absently. "Oh yes. She was in here last week. Looked quite different from how I remember her. I—"

"Wait!" Holly interrupted. "Amelia Cartell was here? Last week? Doing what?"

"Research, I imagine. I didn't really pay attention." Mr. Graham made a move towards another old map.

"What day was that? What time?"

"Hmm? Oh, um, Thursday? Friday? Yes, it was Friday. Just before lunch, I believe."

"But... Mr. Graham, she was murdered on Friday night!"

"I know," the researcher said, shaking his head in disapproval. "Quite shocking. I don't know what this island is coming to!"

Holly stared at him helplessly. "Did you tell the police that she was here?"

"Oh, they already knew," Mr. Graham said. "Our new police inspector was in here yesterday."

Holly spluttered. "Inspector Tucker was here too? Doing what?"

Mr. Graham looked surprised. "He wanted to look at newspapers."

"Are you serious? But that's what I wanted to do!" Holly exclaimed in exasperation. "I wanted to look at some past Bougainvillea Festival accounts!"

"Well, my goodness, Holly, the papers are still here you know. He didn't take them away. You can still look through them." Mr. Graham offered her a soothing smile. "Aisle five. All the back copies of *The Island Gazette*."

Holly huffed in annoyance. "Yes but... Never mind." She forced a smile. "Would you happen to know exactly what papers Inspector Tucker was looking at?"

"Oh, I didn't really pay attention. I helped him find the years he wanted and left him in peace. I'm very busy right now. It's going to take me quite a while to scan all these maps, you know. It's a big project. I really need more volunteers." Mr. Graham frowned at the stack of documents on the table.

"Mr. Graham," Holly pleaded, "can you just show me what the inspector was looking at? Please?" Seething silently, she followed the amiable researcher into the stacks.

19

Mr. Graham rooted around on the shelves of file boxes. "We haven't got around to digitizing these yet. Ah, here you go. The inspector said he wanted to look at accounts from around this time period. I reminded him to put everything back when he finished." He tutted with remembered annoyance. "The Carter woman, you know, left quite a mess for me to put away. I trust you won't do that, Holly."

Holly stared at the boxes. "Amelia—Emily, I mean—was looking through these as well? Which boxes, Mr. Graham?"

"Hmmm. Well, it was this shelf, I believe." The researcher peered at the labels. "Might have been this box— or this—or this..."

"These are from eleven years ago," Holly said, reading the titles on the file boxes. "Are you sure these are the ones she was looking at?"

"Possibly." Mr. Graham sounded doubtful, and Holly smothered a groan as he peered at the shelves. "It could have been this shelf, now that I think about it."

"Twelve years ago?"

Mr. Graham fingered his lip. "I'm not quite sure, Holly, but I do remember she was looking in this general area."

"I guess I'll just have to look through them all." Holly sighed.

"Is there anything else I can help you with before I go back to my maps?"

Holly hesitated. "Did you know Amelia—Emily—when she worked on the island?"

"Not really. She wasn't terribly interested in research. Wrote her articles off the cuff, I'd say. I do recall one ridiculous story about Castlebay Fort. I wrote and complained to Henry Sullivan about it. All about pirates and such rubbish. Completely inaccurate!" Mr. Graham snorted.

"Do you remember anything important that happened on the island during the time she was here? Anything she might have been looking for in these newspapers?"

"From twelve years ago?"

"I guess. Or eleven? If these are the papers she was looking at."

"Hmmm." Mr. Graham pondered the question for a moment. "That's a pretty tall order... Eleven or twelve years ago... Well, that was about the time Hurricane Frank hit. Ripped up a large portion of the south shore road. Terrible erosion, and I remember I lost power for three weeks! I expect you had a generator at the Inn." Before Holly could respond, he shrugged and continued, "I'm afraid nothing is really springing to mind, Holly. Hibiscus Island is a quiet little place, as you know."

Holly sighed. "Thanks anyway, Mr. Graham."

"Happy to be of help." The researcher smiled. "I'll get back to my maps now. Don't forget to tidy everything up when you're done."

~

HOLLY HAD newspapers spread over several tables when the door to the archives burst open and Jamie and Becky tumbled in, both laughing.

"Where are you, Holls?" Jamie called.

Becky shushed her, gesturing toward Mr. Graham, who had looked up with a frown. His face cleared when he saw the young librarian and then he glanced at his watch in alarm. "Is it closing time already? Surely not!"

"No, no, you've still got some time, Mr. Graham," Becky assured him. "The kids are watching *Pride and Prejudice* tonight. I've just popped down to see if Holly found what she was looking for." She smiled at the researcher.

"Ah good, good," he replied, and turned back to his maps.

With a grin, Becky beckoned to Jamie and they tiptoed through the stacks.

"Good grief!" Jamie exclaimed. "What a mess! Have you found anything helpful?"

"It's not a mess," Holly retorted. "It's a system. There's a lot to go through."

Jamie grinned. "Well, put us to work. Becky's got some college kids supervising the movie crowd and said she could help us. I've filled her in on everything we already know."

"I just have to go up at the end of the movie for the discussion period, and to make sure everything is cleaned up," Becky added, moving closer to one of the tables.

"Well, I've only been skimming so far," Holly began. "I looked at some of the earliest things Amelia wrote when she first arrived, just to get a sense of style, and there's nothing slanderous or malicious at all for the first two years. Completely innocuous fluff pieces."

Jamie raised an eyebrow. "So, her blog...?"

"I thought it might have been a private venting platform. You know, the sort of thing where you write everything you'd really like to say to someone before making it more professional. A place to blow off steam. Or just a nasty diary." Holly shrugged, then looked up with a frown. "It's very annoying that the police impounded that computer! It would have been good if we could have compared her diary to what she wrote officially!"

"What happened after the first two years?" Becky asked. "I'm guessing things changed."

"Yeah. She was assigned the *Dear Priscilla* column. It ran twice a week. I haven't read everything obviously, but it escalated. Started with advice and turned into nasty scandal. It only ran for one year."

"It was the best reading in eighth grade," Jamie confided to Becky. "It came out on Mondays and Thursdays and we would spend the whole lunch hour trying to figure out who'd written in. We thought Amelia's responses were hysterical." She shook her head. "I feel kind of guilty about that now."

"The year after that," Holly continued, "was when Amelia started doing investigative articles. So-called, anyway. Again, I've only dipped in and out, but it looks like initially she just raked up old stories about the island and made them sensational. Pirates and things like that. Then they became more personal. The Sanders story was the last thing she wrote, although there's quite a lot about the libel suit after that."

"Hmm." Jamie fingered a newspaper and peered at the date on it before glancing around the room. "So, where do you want us to start?"

Holly leaned back in her chair. "Well, this table has

papers from twelve years ago, which is when that Festival in the blog took place. This pile is June—it doesn't look like the newspaper articles are as bad as the blog posts, from what I've seen so far, but she gets a few digs in. She wrote several articles that week."

"Those papers," she continued, pointing to another table, "are the *Dear Priscilla* columns from thirteen years ago, and those," she indicated a third table, "are the ones that have accounts of the Sanders libel case—which was around eleven years ago and just before Amelia left the island. Her byline stops in April." She looked smug. "See? A system."

"Impressive," Becky said, her eyes twinkling. "You could be a detective. Or better yet, a librarian."

Holly grinned. Waving her hand at the papers in front of her, she said, "I'm focusing on these first, because Mr. Graham told me Amelia was in here on Friday and was looking at these boxes." She made a face. "At least, he thinks it was these. He wasn't completely sure."

"Friday! The day she was murdered!" Jamie exclaimed.

"Yeah. But so far I haven't seen anything that jumps out at me." Holly surveyed the pile of papers on the table. "I've got to say, I'm glad the *Gazette* only publishes twice a week! Imagine if it was a daily! We'd never get through them all."

"It's a great local paper," Becky said. "Very friendly and chatty. It's almost like a newsletter, really."

Jamie nodded. "There's no need for anything more since we get all the world news online now. *The Gazette* just keeps us up to date about Hibiscus happenings."

"And it's the Hibiscus happenings of the past that we're interested in," Holly said pointedly. "Pull up a chair, you two, and get started!"

Jamie grinned. "I'll tackle *Dear Priscilla*." She ambled

across the room, sat down at the appropriate table, and pulled the top newspaper towards her.

"Shall I look at some of these?" Becky asked, gesturing to the papers surrounding Holly. "I'm not sure how useful I'll be since I wasn't here then, but I'm certainly willing to help."

"Well, we were between twelve and fifteen years old when all this was going on, and according to Myrtle, too wrapped up in ourselves to know anything." Holly grinned. "You won't be any less knowledgeable than us."

Becky laughed. "I like Myrtle. I think it's funny she's so involved in all of this and that you guys let her hang out with you. She's kind of like a cool, older aunt."

Jamie snorted. "Great-aunt, you mean. And since when did anyone ever let Myrtle do anything? She just takes over! Insinuates herself into situations and before you know it, you're having a cup of tea with her while she tells you how to solve a murder! And as for being older—that's never stopped Myrtle from doing anything! The woman invited herself to the high school graduating class's boat cruise last year, for Pete's sake! And they all adored her." Jamie scowled. "They'll learn. Wait till she starts poking around in *their* lives!"

Becky was laughing but Holly raised an eyebrow. "Did you see Myrtle today? What did she say?"

"I had coffee with her," Jamie muttered. "At the Bean. She had more information she was dying to share. I meant to tell you as soon as I got here, but got distracted by all this. Myrtle said that her source told her... You know, she still won't tell me who this source is! It's exasperating!" She leaned back in her chair, her scowl deepening.

"The information?" Holly prompted.

"Right. They got more lab tests back. Seems Amelia had other things in her besides scopolamine. They found traces of atropine and hyo... hyo... hyoscyamine as well. They all cause similar symptoms like light phobia, restlessness, agitation, and coordination problems." She paused for effect, giving her friends a meaningful look. "Amelia didn't have too much to drink on Friday night—she'd already been poisoned!"

There was a brief silence.

"So... how long would it take for those symptoms to show up?" Holly asked. "And have they narrowed down the time of death at all?"

"Oh, that's where it gets interesting. Apparently, these things... Hang on, I made some notes." Jamie consulted her phone. "They're called tropane alkaloids. People who take fatal doses usually die of respiratory failure, but the amount needed to be fatal varies from person to person. Myrtle said judging by how people say Amelia was acting at the dinner, they think she was poisoned two hours, give or take thirty minutes, before the first symptoms started. She was slurry at seven thirty, I know, so she could have been poisoned as early as five but no later than six o'clock." She looked at Holly. "Did you find out what time she got back to the Inn?"

"Yes! Lucy said she shot in just before seven o'clock! So, it *wasn't* anyone at the Inn who killed her! Oh gosh, that's great. Gramps can't possibly be a suspect now!" Holly slumped back in relief.

"Well," Becky said cautiously, "I don't think you can rule out the Inn guests completely. The body was hidden, remember?"

"And Myrtle says the medical people now estimate she died no later than ten o'clock," Jamie added, "which means the killer was at the party. Unless, of course, someone else hid the body."

"What on earth for?" Holly exclaimed. "Why would an innocent person hide a dead body?"

Jamie shrugged. "People are weird sometimes."

"Did Myrtle know anything else about the poison?" Becky looked thoughtful. "I mean, where would you get those compounds? They can't be easy to find, or can they?"

"Scopolamine is an anti-nausea drug," Jamie began.

Holly snapped her fingers. "Hey! Atropine! I just remembered. There's an Agatha Christie mystery where someone used atropine eye drops to kill the victim!"

"Oh, yes! You're right! One of the Miss Marple mysteries!" Jamie exclaimed in excitement. "Eye drops and anti-nausea medicine—not that hard to find, I imagine!"

Becky frowned. "But you mentioned another compound —hyoscyamine, wasn't it? What's that? And how would the killer get Amelia to take all these things?"

There was another brief silence.

"We'll figure it out," Jamie said.

"THIS IS INTERESTING." Becky looked up from the paper she was reading. "You know that bougainvillea we saw today, Holly? That pretty pink one with the white center? It looks like it was quite a big deal. The woman who hybridized it got a write-up in one of the big horticultural magazines. That's why there were so many pictures of the plants in everyone's gardens that year. Lady Murray gave small plants to everyone in the Garden Club, and they took photos at that festival to show how they were thriving." She paused. "I wonder if I could find the article that's mentioned here. I'm sure the magazine will have an online archive."

As Becky trotted over to one of the computers in the

room to begin a search, Jamie clutched her head and groaned. "I don't know why we thought this column was funny! I mean, look at this letter to someone called EJ! Poor thing! Amelia's response is really nasty."

Holly glanced over. "EJ? As in Ellen Johnstone?"

"Ellen Johnstone? You mean old Ellen? The one who lives on the edge of town in that weird little house? Why would it be her?"

"The Jones twins mentioned her," Holly replied. "They claimed Amelia faked a letter from her. Said that Ellen would never have written about family business. What's the letter about?"

"Fishing. EJ asked what she should do if she knew someone was setting illegal fish pots. Amelia lectures her on consequences and then goes into a harangue about protecting criminals. Hints at a cover-up! Unnecessarily nasty, if you ask me! And she made the whole thing up?" Jamie frowned.

"Maybe. Hang on a minute," Holly said. "Mr. Graham might remember this. The fish pot ban was one of his projects."

"Ellen Johnstone? What about her?" Mr. Graham asked, looking at the article Holly was holding. "Oh, the fish pot letter! Yes, actually, I do remember this. Ellen wrote in asking what to do if someone she knew was putting down illegal fish pots!" Mr. Graham tutted. "Very silly! She knew quite well what she should have done! She should have reported it directly to the Fisheries department and the police! Everyone knew what fish pots had done to the reefs, and yet people still tried to sneak them into the water! I don't know what Ellen thought an advice columnist was going to tell her!"

"But why was everyone so sure it was her?" Holly asked. "There had to be other people with the initials E and J."

"Oh yes, of course, but Ellen's nephew was a fisherman. And there'd been trouble with him breaking the law in the past. He'd been fined before for illegal fishing within the reef zone, taking fish that were too small, taking lobsters out of season, all sorts of things. It was obvious to everyone who she was talking about. The coast guard and police got involved, illegal fish pots were found, he was fined and got a year's jail sentence—repeated offences, you see." Mr. Graham sighed. "And he lost his fishing license for good. I remember he was very unhappy about it. However, he knew the penalty and we really do have to protect the reefs. Things are getting so much worse now as well, what with the oceans warming and—"

"Yes, I know, Mr. Graham. It's dreadful," Holly interrupted. "Thanks very much." She wandered back to the table, frowning.

"So, you think Amelia faked this letter? Why? What would she get out of it?" Jamie leaned back in her chair.

"Attention maybe. More readers. A way to make Mr. Sullivan notice her and give her a chance at being an investigative reporter. Which she was, in an underhanded kind of way. I wonder how many other letters she faked."

"More to the point," Becky said, joining them with a printout in her hands, "we know that Amelia was spying on people, learning their secrets, and broadcasting them. I wonder how many secrets she knew that she didn't share."

"And if one of them got her killed," Jamie added.

20

The next morning Holly surveyed her grandfather's cutting beds in the slat house. "Gramps, have you seen Sir James Murray's slat houses?"

"What?" Gramps looked up from where he was mixing soil. "Murray's slat houses? Not for some time. Why?"

Holly squatted down on an overturned terracotta planter and watched her grandfather begin to fill small four-inch pots. "I read an article yesterday about Lady Murray and a bougainvillea she hybridized. I know Sir James hybridizes as well and wondered what his slat houses were like. I'd love to see his work."

Gramps snorted. "Good luck to you. Murray acts like he's got all the gold of England in there."

Holly blinked. "I heard he was brilliant. Secretive, but brilliant. Myrtle said he does a lot of hybridization."

Gramps stood up. "He does, but you won't find him sharing anything. Now Clare, on the other hand, she was a generous gardener. Gave away cuttings and seeds all the time. Had a fiery temper, I remember, but generous with her plants."

"She created the White Heart bougainvillea," Holly said. "I saw it yesterday at Wreck Point. Did she give you one?"

Gramps grunted. "Pretty plant, but not very hardy. Clare was still experimenting with that. I said I'd wait for her next round. Myrtle has one. I should get a cutting from her and try to propagate it since it was Clare's last creation. Sad that. Very sad. She's a loss to the horticulture world."

"She died, didn't she? Was she sick?"

Gramps shook his head. "Accident. Happened the spring after that hurricane ripped through. The big one. What was it called again? Frances?"

"Frank," Holly supplied.

"Frank. Yes. Did a number on the south shore, that storm. Massive erosion. It weakened a lot of the cliff areas. Clare was a great bird watcher, you know, and had been out on the cliffs with her binoculars. The edge crumbled. Took three days to find her." Gramps shook his head sadly. "Bad day for the island, that. Clare Murray was a good woman."

"And Sir James became a hermit." Holly sighed. "He must have loved her a lot."

"A hermit? Rubbish. Who told you that?"

"Myrtle did."

"Pah. Romancing as usual. Murray carried on the same as always. Went to court, did his job, went home, and skulked in his slat houses. Oh, I'm not saying he didn't love his wife, but he wouldn't show it. Stiff upper lip and all that —that's Sir James Murray for you. He retired the year after Clare's death, but he'd been planning that anyway. Just bumped it up a bit. Maybe he did withdraw a little," Gramps conceded, "but that's quite natural. Give the man his due— he's good at propagating. Some decent plants have come out of his slat houses, I have to say." A smug look crossed his face. "Hasn't won the Bougainvillea Trophy yet though."

"But Myrtle said he wouldn't open the gardens again. This is the first year since Clare died. She said he couldn't bear the thought of it."

Gramps snorted. "Nothing to do with Clare. Murray didn't want the hassle of visitors, that's all." He shrugged. "Don't know why he changed his mind. Probably just to get Myrtle off his back. The woman has hounded him every year about opening up to the public."

"I'm going there this afternoon," Holly said. "I hear it's beautiful."

"Some nice specimens," Gramps agreed. "You'll like it."

Holly borrowed her mother's car after lunch and took a leisurely drive along the north shore. The north side of Hibiscus Island was rocky, with lots of small inlets and coves to tempt snorkelers and swimmers. Holly grinned when she saw several young teens jumping off the rocks; it had been a favorite pastime of hers when she was that age.

The Murray estate was at the far end of the island and Holly slowed to a crawl as she turned into the wide driveway, her head swiveling from side to side as she tried to take in the extensive grounds with their lush and varied plantings.

"Wow!" she murmured to herself. "This is some property!"

Cliffside House, located at the end of a small peninsula, dated back to the seventeenth century, although the original small cottage was now lost in the mansion that had grown up around it. Holly gaped at the building as she pulled into the paved parking lot. Butter-yellow walls contrasted with the white Palladian-style pillars, wide entrance steps, and upper floor wrap-around balcony that flowed out of sight around the building.

Still staring, Holly picked up the Garden Club brochure and flipped through it until she found Cliffside. "Seven bedrooms, generous room proportions, numerous balconies, two small guest cottages... Four acres of land-scaped grounds... Private pool and beach... And all for one man. Very nice."

Holly climbed the front steps slowly, admiring the over-flowing planters that graced the entrance and gazing up at the delicate fronds of the bottle palms that towered over the doorway. Following voices that echoed from inside the large reception hall, Holly entered to find a Garden Club table, manned by none other than Myrtle, clad today in lime-green with a small black hat perched on top of her immacu-late silver hair.

"You'll find refreshments near the Rose Garden," she was saying to two other visitors, "and make sure you visit the walled garden. There are some magnificent climbing plants there, including a splendid Japanese wisteria, which is just finishing its bloom. It's the only specimen on the island and well worth a look."

She handed them maps and showed the visitors out a side door, then turned to beckon Holly closer. As the young woman approached, Myrtle lowered her voice to a whisper. "Did you hear about the latest lab test results?"

Holly smothered a grin and nodded. "Atropine and hyoscyamine, but they still don't know where the compounds came from."

Myrtle frowned. "No. And my source was puzzled by the combination as well. It's an unusual mix, he said. I called Becky this morning and asked her to do some research for us today. You met her yesterday, I believe? Good. We're meeting tonight to catch up. Jamie is hosting us at the Bean."

Holly blinked. "Um, a meeting? Tonight?"

Myrtle looked impatient. "It's the only night I can manage. The culinary evening is tomorrow, and we'll be prepping for the banquet all day on Saturday. Six thirty tonight. We'll compare notes." She looked up and stiffened. "Hmph. Looks like our new Inspector has decided to visit. Inspector Tucker." She greeted him with a curt nod.

"Myrtle," Rob replied, inclining his head as he approached. "How are you?"

"Hmph." Myrtle eyed the police chief suspiciously. "What do you want?"

Inspector Tucker gave no sign he noticed the combative tone. "I've been made to understand that Ms. Cartell visited this garden on the afternoon of the day she died."

"This garden?"

"What? Who told you that?"

Holly and Myrtle spoke together, and Rob's lips twitched in sudden amusement. "Yes. This garden. And I can't reveal my source, I'm afraid."

"What do you want, Inspector?" Myrtle bit the words off.

"I just have a couple of questions." The inspector paused. "And since you're here as well, Miss Gold, I'd appreciate it if you could join us."

Myrtle scowled. "I'm on duty."

"Could you take a short break?" the inspector asked, keeping his tone pleasant. "It will only take a minute."

Myrtle glanced across the foyer as more visitors arrived and sighed heavily. "Let me get someone to take over here and then I'll join you. There's lemonade in the Rose Garden. Holly, here's a map. Take the inspector through that door. The Rose Garden is straight ahead."

Holly opened her mouth to protest, but Myrtle barreled on, "I can give you five minutes, Inspector. No more." She bustled away.

Holly tightened her lips, then gestured toward the French doors leading to the garden. "I think we go this way."

"You haven't been here before?" Rob asked, walking beside her. He glanced around with appreciation. "It's a beautiful spot."

"It's been closed for the last ten years," Holly said, clipping her words short. "Since Sir James's wife died."

"Ah yes. Clare Murray. She fell off a cliff, I believe. Someone mentioned her."

Holly looked sideways at him, narrowing her eyes. "People seem to be mentioning an awful lot to you."

Rob's mouth quirked at the tone, but he responded seriously. "Unfortunately, they're not." He ran a hand through his hair. "It's been made clear to me that I'm not an islander."

"So what? Where you're from has nothing to do with investigating a murder. You can either do your job or you can't." As the words left her mouth, Holly cringed and cast a sideways look at the inspector, who returned the glance with an impassive one of his own. She flushed. "Sorry. I didn't mean that the way it sounded."

"No problem."

There was a short silence as they walked along. Holly wrestled with herself for a moment before giving up. "Who's made it clear that you're not an islander?"

Rob glanced down, then shrugged and rubbed the back of his neck. "Everyone. I've come across it in small communities before. People talk about things that happened a hundred years ago as if it was yesterday; they quote people who died thirty years ago as if they just had coffee with them that morning; they even give directions using landmarks that don't exist anymore!"

Well, that's true, Holly thought to herself. She felt a grudging sympathy for the inspector, remembering how she'd felt when she first moved to the mainland and had experienced similar situations.

"Yesterday, for instance," Rob continued, "someone told me to turn left at the old Bleak House by the rubber tree that was hit by lightning, and I couldn't miss finding Sunset Cove. Well, I didn't find the cove because there's no rubber tree and there's no Bleak House!"

His face was gloomy, and a reluctant laugh escaped Holly. "Bleak House is the old ruin on the side of the road before the turn off. It's been called that for years, but I bet it's completely overgrown now. The rubber tree came down in a storm when I was in primary school."

"Yeah, you know these things. I don't." Rob glanced down at Holly. "That's just one example. When it comes to investigating this particular murder, I'm coming up against events that happened a dozen years ago. People either don't remember them clearly, don't want to talk about them, assume I know things that I don't, or they go to the other extreme and hypothesize wildly!"

Holly gave the inspector a measuring look. "Uh huh. You could probably use some assistance from people who live here. Oh wait. We offered and you said no." After giving him her best Myrtle-like harumph, Holly checked the map in her hands. "We go this way. The Rose Garden is straight ahead. That must be it—inside those walls."

Rob frowned, then a tiny grin tugged at his mouth. Holly ignored it and marched ahead to open the wrought iron gate that led into a small garden.

21

Once inside, Holly paused. "Wow! This is gorgeous! Look at all the varieties! He must have been collecting them for years!"

Narrow grass paths neatly dissected rectangular beds filled to bursting with rose bushes of all sizes. A tiny fountain burbled at the far end of a walkway, framed by an arch that held pink and white ramblers; roses climbed the walls, supported by wooden trellises; and here and there ornate benches invited visitors to sit, relax, and enjoy the quiet, broken only by the deep, sonorous buzzing of bees.

"Interesting," Holly mused. "These walls must create a little microclimate in here to have so many roses still in full bloom this late in the summer. I wonder if we could do something like this at the Inn..."

"Do you know what they're all called?" Rob asked, studying a deep, red bloom with a frown. "I'm surprised roses even grow on a tropical island. Don't they need a frost or something?"

"They need protection from frost," Holly replied shortly. The inspector raised a curious eyebrow and she sighed.

"Most of the roses on Hibiscus Island are old garden roses—China roses, Damask roses, some tea roses, briars, that kind of thing. We don't do so well with the hybrid teas, although I know some people still try to grow them. There's a Rose Society if you're interested in learning about them."

"Do you like them?"

"Me?" Holly asked, straightening up from the rose she was inspecting. "Yeah, they're pretty. And they flower almost all year here. October through till May, anyway. You get some blooms in the summer months, but this is quite spectacular for this time of year. It must look incredible when it's in full bloom!"

"Where do the roses come from? I can't imagine they're indigenous to the island—or are they?"

Holly eyed the inspector suspiciously. "Are you really interested? Or are you just making small talk?"

"Surprisingly," Rob said with a small grin, "I *am* quite interested."

"Huh." Holly stared at him and then shrugged. "Well, I'm not an expert by any means, but most of the island roses came from Europe when people started collecting them back in the 1800s. There was a craze for all things oriental in the 1700s and the original *Rosa chinensis* was shipped from China to the west via India. Look, see this one?" She cradled a pale pink semi-double rose in her hand. "This is Old Blush. It's one of the original China roses from the eighteenth century. It practically grows wild here now."

"Do they seed themselves?" Rob asked, staring at the rose. "Don't roses have hips or something like that?"

A reluctant grin escaped Holly. "You can grow them from seed, but we generally take slips." Seeing the confused look on Rob's face, she clarified, "Cuttings. Gramps usually starts his in December. There's a big plant sale in February or March and roses are popular. We have a couple of mystery roses at the Inn that are really gorgeous too."

"Mystery roses?"

"Yes, they're fascinating." Rob smiled again as he watched Holly's animated expression, her enthusiasm unmistakable. "They've been grown in Bermuda for over a hundred years and Gramps managed to get hold of some plants from a friend there. They bloom all year round, but no one knows what they are. Their proper historical names have been lost, so they've just been called after the places they were found or the people who grew them. We have a Trinity rose, a Smiths Parish, and an Emmie Gray up at the Inn." She grinned suddenly. "And Gramps planted a whole pile of Portuguese ramblers at Sunset Cove years ago. They only bloom once a year but they're spectacular when they do! You should go see them in April."

Rob made a face at her mention of Sunset Cove as she had intended, and Holly smirked. "To get to Sunset Cove," she said in a sweet voice, "you need to look for the sign that says Blue Hole. Turn left there and then turn left again on Kiskadee Road. You can't miss it."

"Uh huh. I'm sure," Rob said dryly. "Maybe you can take me there some day." He ignored Holly's look of surprise. "Hey, there's lemonade over there. I'll treat you."

"It's free," Holly said, finding her voice. "And I can get my own lemonade, thank you."

Rob studied her with a speculative air as they walked toward the gate. "Shall we declare a truce, Miss Gold?"

"A truce?"

"Yes."

"Why?"

"Because..." Rob sighed. "As much as I hate to admit it, I do need help. From people who know the island." He grimaced before continuing in a hurry. "That doesn't mean I'm going to deputize you into the police force! I just need to understand how this island works and, from what I've been told, it seems that you, Jamie, and Myrtle are my best bet." He looked curiously at Holly. "You're quite an odd group, you know. Has anyone ever told you that?"

"Frequently. But we're not actually a 'group,' Inspector."

Rob raised an eyebrow. "Myrtle gave me the very clear impression that you are. When she was still speaking to me, that is."

Holly quickened her pace towards the refreshments. "This way, Inspector."

A tiny patio was set up with wrought iron tables and two Garden Club members dispensed frosty glasses of lemonade and plates of cookies to visitors.

They each picked up a cup of the icy beverage and Rob took a plate of cookies for them to share. Sitting down at a table under a tree, Holly sighed with pleasure at the first sip. After a moment, she eyed Rob over her glass. "So, Myrtle is snubbing you, is she, Inspector?"

Rob picked up a cookie. "I've been demoted from 'Rob' to 'Inspector', and I can practically feel the icicles forming when she deigns to speak to me."

Holly tried not to grin. "Well, you couldn't really expect her to be pleased with the way you treated her, you know. It's not what Myrtle—or any of us, actually—are used to." Remembered indignation colored her voice and she frowned at the inspector.

"I've figured that out," Rob said wryly. "In my defense, this island isn't what I'm used to either."

"Uh huh." Holly's reply was noncommittal.

"I've never been in a place that's so... so..."

"Friendly? Community-minded? Helpful?"

Rob narrowed his eyes and then a small grin crossed his face. "I was thinking inquisitive, meddlesome, interfering, and prying, to tell the truth."

An inadvertent laugh escaped Holly. "You mean public-spirited," she corrected, feeling herself relax a little. She waved a cookie at Rob. "Well, I hate to tell you, Inspector, but this is Hibiscus Island. You won't change it so you'll either have to learn to live with us or find another place to go." She crunched her cookie with relish.

"Is that why you left?"

"What? I didn't leave!"

"You lived on Grand Island for a few years, didn't you?"

"Yes, but it had nothing to do with wanting to leave Hibiscus," Holly protested. "I just needed to be away for a while. Stand on my own feet. That's all. I always knew I'd come back. I love the island."

"My sister does too," Rob said musingly. "She's the one who convinced me to come down and interview for the job, you know. It's a beautiful place but... I'm not sure it's for me." He sipped his lemonade and gazed around the garden.

Seeing his pensive expression, Holly reluctantly realized she was starting to feel sorry for him. Hibiscus Islanders were friendly to a fault, but they were also known to hold a grudge. If Rob had upset people, it could take a while to regain his former footing with them. Her mother's words about giving him a chance came back to her and Holly gave a huff of resignation.

"Well, maybe you need to change the way you look at things."

Rob raised an eyebrow. "Change?"

Holly stuffed the last of her cookie in her mouth, using the time she chewed to pick the right words. "Look Inspector, I know you think we've been interfering in your case..."

"You have," Rob agreed.

Holly paused, then gritted her teeth and continued, "... but it's kind of what people do here. Take Myrtle, for instance. I know she's bossy and opinionated and drives us all crazy half the time but she's a Hibiscus Islander through and through. She'll do anything for anyone, and this community means everything to her. She's a fixer. You know, the kind of person who has to solve any problems that come her way."

"That type of person is known as a busybody where I'm from," Rob said dryly.

Holly glared at him. "Do you want help or not? Because I'm trying to explain some things here!"

Rob held up his hands. "Sorry. I'm listening. Go on."

Holly frowned. "You've never lived on an island before, have you?"

"Only the British Isles," Rob said with a small grin, then flinched at Holly's glare. "No, I haven't. Not on an island as small as this. I've worked in towns before, and in the cities. This is more like a village, population-wise."

"True," Holly agreed. "Hibiscus is like a village. Not just in size, but in the way the community works."

"I'm not all that fond of villages," Rob muttered. Holly narrowed her eyes at him, and he straightened up. "My apologies. Continue. Please."

Holly hesitated a moment, frowning, and then shrugged mentally. "My dad was born here, you know."

Rob nodded. "I've been told."

"Oh." Holly paused. "Well, because he was born here, he didn't have to learn to fit in, like you will. But when he took over as police chief, he still had to adjust a bit. He told me he had to learn to go with the flow and use the island's public-spiritedness to help him do his job."

Rob opened his mouth, but Holly waved him quiet. "Yes, yes, I know what you're going to say. People are nosy, gossipy and so on. My dad knew that. The thing is when he called it public-spiritedness, he started to think of it like that. Instead of getting annoyed with people because they interfered, he used it to his advantage."

She hurried on. "So, he would check in with Myrtle every now and then, because she's a member of just about every group on the island, knows nearly everyone and would tell him what was going on. He joined Mrs. Eastham at the library for some of her Wednesday activities so he got to know the high schoolers before they got into trouble. He had coffee with old Mrs. Howard every week because he knew she would keep him up to date on any issues happening in the senior community. And boy, did she love her weekly 'police meeting'!"

Holly smiled in remembrance. "He still walked the beat, as he called it. It didn't make all the problems go away, but people knew they could go to Solid. Dad used to tell me that you can't police from the outside; you have to be part of the community."

"Solid Gold was a good cop, and I've heard nothing but praise for the way he did things here. Your dad is definitely still missed."

The inspector's voice was kind and Holly's eyes filled with sudden tears. She looked away, blinking rapidly.

"And I understand what you're saying, I really do. But... well, there's a difference between asking for community support and involvement and allowing citizens to run around trying to solve a murder!" Rob looked shrewdly at Holly. "Would Inspector Gold have let your little group help him try to find a killer?"

Holly cleared her throat. "We aren't a group, but actually,

my dad did ask for help sometimes. Myrtle was part of figuring out what happened to a fisherman who went missing, and Jamie and I helped him with the case of the stolen palm trees. He got us to stake out the Botanic Gardens one afternoon. It was really cool." Her grin at the memory turned to a scowl when she saw Rob's smile. "We aren't a group! Those were separate incidents and it's not the point, anyway. Look, do you, or do you not, want help?"

"I do," Rob admitted, "but I don't need on-the-ground detectives so much as... as... cultural consultants! Yes, that's exactly what I need. Cultural consultants! People who can help me with all the little island things I don't know. For instance, people who can tell me which seats in the park are reserved for certain seniors; make sure I understand it's okay to hold the door open for Mrs. Smith, but Mrs. Jones will have an absolute fit if I do the same for her; explain to me why you can fish off the rocks on the north shore but not on the south shore—I could go on for ages!"

"And how will knowing all that help you solve this murder?" Holly enquired, trying not to laugh at what was clearly a list of issues he'd already experienced.

Rob sighed. "It would help me not to antagonize people unnecessarily, which would mean they'd be more willing to answer questions and volunteer information. It isn't just your little group I've inadvertently offended."

"Well, frankly, it would be more helpful to have good informants on your side," Holly said bluntly. "You're an outsider, Inspector, and you're going to be one for some time until people get used to you."

Rob looked taken aback and she continued, "Now, Myrtle can get information out of anyone, and the Bean is a virtual hotbed of gossip, so Jamie knows everything that's going on. If I were you, I'd grovel. They might still be willing to help!"

"They might? What about you? From what I've seen so far, you come as a set of three."

Holly gave him a withering look. "Oh please. I told Jamie right from the start I wanted nothing to do with any of this. The only reason I got roped in was because you suspected Gramps." She paused. "It's actually your fault I'm involved at all."

Rob straightened. "Excuse me?"

"It is," Holly said, pushing her hair off her face and grimacing at the indignant inspector. "Jamie has always been obsessed with solving mysteries and Myrtle has a finger in every pie on the island. And I can't say no to either one of them. And now they've roped in poor Becky as well!"

"What? Becky?" Rob sat up with a jerk. He stared at Holly, then groaned. "Are you telling me that my sister is..." His voice trailed away.

"I'm afraid so, Inspector," Holly said in mock sympathy.

Rob's eyes narrowed. "You're not remotely sorry, Miss Gold," he retorted, tapping his fingers on the table.

"Your sister's great," Holly offered with a grin. "I really like her."

The inspector stared at her in disbelief for a moment and then his mouth suddenly quirked. He leaned back in his chair, relaxing with a flicker of a smile. "I do too. And I suppose I should be grateful Becky is adjusting so well to island life. Making friends, getting involved, becoming—what was it you said? —more public-spirited."

Holly was surprised into a laugh. "Well, I have to say I didn't expect *that* reaction. Maybe there's hope for you yet, Inspector."

Rob nodded. "I don't know the island and you don't know me. That'll change."

Holly blinked. "Uh... okay... I think." She narrowed her eyes. "So, does that mean you'll let us help?"

"Within limits, yes. As consultants." He grinned. "And maybe informants."

Holly rolled her eyes as she glanced across the patio. Her face lit up in sudden amusement. "Well, Inspector, get ready to grovel. Here comes Myrtle!"

22

Myrtle had a scowl on her face as she reached the table and sat down on one of the chairs with a thump. "Well, Inspector? Let's make this quick. What's your question?"

"The inspector has asked for our help, Myrtle," Holly said, with a sidelong grin at Rob.

"Is that so?" Myrtle frowned, then took a deep breath and launched into a prepared speech. "I have to tell you, Inspector Tucker, that I've never been so disappointed in all my life as I was at the way I was treated the other day!" With a disapproving glower fixed on Rob, she took another deep breath before continuing. "On Hibiscus Island, young man, we are a community. We help each other. Accusing helpful citizens of obstructing justice and getting in the way of an investigation is *not* the island way, and I must say—"

Rob shot Holly a desperate glance, and her lips quirked in amusement. Taking pity on him, she interrupted Myrtle's harangue. "He's very sorry. Aren't you, Inspector?"

Rob shot her a look of mingled gratitude and annoyance, but nodded as Myrtle stopped talking. "I sincerely apologize for offending you, Myrtle."

"He's realized the error of his ways," Holly continued solemnly, "and has begged us to reconsider and help him with the case."

Gratitude disappeared completely. "I did not say that! I merely said I could use some help understanding the island!"

Laughing, Holly explained to Myrtle. "He wants us to be cultural consultants."

Myrtle blinked. "Cultural what? What are you talking about, Holly?" She looked Rob up and down. "I promised you five minutes."

As Myrtle folded her arms and sat back, Rob sighed. "I need a list of all the volunteers who were here on Friday. I was directed to you as the president of the Garden Club."

Myrtle waited for more, then lowered her arms. "That's it? That's the help you need? You could have called me for that."

"True," Holly agreed. "Why'd you drive all the way out here?"

"It's only five miles or so from Bridgeport," Rob protested. "Hardly a long drive."

"No, you wanted to see the actual garden. Interesting. Why? Is there a clue here? Why do you want to talk to the volunteers?" Myrtle stared at him, her eyes narrowed in interrogation.

Rob drew in a deep breath, then slumped back and met Holly's eyes ruefully. "When on the island..." he began.

Holly grinned in amusement. "...do as the islanders do. Very good, Inspector! As a cultural consultant, I couldn't have said it better myself!"

Rob's lips twitched, and an answering smile tugged at

his mouth before he turned to Myrtle. "On Friday, Amelia Cartell ditched her security guard and secretary, went to the library, and then came here. I want to know what she did and I'm hoping that whoever was on duty when she was here might be able to tell me."

Myrtle's eyes sharpened in interest. "How do you know she came here? Who told you?"

"I can't tell you," Rob said, raising his hands placatingly when Myrtle scowled. "I can't. It was an anonymous call."

"An anonymous call!" Myrtle exclaimed. "Man or woman?"

"The voice was distorted. Sergeant Hollis didn't recognize it. Myrtle, all I'd like to know is—"

"Why would someone think telling you Amelia visited a garden on the Festival Tour required anonymity?" Myrtle mused. "A normal person would just have told the police upfront. This caller was afraid so she—or he—must know something about the crime. Or possibly they thought you would know them. Some of our elderly people forget to introduce themselves on the phone, you know. Hmmm. Perhaps someone on a bus saw her? Possible, possible..."

"What time was Amelia here?" Holly interjected.

"She was seen entering the main drive at about four o'clock," Rob replied.

"That's when the tours stop." Myrtle frowned. "Whoever was on duty at that time might still have been handing out some last drinks, but they would have started to pack up. Sir James is very insistent that we vacate the property by five thirty at the latest each day, and since it's too difficult to find visitors in all the nooks and crannies, we don't allow anyone past this area after four."

"Wait a minute," Holly said in sudden excitement. "If she got here at four, maybe she was poisoned *here*! Before she got back to the Inn!" She looked at the inspector. "What time did she leave?"

"I don't know when she left." Exasperation tinged Rob's voice. "Amelia Cartell was seen entering the main gates of the property just after four o'clock on Friday. I don't know why she was here or what she did while she was here, and I want to find out. Who was here at the end of the day? Maybe someone saw her." He paused. "And how do you know she was poisoned? That information hasn't been made public."

Poor thing. He has so much to learn, Holly thought. Taking pity on him, she said, "The whole island knows, Inspector."

Myrtle pondered for a moment. "I believe our afternoon volunteers were Violet Greenley and Karen Hopkins. Violet is over there right now actually. I'll just go fetch her and we can see what she has to say."

"No, that's okay. I'll—" Rob was too late. Myrtle was already bustling away.

"Relax, Inspector. Just go with the flow. Let Myrtle do her stuff." Holly hid her amusement at the frustrated look on his face by taking a sip of her lemonade.

Rob stood up politely as the two ladies approached the table. Miss Greenley simpered as he pulled out a chair for her, and thanked him in a high-pitched fluttery voice.

"Miss Greenley," Rob began, "you were here on Friday doing the afternoon shift, I understand."

"Yes, that's right, Inspector Tucker," Miss Greenley responded. "I was *supposed* to be on duty on Thursday but then Dora Whittier came down with a rather *nasty* cold and she asked if I would trade places with her. It was a little awkward of course, because Friday is *usually* my day to exchange my library book in the afternoon—I work at my little shop in the morning, you know, but my niece takes over for me at lunchtime and then I spend a pleasant hour or so in the library. Your sister has been *so* helpful to me, Inspector." She stopped to take a deep breath before launching back into her story. "But of course, when Dora called with her request, I was only *too* willing to help out. Such a nasty cold she had, and—"

"For goodness' sake, Violet! Stop dithering!" Myrtle snapped. "The inspector doesn't have time to listen to a long and involved story. He wants to know if you saw Amelia Cartell on the property around four o'clock. Did you?"

Miss Greenley looked blank. "Amelia Cartell?"

"Yes, Violet. The woman who was murdered up at the Inn!" Myrtle was exasperated. "You must remember her! For heaven's sake! You discovered the body on Saturday!"

"Ohhhh, *that* woman!" Violet Greenley gave a violent shudder. "Oh, that was just *dreadful*! I can still remember seeing that foot sticking out from under the branches. We'd taken a shortcut through the gardens to get to the slat house tables, you know, and at first I quite thought that someone had just lost their shoe, but then I realized there was *still a foot in it*!" She fanned her face with her hand. "Such a *shocking* thing! Murder! It's not what one *expects* to see at a garden party, is it?"

"No Violet, it isn't," Myrtle responded with commendable restraint. "However, it's not Saturday at the Inn the inspector is interested in. He wants to know about last Friday when you were on duty here. At this garden. Did you see the victim while she was still alive?!"

"Well, let me *think*, dear," Miss Greenley replied, tapping her lip thoughtfully. "I was on duty with Karen Hopkins for the *first* part of the afternoon, but she had to go pick up her grandson halfway through because he had a fall at school and, of course, his mother *works*, so she phoned Carolyn Sullivan and asked *her* to come and take her place because it would have been *quite* difficult for me to manage alone." She sniffed. "Carolyn was *quite* snippy about it, but as I said to her, it wasn't *my* fault the child fell, and she didn't need to take out her temper on *me*. Of course, she *had* been working hard on the Bougainvillea Exhibit, and naturally, I *do* understand it was annoying to have to go home first and then come here, but we had *such* a lot of visitors that day and it really does need at *least* two people to manage the refreshments. It's such a large property and people do get so warm when they're touring…"

Holly's eyes met those of the inspector, and she choked back a giggle at the look of stunned incredulity in them. Beside him, Myrtle appeared ready to explode as Miss Greenley twittered on.

"… but it all worked out because she needed to get something for Henry, and she said they would go straight to the Inn after—"

"Miss Greenley," Holly managed to speak before Myrtle, "were you still here on Friday at four?"

Violet Greenley beamed at her. "Oh yes, dear. I was *just* starting to clear away because, of course, you know that Sir James likes us to be off the property by five thirty and it was the opening dinner at the Inn that night and I wanted to be on *time* for that, so—"

"Miss Greenley!" Holly interrupted again. "Did anyone arrive at four?"

Miss Greenley pursed her lips. "Well, not to say *arrived* as such, dear, but I *did* think I caught a glimpse of *someone* in the garden around that time, down near the pond—you can just see it through the shrubbery there if you look carefully —but when I looked again, they had gone."

"What do you mean you *thought* you caught a glimpse of a glimpse?" Myrtle snapped. "You either saw someone or you didn't! Was Amelia Cartell here at four o'clock or not?"

Miss Greenley pursed her lips in disapproval this time. "Well *really*, Myrtle, I don't think there's *any* call to use *that* tone of voice. There were still *quite* a few visitors here at four, but of course, they had already *finished* their garden tours and were sitting just where you are now, enjoying some lemonade. Ms. Cartell wasn't here on the patio, I know *that*."

"But you think she was in the garden?" Holly asked quickly, forestalling another explosion from Myrtle.

"Well, dear, my eyes aren't *quite* as good as they have been. I just caught a *glimpse* of someone in the garden—a flash of red, really—and I was really quite cross because, of course, that would mean I would have to go and *find* the person, and although the garden is *quite* lovely, it's also *very* large and the paths just *meander* around, and although the lawns are quite beautiful with their herbaceous borders... Well, it's just such a *large* property, isn't it, and I was trying to tidy up, and when I didn't see anyone appear, well, I just thought I'd made a *mistake* and so I... well, I didn't—"

"—you didn't go look," Rob finished.

"Well... no... I *should* have, of course, but as I said, there was a *lot* to do, and I wasn't *sure* that I'd seen something..." Miss Greenley's flustered voice trailed away, and a look of intense curiosity appeared on her face. "You think it was the *victim* that I saw in the garden? How very *intriguing*! What was she doing here? And so late in the day? I mean, *surely* she knew the tours stopped at four. It's quite *clearly* signposted at the main gates because we really *do* need to make sure that people aren't on the property after five thirty, you know."

Hearing Myrtle take a deep, ominous breath, Holly

quickly intervened. "Miss Greenley, you said Mrs. Sullivan was here with you. Could she have seen Ms. Cartell?"

Violet Greenley pondered. "Well, *possibly*, dear. I left before she did. She was waiting for her husband, you know, and he was delayed at the office. I *offered* to drive her, but Carolyn said she didn't mind waiting, so I left her here. She said she would finish clearing away. I must say, I was surprised that she was so accommodating because she really had been *quite* grumpy all afternoon and—"

"Right. Well, thank you very much, Miss Greenley," Rob said, getting to his feet abruptly. "You've been very helpful. We'll let you get back to your duties now. It looks like you have some more customers approaching." He gave a smile and nodded towards the house.

As Miss Greenley fluttered back towards the lemonade table, Myrtle let out an explosive breath and cast her eyes upward. "May all the saints in heaven grant me patience. What a twittering old maid Violet Greenley has become! How she manages her business, I'll never know!"

"Well, she did give us some information," Holly said with a grin. "Maybe Mrs. Sullivan can fill in the gaps for you, Inspector. Will you go see her today?"

Rob glanced at his watch, then at Holly. "It's a bit late now. I think I'll wait until tomorrow morning. Right now, I'd like to see a bit more of this garden. I'm curious about why Amelia would come here, so perhaps a tour will shed some light on the situation. Would you be willing to be my guide, Miss Gold?"

"Oh... well... I don't even know the place," Holly began to demur, but Myrtle interrupted.

"Certainly, she will. I'd take you round myself, Inspector, but it's been made abundantly clear to me," she glared in Violet Greenley's direction, "that better organization is required in some departments of the Garden Club, and as the president, it's my job to make sure that happens! Holly, you have the map. It's quite easy to follow. Make sure that the inspector sees the Japanese wisteria and the bonsai display. It's the only slat house open to the public. At least I got James Murray to agree to that!"

As the inspector returned the empty lemonade glasses to the volunteer table, Myrtle appraised Holly. "You seem to be getting on quite well with Rob. Make sure you ask him about the case while you're taking him around—I'm particularly curious to know whether he has any information about what form the poison was in and how it was administered—and you can report your findings to us tonight. Hmm. I must remember to check that Becky has done the research I asked her to do..."

"Report my findings?" Holly stared at her flabbergasted. "Myrtle, I can't interrogate him about the investigation!"

"Of course you can. He's asked for our help, hasn't he? I'd start with the walled garden, if I were you, Holly, and then go through here," Myrtle drew a line on the map, "and then here. Finish at the slat houses. You have about an hour, which is rushing it a bit, but you can see the main attractions quite easily."

Myrtle smiled at the inspector, who had just returned. "Enjoy the tour, Rob."

23

_____

Holly glared after her as Myrtle bustled away. "That woman. Honestly, sometimes she just drives me crazy. I swear, I'm the one who needs patience, not her."

"Surely you're not complaining about islander public-spiritedness, are you, Miss Gold?"

Holly transferred her scowl to the Inspector. "What?"

He was grinning. "You need to relax, Miss Gold. Go with the flow. Isn't that what you just told me?"

A reluctant laugh escaped Holly. "Touché, Inspector."

"You know, I think we started off on the wrong foot. How about you drop the 'Inspector' stuff, and call me Rob? In the spirit of Hibiscus Island friendliness?" He held out his hand.

"Uh..." Holly stared at him. "Well... I guess so." After pausing for half a beat, she shook the offered hand.

"Your enthusiasm overwhelms me."

His wry observation made Holly flush, and she gave him a sheepish grin. "I guess you can drop the 'Miss Gold' stuff as well—and call me Holly."

"It's a deal. Shall we start our tour? Which way first, Holly?"

"That way, I think," Holly said, pointing away from the patio. "That should take us through some herbaceous borders to the pond Miss Greenley was talking about. And then we can go check out the slat houses." She sighed wistfully as she led the way. "I do wish they were open to the public. I would love to see Sir James's bougainvillea hybrids!"

"I understand he's quite well-known for his work."

"Apparently so. Gramps said he's good. And that's high praise from him. He and the judge have quite a rivalry!"

Rob grinned. "Mr. Mack is a character," he agreed, and Holly blinked in surprise at his comfortable use of the island name for Gramps. The inspector paused. "Holly, you know I had to check up on him, right? It wasn't personal. I like your grandfather."

Before a startled Holly could speak, Rob continued hastily, "Ah, this must be the walled garden Myrtle was talking about. Home of the famous Japanese wisteria, I believe."

Distracted from his unexpected comments about Gramps, Holly stared in delight at the ivy-covered walls in front of her. "It's like *The Secret Garden*! If the door was covered too, it would be perfect!" She pushed open the little wooden door set in the walls. "Oh wow! Look at that!"

In front of them, a long, arched walkway, shrouded in a light mauve haze, stretched into the garden. The effect was both magical and mysterious, and Holly took a deep breath. "It's wonderful. It must be just incredible when it's in full bloom! And Myrtle says this all started with layered cuttings! I had no idea there was anything like this on the island!"

"It's spectacular," Rob agreed. "You'd think more people would grow this in their gardens."

"It needs a lot of space. Not many people have room for a forty-foot vine in their garden." She gazed up at the flowers. "I wonder if Gramps has ever considered it. I would love a walkway like this at the Inn!"

"You could ask Sir James for some, what do you call them? Cuttings?" Rob nodded towards the corner of the garden. "He's right over there."

Holly followed his gaze. Sir James Murray, dressed in clothes that rivaled Gramps's in disreputable appearance, was grubbing away with a trowel in one of the garden beds. As Holly watched, he lifted some small seedlings from a tray, upended them from their pots, and carefully planted them beneath a large rose bush.

Rob hailed him. "Sir James!"

"Inspector Tucker!" The judge sounded pleased. Clambering to his feet, he dusted off his hand and held it out, then looked down with a grimace. "Excuse my appearance, Inspector. Perhaps we should avoid the handshake today." He smiled at the younger man. "I hear you had a very good round the other day. Near par, wasn't it?"

Rob grinned. "Two over. Not too shabby."

"Not at all!" Sir James exclaimed. "We must set up another game soon. Perhaps when you have more time on your hands. I expect you're quite busy right now with this murder to solve."

"Just a bit," Rob agreed.

"Are you here to see me? I already told you about my unpleasant altercation with the woman on Friday night. Do you have more questions for me?"

Unpleasant altercation? Holly stared at the judge in sudden speculation. Had he been the person Bob Schafer had heard in the Bougainvillea Exhibit?

"No, we had a report that Ms. Cartell was seen here at

four o'clock on Friday. I'm just following up on the lead," Rob replied. "You didn't see her, did you, Sir James?"

Sir James tapped his lip as he considered the question. "I didn't, but... well, that does make part of her confused rambling on Friday night more meaningful. She mentioned my wife's slat house, as I told you previously. Perhaps she was comparing it to the ones she saw here. They may have made an impression on her. They'd be new since her time on the island. I remember she visited here once when she was working at the newspaper. A Garden Club piece, perhaps? Hmmm. I can't quite recall when that would have been... Not that it's relevant, I'm sure." He shrugged and looked apologetically at Rob. "I'm sorry I can't be more helpful, Inspector. As I told you, she was an unpleasant woman when she lived here and didn't seem to have changed much in that respect. I thought she'd had too much to drink, extricated myself quickly from an uncomfortable situation, and left her in the tent."

"Well, if you remember anything else, just give me a call." Rob smiled at Sir James. "You've built new slat houses recently, have you?"

"Oh, I've had them for a few years now. Haven't you seen them yet?" Rob shook his head and Sir James's face lit up. "Oh, you must! I'm a self-taught gardener, but I pride myself on having reached a certain level of professionalism, particularly in the hybridization field. You must come and see my specimens!" He looked down at his seedlings. "These will be quite safe here for a while. Come along, Inspector. You too, Miss... Miss..."

"Gold," Rob said with a grin. "Holly Gold."

Sir James's face showed sudden comprehension. "Oh, you're Solid's daughter! Of course! I knew your dad well. He was a good man. I don't think I've seen you for years. Not since you were just a little thing." He eyed Holly with cheerful interest. "Although I saw you at the seminar the other night, didn't I? Someone told me that you're a horticulturist. Where did you do your training, if you don't mind my asking?"

Holly stared, flabbergasted, at this new smiling judge, then regained her voice. "I went to college in England. In Kent."

"Ah, then you'll know all the lovely old gardens down there!" Sir James beamed as he led the way out the wooden door. "Like Sissinghurst Castle, for instance. Did you ever go there? What a superb place that is. I've drawn on that for some of my inspiration here, you know. What do you think of my gardens so far?"

"They're stunning," Holly replied, looking back over her shoulder. "That one reminds me of the secret garden that Mary Lennox found, and the wisteria is amazing!"

"Yes, the wisteria has done very well," Sir James agreed, pleased at Holly's obvious admiration. "I'm a fan of walled or hedged gardens, as you can see. Your gardens at the Inn are beautiful as well, of course. Stuart and I butt heads frequently, but I can't deny that he's a superb landscaper. And he knows his plants, I'll give him that. Come along. I'll show you some things that will make him blind with envy." He chortled with delight at the thought and led them away from the walled garden.

Holly clutched Rob's arm as they followed the judge. "He's the one who was talking to Amelia on Friday, in the Bougainvillea Exhibit," she hissed. "Right?"

Rob blinked. "How did you know Sir James saw her in the Exhibit?"

Holly ignored his question. "And how are *you* so friendly

with him? He doesn't show anyone his slat houses! At least that's what Myrtle said."

"We play golf together," Rob replied. He chuckled at the expression on Holly's face.

"Play golf. I... I... Play *golf*? Words fail me, Inspector." She gave a gurgle of laughter. "I can't wait to tell Myrtle!"

Sir James led them down a narrow path that circled towards the back of the mansion. A small slat house came into view, but Sir James kept walking. With a glance at Holly, he explained, "This is just for hardening off plants for the borders and ornamental gardens. It's a traditional structure, as you can see. My working greenhouses are around here."

As they rounded the house, Holly's mouth dropped open. "Wow," she managed finally.

Sir James looked pleased at her reaction. "Two of them are relatively new. I've tested some state-of-the-art technologies over the years, looking for something that would help to control the greenhouse environment. You probably know that's quite challenging on a tropical island. They're not large, of course, but they suit my purpose admirably."

"I worked at a plant nursery on Grand Island for a couple of years. We didn't have anything like this. It's amazing."

Rob looked confused as Sir James ushered them inside the small glass and metal structure. "What's so special about it? It looks very similar to the glasshouses I've seen in other countries."

"But this is a *cooled* conservatory," Holly said, surveying the building in awe. "It makes it possible to control the temperature, which is really hard to do in tropical places. This is like a Mediterranean climate."

"Yes, it's modeled after the conservatories in Singapore," Sir

James said, "but on a much smaller scale, of course. I've used coated glass, which lets in light but reduces heat. And there are additional shade structures that can be remotely controlled if necessary. I have to use them in July and August usually."

Holly nodded. "What about air movement? And do you collect rainwater? How do you power the systems?" She looked around eagerly. "It's amazing!"

Sir James smiled at her enthusiasm. "I collect water of course—that's a given on Hibiscus Island—and recycle it for the misting units. Fans at floor level move air around and a dehumidifier helps with cooling. There are solar arrays outside that power the place so it's fairly sustainable. It's quite a good model for tropical locations although the materials are expensive." He glanced at Holly. "My other greenhouse is a completely different model. I'm trying out an NVAC greenhouse. Have you heard of that?"

"Yes. Natural ventilation augmented cooling." Holly's face lit with interest. "I visited one of them last year. It had a triple roof and was covered in UV-resistant plastic. Is that what yours has? I'd love to see it, if you don't mind."

Rob had been staring around as Holly and Sir James talked. "How does all this glass stand up to hurricanes?" he asked, looking up at the roof in curiosity. "I've heard they can be quite bad here."

Sir James shrugged. "We haven't had a really strong storm since I put this up, but the panels are small, as you can see, and it's hurricane-resistant glass, so I'll just hope for the best." He gestured for them to continue on. "My bougainvillea hybrids are this way."

Holly and Rob followed Sir James into the main part of the conservatory, threading their way through the narrow aisles between the misting benches.

"These are bougainvillea cuttings," Sir James said, indicating a bench full of little pots. "They're about two months along now. I'm expecting to see flowers on them soon and hopefully they'll be in decent shape for the plant sale in the spring."

"What varieties are they?" Holly asked.

"Oh, just some of the more common ones," Sir James replied. "They grow well here, and people like them. These are lantanas. I did the cuttings in the spring so they're well along now. Pretty, aren't they?"

"Beautiful," Holly agreed, admiring the hot pink, orange, red and yellow starry flowers.

"Now, through here," Sir James led them into a smaller section at the end of the conservatory, "are my bougainvillea hybrids. I have some hibiscus I'm experimenting with in another slat house, and of course, I have my bonsais as well, but these are my newest experiments. What do you think?"

Holly stared at the row of pots. Purple, white, pink, orange, and deep red bougainvillea plants sat proudly on benches, while in another section, she could see small pots with tiny seedlings in various stages of growth. Still more pots held small plants, just beginning to flower.

"It's amazing! These are all your own work?" As Sir James nodded, smiling, Holly pointed to a deep pink flower with a white center. "I recognize that one. Isn't that the White Heart hybrid?"

Sir James looked impressed. "It's not, but I used the White Heart as one of the parent plants. My wife created the White Heart variety, but it wasn't very hardy. I've spent years trying to improve it, while keeping the colors she loved, and I've finally succeeded. This one will be called Clare's Heart. I'm planning to present it at the Bougainvillea Banquet on Saturday. You're the first people to see it!" He gently fingered one of the blossoms, then shot them both an anxious look. "You'll keep it a secret, won't you?"

"We won't say a word," Rob agreed. "It's a beautiful plant and we're honored to have been the first to see it. I'm sure Lady Murray would have been very pleased to have such a tribute paid to her."

Holly stared at him. The words should have sounded pompous, but, somehow, they worked.

"Thank you, Inspector," Sir James said quietly. He sighed and looked around the small conservatory. "Clare would have loved this greenhouse. She did her propagating in an old wooden and shade-cloth structure, you know. I can still remember her rage and despair when it burned down. All her notes and seedlings—gone." He sighed again.

"Gosh, what a shame!" Holly exclaimed. "When did that happen?"

"Eleven years ago, in the spring," Sir James replied. "I remember it well. Clare died that same week."

24

Much later, Holly hugged a small pot to her chest in ecstasy as she and Rob returned to the front of the house. "A Japanese wisteria," she gloated, then glanced at the tray the inspector carried. "And some of Sir James's own bougainvillea! Gramps won't believe it. Heck, I don't believe it! Everyone told me he doesn't share plants and look at all these that he's given me!" She beamed at Rob.

"He was quite taken with you," Rob agreed.

"Taken with me?" Holly grinned. "You know, you're awfully formal sometimes, Inspector. You need to loosen up a bit."

"What do you mean, 'formal'?"

"Oh, it's nothing bad," Holly said in a rush. "It's just your choice of vocabulary sometimes. It's kind of... of... stuffy."

"Stuffy?" Rob exclaimed indignantly. "I am not stuffy!"

"A little stiff then," Holly conceded. "My car's right there. Can you put that tray on the back seat for me?" She opened the passenger side door and placed the wisteria plant on the floor, then fished out her phone. "Good grief! It's quarter to six! We've been here for ages! I'm going to have to race! I'm meeting Jamie, Becky, and Myrtle at six thirty, and I don't want to be la..."

Her voice trailed away as the inspector's head snapped around.

"Are you indeed? And why, may I ask, are you ladies meeting?"

"None of your business," Holly retorted. "And you're being stuffy again."

She rushed around to the other side of the car and Rob, still glowering, automatically opened the door for her. Holly smiled as he closed it again once she was in. The inspector's old-fashioned courtesy was starting to grow on her.

"Thanks!" She waved at Rob and shot out of the driveway.

~

HOLLY WAS late to the café meeting.

She had driven home at full speed, deposited her precious plants safely on the small patio outside her apartment, collected Truffle, shouted goodbye to her mother, and leapt back in the car.

Now she and Truffle waited impatiently for Jamie to let them into the Bean. Holly craned her head back to look up at the lighted windows on the top floor. Jamie should have had her text by now.

A light flicked on inside the café, showing Becky threading her way through the café tables. She opened the door with a smile. "Oh good, you're here. Myrtle has been bemoaning your absence for the past ten minutes."

Holly giggled. "Bemoaning? You sound like your brother."

"Well, you would know," Becky drawled as they walked

up the stairs. "I hear you had an enjoyable time together at Sir James's garden today." Her eyes twinkled at Holly's expression. "Rob and François are having dinner tonight. Did you really call him 'stuffy'?"

Holly blushed. "I may have. I didn't mean it badly though."

Becky laughed outright. "Oh, I don't mind. He asked if I agreed with you. Seems you've made quite an impression on him, Miss Gold."

"Well, finally," Myrtle exclaimed, as Holly entered the room. Her disapproving expression morphed into sudden fatuousness when Truffle pranced in as well. "Oh, you've brought Truffle. Come here, Truffle darling. Come and see Auntie Myrtle. Look, I have a treat for you," she cooed.

Truffle galloped over at full speed, flinging herself on Myrtle, who laughed with delight and fished a small treat out of her purse. Teddy the poodle, realizing that food was being dispensed, sat up alertly and then trotted over to Myrtle as well.

"Good dogs," she exclaimed. "Such clever, clever dogs. Sit, Teddy. Good boy. Here's your treat. Your turn, Truffle darling. Can you give me your paw? Paw, Truffle. Oh, good girl."

Holly grinned as she watched Myrtle play with the dogs. She'd forgotten how much the older woman liked them.

"You should get a dog, Myrtle," Jamie said, as she delivered a plate of cookies to the small coffee table. "You're really good with them."

Myrtle glanced up, shaking her head. "Oh, I'm afraid Napoleon wouldn't like that at all, Jamie. He's very territorial." Napoleon was a Himalayan Persian—an unbelievably spoiled and snooty cat who ruled Myrtle with a velvet paw.

"Truffle's quite good with cats," Holly offered. "Has she met Napoleon yet?"

"Once. Poor little Truffle was bullied terribly. No, I'm afraid Napoleon will have to remain an only cat." Myrtle gave both dogs a final cuddle and sat up. "Now that we're all finally here, let's get on with the business at hand." She looked appraisingly at Holly. "You and the inspector were a long time touring the garden today, so I assume you were able to obtain some information for us?"

Holly looked sheepish. "Well... uh... I'm afraid not," she confessed, then hurried on before Myrtle could speak. "We met Sir James and he showed us his slat houses and I kind of got caught up in that."

"He showed you his slat houses?!" Myrtle sat bolt upright, flabbergasted. "James Murray? Well, I never! Good heavens, Holly, what an... an... honor!"

"He gave me some plants as well."

Myrtle's mouth dropped open further. "Plants?" she repeated weakly.

"A wisteria and some bougainvillea." Holly beamed at the thought.

Myrtle moaned. "You have one of Clare's wisteria plants? That's like gold, Holly! And bougainvillea? Which ones?"

Holly named two of the varieties Sir James had given her and then added, "And he gave me one of his new plants. He calls it Sunset Cove." She giggled, remembering Rob's expression when he heard the name of the bougainvillea. "It's a gorgeous deep reddish orange!"

Another groan escaped Myrtle. "Sunset Cove," she repeated. She looked at Holly, shaking her head again in disbelief. "He must have taken a shine to you. James Murray. Giving away plants. I can't believe it."

"Actually, I think it was Rob's doing," Holly admitted. "He and Sir James are golf buddies."

"Golf buddies!"

"Oh, it's Rob now, is it?"

Myrtle and Jamie spoke together. Stunned indignation laced Myrtle's voice, but Jamie was grinning.

"Anyway," Holly said quickly, "I didn't get to ask about the poison. Sorry, Myrtle."

"Oh, I found out about that," Becky interjected. "I did some research today." She leaned forward and helped herself to a cookie from the table, then pulled out a note-book, grinning at Jamie. "I prefer paper for my note-taking. I'm old-fashioned that way."

Jamie laughed as she settled herself on the sofa beside Becky. "Whatever works. What did you find out?"

Having recovered from her shock, Myrtle sat up, listening intently.

"Well," Becky started, "all three of the compounds found in the victim are, interestingly enough, plant alkaloids. Atropine and hyoscyamine are very closely related. I'm not a scientist, so I honestly didn't completely understand the ways that they're linked, but suffice to say, they're similar. Scopolamine is also known as hyoscine, and can be fatal in small doses. When I looked them up, I learned they're only found in some plant families, including *Brassicae* and *Solanacae*. That would include plants like cabbage, kale, and cauliflower as well as tomato and eggplant."

"Wait! Are you telling me Amelia might have been poisoned by a cauliflower?" Jamie stared at Becky, in mock amazement.

"No, of course not, Jamie," Myrtle interjected impatiently. "We can obviously eliminate all common food plants."

Holly bit the inside of her cheek as Jamie grinned and sent a wink her way.

"And there are a lot of sub-sections within the overall groups. Not every sub-section has the plant alkaloids. For instance, scopolamine is found in the *Datura* and *Hyoscyamus* sub-sections," Becky said, a smile tugging at her mouth.

"Oh, so helpful," Jamie said in a withering voice as she rolled her eyes. "You know I have no idea what you're talking about, don't you?"

"Well, for instance," Becky clarified, "henbane is a member of the *Hyoscyamus* genus, which is part of the overall *Solanacea* family. Henbane has scopolamine inside it."

"Uh huh," Jamie said. "Henbane. Of course. And what, pray tell, is a henbane?"

Holly grinned. "And you call yourself a detective! You've heard of deadly nightshade, haven't you? That's a henbane."

"Yes, that one does get a lot of press," Becky admitted. She consulted her notes. "*Atropa belladonna* is its botanical name. It was a favorite plant of poisoners throughout history, but it's also been used for medicinal purposes. Sparingly, I might add. It's pretty lethal. There are a lot of cases of accidental poisoning from children eating the berries. Apparently, they taste quite good." She looked up. "It causes the symptoms Amelia had."

"Well, that sounds promising!" Jamie said.

"Yes, but it doesn't grow here," Holly told her. "At least, I don't think it does."

"It doesn't," Myrtle agreed. She looked slightly disappointed. "We do have a Garden Nightshade, a member of the *Solanum* family. It's poisonous but rarely fatal. You'd need enormous quantities to kill someone." She looked at Becky. "What else did you discover?"

"Well, the only man-made substance I could find that had all three compounds was an anti-spasmodic drug, used to treat ulcers among other things. But it also has phenobarbital and that wasn't present in Amelia's tox screen results, was it?"

Myrtle shook her head and Becky continued, "I don't think it's feasible that the killer somehow got both eyedrops and an anti-nausea drug into the victim, so, it really does seem as though a plant poison must have been used. The problem is, as you said, Myrtle, other than belladonna, which is lethal in small doses, most of the other plants that contain these compounds would need to be ingested in huge amounts."

"What other plants?" Jamie asked, looking slightly appalled. "How many poisonous things are on this island, anyway?"

Holly laughed. "There are tons, but since you don't go around eating them, you should be fine. Oleander, yellow oleander, castor bean plant, bird of paradise, poison ivy, angels trumpet, Brazilian pepper, poinsettia—"

"Got it," Jamie interrupted. She grimaced. "I knew there was a reason I didn't like gardening."

Becky looked thoughtful. "How many of those would contain these *particular* tropane alkaloids?"

"Hmm." Holly paused. "Good point."

Becky made a note. "It would be helpful to have a list of plants that grow here, so I can cross-reference. Is there such a thing? A directory of Hibiscus Island flora, perhaps? There's nothing in the library—I already checked."

"I can consult the Garden Club library," Myrtle said. "We keep detailed lists of all the plants in members' gardens. Of course, that only covers a portion of the population on the island. There could be plants we don't know about."

"I wouldn't think the non-gardeners would be harboring rare plants," Jamie said. "I know I'm not. At least, I don't think my garden has anything special in it."

Holly rolled her eyes in amusement. "How would you know? Your garden, unless it's changed drastically in the last two years, is a hideous jungle apart from some grass and a stunted hibiscus bush."

Jamie pretended to ponder, then laughed. "Yep, that's about right. You should redesign it for me, Holly. Create something that will look good all year but be low maintenance."

"It would have to be *very* low maintenance," Myrtle said dryly. Before an indignant Jamie could respond, she sighed and continued, "I'm sorry to say it but if a plant poison was used, we have to presume that the killer is knowledgeable, horticulturally speaking. And that means—"

"—it's likely a Garden Club member is involved somehow," Jamie concluded, her face somber.

Myrtle's nod was grim. "I'm afraid so."

25

Jamie broke the short silence that had ensued. "What else have we found out? There's been nothing that's stood out in any of the gardens, has there?"

"Not that I've seen." Holly picked up a cookie and nibbled on it. "It's been fun visiting them though. Sir James's garden is amazing and his slat houses are to die for! Wait a minute! I forgot to tell you something. Apparently, it was Sir James that Amelia was talking to in the Bougainvillea Exhibit on Friday night. Remember Bob Schafer thought it was Gramps? Well, it was Sir James. He said Amelia was talking about his slat houses."

"His slat houses?" Myrtle frowned. "Why?"

Holly glanced at the older woman. "I don't know, but Sir James told me his old slat house burned down eleven years ago, just before his wife died. Do you remember that?"

"Oh goodness, yes!" Myrtle exclaimed. "Clare was devastated. All her notes, seedlings, propagation records—all gone! And then Clare died a week later. It was just a tragedy all around."

"How did she die?" Becky asked.

"She fell from a cliff," Holly said. "Gramps said the edge had eroded during the big hurricane and the rock face crumbled. He said it took a few days to find her."

"Oh, that's awful! Poor Sir James." Becky's face fell in sympathy for the judge.

"It was a terrible time. The whole island turned out to search. We didn't find her body until the fifteenth; she went missing on the twelfth." Myrtle's voice was sober. Her mouth quivered and she had to take a deep breath. "So that would mean the slat house burned down on the fifth of May or thereabouts. I can't think why Amelia Cartell would be interested in it."

"Maybe Amelia knew something about the fire, although I don't see why that would make someone want to murder her." Becky frowned. "Come to think of it, I remember seeing something about arson and slat houses in those old newspapers... Hmmm... I can't quite remember what it was. I'll pull them out again tomorrow and have a look."

"It was big news at the time," Myrtle said, "but no one ever came forward with any evidence, and certainly no one was charged with arson! Are you suggesting that Amelia Cartell knew something and didn't speak up? I find that hard to believe."

"Yeah, I don't think Amelia was the sort of person to hold back knowledge like that," Holly said. "Not if her *Dear Priscilla* column was anything to go by."

"But maybe she didn't *know* she knew anything!" Jamie exclaimed. She looked eagerly around. "Remember, her byline at the newspaper stopped in April. She left the island right after the Sanders libel case, so it was only when she came back she realized she knew something! That's why she was looking through the blog and the newspapers!"

"She was looking for confirmation of something," Holly said, nodding in comprehension. "So, she did see something when she was touring the island! Something that reminded her of the fire, maybe." She pursed her lips. "Becky, you said you saw an article that mentioned arson. If the slat house was burned deliberately, and Amelia knew who did it, the arsonist could have killed her."

"Maybe. I'll look up that article and see if arson was ever confirmed. There's another possibility though." Becky, almost diffident, hesitated. "Amelia went to Sir James Murray's house on Friday at around the time we believe she was poisoned. In addition, Sir James admits to being in the Bougainvillea Exhibit with her later that night. Is there a connection between him and Amelia we don't know about?"

Holly shook her head. "But Sir James said he didn't see her on the property on Friday."

"We only have his word for that," Jamie pointed out. "It's possible he killed Amelia, I suppose."

"What motive would he have?" Holly protested. "It can't be Sir James!"

"You just like him because he gave you plants," Jamie rolled her eyes at her friend. "We should check his garden, though, to see if he has anything poisonous in it."

"It's just an idea," Becky said.

"It's a bit weak, but we'll hold it in reserve just in case. You know," Jamie carried on, ignoring Becky's sardonic 'thank you', "I am so disappointed in Rob! All he had to do was let us help and we'd know everything the police know, and this case would be so much easier! He's just—"

"Stuffy?" Becky interrupted.

"A stick-in-the-mud?" Holly said at the same time.

Jamie paused, her lips twitching into a wry grin. "Both of those."

"He did say he wanted us to be consultants," Holly said in appeasement. "Not that I'm defending him or anything."

Becky cleared her throat. "Uh, on that note. Rob spoke to me just before I left the house."

"About what?" Jamie perked up. "Has he changed his mind?"

"Sort of," Becky replied, her eyes twinkling at Holly. "Rob said he'd chatted with Holly this afternoon and it had been enlightening. His words."

Jamie's head whipped around. "Chatted with you? About what? What have you not told us?"

"I'm not sure exactly what you said to him, Holly," Becky continued with a grin, "but he's definitely seeing Hibiscus Island in a different light now. He told me he realized he might have to adjust the way he approaches his work here. He actually used the phrase 'go with the flow.' I'm stunned! This is my brother we're talking about. He does everything by the book, so the fact that he's even willing to consider consulting with civilians is unreal!"

Jamie and Myrtle eyed a now-blushing Holly with unqualified approval.

"Good job, Holls!" Jamie exclaimed.

"Of course," Becky interjected, "Rob also reiterated that we were to stop interfering in police matters and, I quote, 'stay out of trouble and not do anything foolhardy.'"

The pleased expression on Myrtle's face vanished as quickly as it had appeared, replaced by indignation. She sniffed. "Foolhardy indeed! That young man needs to make up his mind. Does he want help or not?"

Becky grinned. "He does seem to be a little confused right now. I think the island is working on him."

Jamie's eyes had narrowed in calculation. As she turned

her gaze on Holly, the other woman flinched. "Wait a minute," Holly began.

Her friend grinned at her. "Now, Holls, don't start getting all uptight. You don't even know what I'm going to say!"

"I know I won't like it, no matter what it is!" Holly retorted.

"Oh, come on, Holls," Jamie wheedled. "You're obviously the golden girl with the police right now. You should be the one to tell Rob all this stuff about the plants. You know, the killer cauliflower and all! And then you can ask him about the case!"

"There is no killer cauliflower!"

"I am not a 'golden girl'!"

Myrtle and Holly spoke at the same time.

Jamie waved an airy hand. "I'm joking about the cauliflower, Myrtle. Joking!"

"It's not a joking matter, Jamie," Myrtle replied severely. "Once Becky and I have cross-referenced all the plants, however, I do agree Holly should be the one to present our findings to the inspector." She nodded in approval at the now flustered Holly. "You do seem to have a way with that young man."

Jamie winked at Holly. "Tell Rob all about the henbane or whatever it's called and then bat your eyelashes and see what you can get him to tell you about the case."

"Meanwhile," Myrtle continued, before Holly could react, "I think another visit to the library archives is required. Becky, I'm assigning that job to you since you work there. I'd like you to look for reports on the Murray slat house fire. See what you can find out."

She made a note in her notebook and looked up again. "Also, Becky, if it's convenient, I will bring the Garden Club plant records to you in the library tomorrow and we'll see if we can make a shortlist of plants that could be the potential culprits." Becky nodded as Myrtle transferred her attention to Jamie.

"Now, wait a minute, Myrtle," Jamie began, but was cut off.

"Jamie, aren't you helping to cater the Bougainvillea Culinary Evening tomorrow?"

Jamie made a sour face. "No. Apparently I use too many refined substances in my food, so they've gone with the health food store from Castlebay." She looked indignant. "They made it sound like I was lacing my muffins with arsenic instead of honey! You know, the problem with these back-to-the-land types is they just go too far sometimes! I mean, it's not as if honey is a bad thing—"

"Yes, yes! Very trying indeed," Myrtle interrupted. She eyed the young woman for a moment. "Just remember, Jamie, that the Bean is the most popular place on the island, and your baked goods are second to none. You also make the best lattes. Ignore the naysayers."

Jamie gaped at her like a stranded goldfish, then flushed in stunned gratification.

"Now that's what I call masterful manipulation," Becky whispered into Holly's ear. "Flattery will get you everywhere."

Holly smothered a giggle.

Myrtle continued, "Well then, perhaps you and Becky can combine forces in the library? I think that would be helpful. If you're able to take some time, that is, Jamie? I know the café keeps you very busy."

Recovering, Jamie nodded. "I can do that. You really think our baked goods are the best? And that we're the most popular?"

"I wouldn't patronize the Bean if it were otherwise," Myrtle said matter-of-factly.

Jamie beamed as Myrtle turned her attention to Holly.

Before Myrtle could order her to bat her eyelashes at the inspector, Holly rushed to forestall her. "I'm going to take a drive out to Spanish Cliffs tomorrow."

Myrtle paused. "Spanish Cliffs? Why?"

"Because of something Lucy said earlier. Amelia visited the Cliffs last Thursday and Lucy said she wandered off at one point. I thought I'd like to see the place." Holly peered at Myrtle. "What's the matter? Is there a problem with that?"

"Nooo," Myrtle said slowly, "but... well... Spanish Cliffs is where Clare Murray died. At the Lookout."

The young women all stared at her and then Jamie gave a low whistle. "The plot thickens. Tell you what, Holls, I'll get Angie to do my shift tomorrow and come out with you. Becky can handle the research by herself, can't you, Beck? And Holls, you talk to Lucy and see if you can get a little more information about what they did out there."

Holly nodded absently, still watching Myrtle. The older woman was fingering her lip, her forehead furrowed. Feeling Holly's gaze on her, Myrtle smoothed out her face and started to gather her purse and notepad.

"Tomorrow is the culinary evening," she said. "Are any of you going?"

"I am," Becky replied as she gathered her belongings. "I'm dragging François along and Rob said he'd be there too."

Holly clipped Truffle's leash to her collar and stood up. "I'll be there."

"And I'm definitely going," Jamie announced. "I want to see what the catering's like. I can't imagine they don't use any sweeteners at all! We can all sit together. Tell Rob to join us, Becky. Holly can always tell him about the poisonous cauliflower over dinner."

She grinned at the twin huffs of annoyance from Myrtle and Holly and flicked off the lights as the group threaded their way through the tables to the café's front door.

26

"Did Myrtle seem worried to you last night?" Holly asked, leaning back in Jamie's car.

Jamie shot her a quick look before returning her attention to the road. "Hang on a minute, Holls. Look at this wobbly creature in front of me! Honestly, tourists should have to pass a road test before they're allowed to rent a bicycle!" She tsked. "And who wants to ride a bike in this weather anyway? Look at the poor thing. Exhausted. And red as a lobster!"

"I think that might be sunburn. They're riding electric bikes," Holly pointed out. "I was thinking of getting one, actually. It would be handy when I can't borrow the car."

Jamie flicked on her turn signal and pulled out to pass, giving the puffing bikers a wide berth. "I wouldn't be caught dead on one of those. You should get a little buggy instead. They're electric as well, and since the Inn has solar power, you'd be able to charge it with clean energy. Plus, they have roofs. You don't want to be riding one of those bikes in the rain, Holls."

"True," Holly mused.

"What were you saying about Myrtle?" Jamie asked, then beamed in remembrance. "Hey, did you hear what she said about the Bean? I have to say, the woman is growing on me. She's not been as bossy as I thought she'd be. We might want to consider making her an honorable member of the Hibiscus Island Detective Club. A consultant, so to speak. She definitely has useful connections, that's for sure."

"Consultant! Ha!" Holly snorted in derision. "Myrtle's totally in charge and we all just do what she tells us. People keep saying we're a weird group and they're absolutely right. Anyway, I'm hoping that this is the last case the Hibiscus Island Detective Club ever has."

"Liar," Jamie said, her eyes twinkling. "You're loving every minute of this investigation, and you know it. Not to mention you're getting to hang out with our super cute police inspector. I knew you two would hit it off. You should practice your eyelash batting today. Oh, blast it!" She ignored Holly's spluttered denial and slammed on the brakes. "I missed the turn. It's been ages since I've been out this way."

Looking back over her shoulder, Jamie backed up and turned onto the narrow track leading to the Spanish Cliffs nature reserve. "Good grief!" she muttered, as the car bounced over ruts and holes in the road. "This road is dreadful! My poor car! And it's new too! It's electric, you know. New law. All new vehicles have to be zero-emission."

Holly resigned herself to the fact that there was no point in pursuing the subject of her lack of interest in the police inspector. Jamie had already moved on. She hadn't changed a bit, Holly mused. Even when they were children, Jamie had always had a quicksilver mind, moving from one subject to another faster than most people could keep up.

"Ow!" They both bounced as the car hit a large pothole.

"Seriously," Jamie snarled. "I'm going to write to someone about this road. It's ridiculous that it's so bad. This is a national park, for goodness' sake!"

From the back of the car came two complaining woofs and Holly twisted around. Truffle and Teddy stared back reproachfully, swaying as the car bounced.

Spanish Cliffs was a large nature reserve popular with dog walkers, so the parking lot was quite full when Jamie finally pulled in. The girls grabbed their small backpacks, clipped leashes to the now-excited dogs, and headed down the small trail that led into the park proper, pausing at the sign with a map of all the trails through the reserve.

"Which way shall we go?"

"Oh, let's go by the shore trail," Holly said. "I love it. We can look for land crabs as well."

Jamie grinned. "There aren't as many as there used to be. The night herons are eating them. It's a shame really. I know there needed to be some population control, but I have to say I miss seeing all the crabs. Remember when they used to cross the roads at the beginning of the summer?"

"Yes! Dad used to stop the car and Mama would tell him to keep going. He didn't want to squash them, but there were just so many, you couldn't help it."

"Spawning time," Jamie said. "The Hibiscus Eco Club did a talk about them last year. We had a good turnout." She glanced at Holly. "You're welcome to join us, you know."

"I might. I'd like to get back to scuba diving and I want to try lionfish hunting. Have you done it?"

"Have I hunted lionfish? Please! You're talking to the reigning champion! I won the tournament last year." Jamie's smile was proud. "I caught over one hundred of the pests. We're doing it again this November. You'll have to sign up. It's a month-long tournament and we really need to control those fish. They're completely messing up the reef ecosystem!"

She clambered over a large boulder and onto a narrow path. Teddy sniffed excitedly at the nearby buttonwood bushes, then trotted ahead, tail waving high. Truffle whined as she tried to follow.

"You can let Truffle off her leash. She won't leave the path. She's very well-trained. I saw her here with Maggie once," Jamie said, in answer to Holly's enquiring look. "Unfortunately, *my* dog still hasn't grasped the niceties of walking to heel!" The big poodle looked back, his tongue hanging out, and Jamie grinned. "But you're a good boy, aren't you, Teddy?"

They climbed up onto the grey, weathered limestone rocks that edged the sea, and Holly sighed with delight as she looked out over the north shore water. "Gorgeous."

Cup reefs lined the edge of Hibiscus Island's north shore, within easy swimming distance of land, and at low tide on a calm day, they protruded out of the water resembling miniature swimming pools. Large schools of parrot fish grazed on algae in the shallower water near the shore, drifting around like a flock of brightly colored sheep.

Holly jumped across a small rift in the rocks looking toward the higher cliffs in front of them, where white gashes stood out in the grey limestone. "Do you remember Hurricane Frank?"

"Vaguely," Jamie said. "I remember it was boring. We lost power so there was nothing to do but sit and stare at each other. My parents split up that year, remember? I was at my dad's for the storm."

Holly hesitated, knowing that Jamie didn't always like to talk about her parents.

Jamie looked sideways at her and smiled. "It's okay,

Holls. The last I heard, mom was somewhere in Arizona looking for mystical gateways or something like that. Dad and Bunny," she grinned as she named her stepmother, "are still living the good life in Florida. They're happy so I'm happy. I've got Aunt Rosie's cottage and the café, and now my best friend is back home and we're solving a mystery. Life couldn't be any better!" She laughed. "Enough about me. Why were you asking about the storm?"

"Oh, just because I can see some erosion over there on Lookout Point. Gramps said Lady Murray was watching birds when the cliff crumbled."

Jamie gave a shiver, then looked at Holly curiously. "What were you saying earlier about Myrtle being worried? Worried about what?"

"I don't know," Holly admitted. "It was when I said Amelia had been here. She looked like she'd suddenly thought of something. Maybe I just imagined it."

"I didn't notice."

Holly paused to catch her breath. "You know, I can't believe that Amelia Cartell hiked this path! This is a tough walk, and she wasn't exactly fit!"

"Oh Holls, you really have been away too long! Amelia wouldn't have come this way! There's a parking lot up by the Lookout for the tourists who just want to take pictures. She'd have gone straight there." Jamie grinned at her wheezing friend. "We have to get you in better shape! You used to be able to run up this hill!"

"When I was ten," Holly huffed. She eyed Jamie resentfully, taking in her friend's black bike shorts and bright red running shirt. Jamie's long hair was tied back, big gold hoops glinted in her ears, and she glowed with health and vigor. "You make me sick. Look at you, all athletic and energetic."

"Good island genes." Jamie preened, then laughed at Holly's expression. "You can't have done much hiking on the mainland."

"None," Holly admitted, taking a long sip of water. "I didn't do much of anything except work. I loved the job—which is why I stayed—but I didn't know what to do with my time off. It's a different type of place from Hibiscus. I didn't really fit in, I guess."

"Well, you wouldn't have known it wasn't for you if you hadn't tried," Jamie said matter-of-factly. "I'm glad you're back though! Now, if you've rested enough, we've got a hill to climb. If Truffle can do it, you can too!"

∼

JAMIE WAS LOUNGING on the large flat rock at the top of Lookout Point when Holly finally puffed her way to the crest of the hill. Truffle, traitor that she was, had deserted her halfway up, and now both dogs and Jamie looked around idly.

"Well, about time!" Jamie said with a grin as she held out a water bottle to her friend.

Holly grabbed it, scowling at them. "Don't speak to me. I hate all of you!" She gulped down several mouthfuls and then sank onto the rock beside Jamie, pushing her red-gold hair off her face and breathing deeply. Together, they stared out over the ocean.

Lookout Point was high enough that visitors could see over much of the western part of the island as well as all the way out to the horizon. An occasional house dotted the shoreline, but for the most part, this end of the island was rugged, wild land.

As its name suggested, the Point had been a lookout in

the early part of the island's history—a place to watch for ships, both incoming trade vessels and the marauding ships of the buccaneers who used to roam these waters. It was also a favorite spot for wreckers, who had lured unsuspecting ships onto the reefs below by shining a light from the hilltop.

Holly looked at the fence that edged the cliff. "I never realized the fence was put up because of Clare Murray."

"No," Jamie agreed. "I remember being annoyed when it first appeared. It was fun to stand right on the edge and look out."

"Yeah, and we could see the little beach at the bottom." Holly got up and went to the fence. "I guess that's where Clare would have fallen. You can't even see it now."

"It's no wonder she wasn't found for a few days," Jamie said with a shudder as she joined Holly. "Imagine falling all that way. I suppose there's one good thing—she'd have died immediately. No one could have survived that fall."

Holly glanced around. "I asked Lucy what Amelia did up here when they visited. She said Amelia told her and Pete to take photos of the view. When they turned around, Amelia had disappeared. Lucy said they went down a couple of trails but were afraid to go too far. Finally they just went back to the parking lot and waited for her to return. Amelia was gone for about half an hour."

"Was there anyone else here?"

"I asked that too," Holly said. "There were quite a few people up here that day. It's a popular tourist spot so you'd expect that. Lucy and Pete got to chatting with a family which is why they didn't notice where Amelia went."

"There aren't that many ways she could have gone from here," Jamie pointed out. "There's the way we came, up the hill—and, as you said, I can't see Amelia doing that hike;

there's the path to the parking lot; there's a small trail that leads down to the rocks over there, but it dead ends at the cliff, and besides, it's pretty visible from here. And there's the path that goes to the salt marshes but again, that's wide and once she got down the steep bit, she'd have been visible."

Jamie looked around, thinking. "There used to be a small trail that went through the woods, but it's been neglected for years. Do you suppose she found that? I can't remember where it goes, but it's the only other possibility. If she really did disappear, that is. Are we sure she didn't just sneak off for a bathroom break or something?"

"Amelia Cartell? I sincerely doubt it! And a bathroom break wouldn't take half an hour!" Holly put her water bottle back in her backpack and slung it across her shoulders. "Where's this trail? We should check it out just in case."

Jamie pursed her lips. "It's been ages since I've been here. I think it was over there somewhere." She pointed towards a grove of bay grape trees. "If memory serves me, there's a small overhang of rock and then the trail went west down the hill. Come on, we'll try it anyway." She unhooked Teddy's leash from a small post and they set off.

27

J amie led the way off the point, jumping down from a large slab of rock onto a tiny, worn path. Large bay grape trees crowded the trail, their thick, saucer-shaped leaves brushing against the girls' faces as they pushed their way along.

"Watch out for the prickles," Jamie warned, pointing to the spiny cactus at ankle level.

"They're prickly pears," Holly corrected, swerving to avoid them. "No fruit yet. They don't flower till later in the year."

"We might get some jelly tonight at the culinary thing though. Quite a lot of people make jams and sauce from them. I've always wanted to try it." Jamie paused and looked back at Holly. "Actually, I'm quite looking forward to this evening. Foraging is becoming a big thing nowadays. There's a foragers club on the island now, you know."

"Really? That would be fun, I think." Holly grinned at her friend. "We might make a botanist out of you yet."

"Yeah, no," Jamie responded. "I'd like to know what I can safely eat—particularly since there seem to be so many lethal plants on this island that I knew nothing about—but otherwise I don't really care what the leafy things are called." She pushed forward again and then stopped. "Oh, I think this is it. See that cave?"

Holly peered into the trees. "It's hardly a cave," she scoffed. "It's just an overhanging rock."

"Yeah, but I thought it was a cave when I was little," Jamie said with a grin. "It's this way. Come on. Look, you can just see the path. Looks like it's still getting used a bit."

Holly followed Jamie through the trees. There was a very faint trail that meandered between the bay grapes heading downhill into a wood of whistling pines. The path itself disappeared under a thick layer of needles, but faded red paint on tree trunks, as well as the evidence of previously cut branches, showed a trail had once existed and, judging by the body-sized skid mark left behind in the needle-carpeted floor, someone had recently come this way—and fallen.

Holly and Jamie exchanged glances.

"You think Amelia went down this hill?" Holly asked. "But why?"

"Looks like she slid down the hill," Jamie said with a smirk. She trotted carefully ahead and examined the first skid mark. A light sprinkling of needles was scattered over the soil. "Ouch. She must have tripped over this root here, caught herself, then sat down. Hard. And skidded."

Holly grinned. "Jamie the Ranger. You remind me of Aragorn when he tracked the hobbits in *The Lord of the Rings*."

"I'd rather be an elf. Way cooler," Jamie retorted immediately as she headed down the hill. "Be careful, Holly. Don't fall and destroy the evidence."

Holly glared at her back. "I'm not going to fall."

The two girls and dogs slipped and slithered down the hill until they reached the bottom and emerged once more onto rocky ground.

Holly brushed off the needles that clung to her leggings, ignoring the grin that Jamie sent her way. She'd only fallen once, and it had been Truffle's fault! The little cavapoo had darted across her path chasing a bird and Holly had lost her balance trying to avoid her. Anyone would have fallen!

"There's no way Amelia Cartell climbed back up that hill!" she exclaimed. "I'm shocked she even got down it, based on what I saw of her. If it was her that came down, that is."

"Had to be. It's the only way she could have vanished as Lucy claims she did. And she wouldn't have to climb back up," Jamie replied. "The main road is over there. All she'd have to do is walk along it for less than a quarter of a mile and she'd be back at the car park. It's uphill, but an easy stroll otherwise. I wonder if Lucy noticed which way Amelia came back. We'll have to ask her."

Holly looked around, frowning. Ahead of her was a low stone wall, and beyond it she could see the white roof of a house overlooking the north shore. Between the whistling pine wood and the wall, an occasional buttonwood sprouted up between the bright yellow flowers of seaside goldenrod that carpeted the ground. There was a small gate set in the wall but no road that Holly could see, so she deduced it was a back entrance that the occupants used to access the national park land.

"Where are we?" she asked. "Whose house is that?"

"You don't recognize it? It's Sea Bright. The Sullivans' place."

Holly stared. "I've never seen it from this angle before. I didn't realize they backed on to the Lookout. Hmm. Pete told me they visited Sea Bright, but I wonder if they came before or after going to the Cliffs?"

"No idea. But it doesn't really matter what order they did things in!" Jamie's voice rose in excitement. "It's the fact that they came here at all that's important! Holly! I know who did it!"

"Did what?"

"Murdered Amelia, of course," Jamie said. "What else would I be talking about? It's Mr. Sullivan! He's the murderer!"

Holly blinked. "Whoa. That's a big leap. Where do you get that from?"

"It's so obvious!" Jamie exclaimed. "First of all, he's the person who fired Amelia eleven years ago; second, he was fined a lot of money because of her unethical writing and third," she paused for emphasis, "he was in Sir James's garden on Friday when Amelia was there! Remember Miss Greenley said he picked up his wife? Means, motive, and opportunity! Boom! He did it. We've solved the case! We have to go tell Rob."

"Slow down there," Holly said. "*Possible* motive and *possible* opportunity, okay, but what are the means?"

"Huh?"

"How did he poison Amelia?"

"I don't know. With a plant of some kind, obviously," Jamie said impatiently. "Come on. We've got to get to the library and let Myrtle and Becky know what we've discovered before tonight's event!" She stopped short. "Tonight's event! Henry Sullivan is a forager! He knows all about what to eat and what not to eat. Oh yeah! He's totally the murderer! Let's go along the road—it'll be faster than hiking all that way back. Ready to run, Teddy?"

The big poodle wagged his tail furiously, prancing around his owner but Holly gave Jamie a withering look.

"I'm not running!" She moaned as Jamie and Teddy took off at a jog. When Truffle looked up at her with a whimper, Holly looked down at the little dog. "Don't worry, Truff. We're not running!"

~

JUST UNDER AN HOUR LATER, Jamie burst into the Bridgeport Library archives.

"Myrtle! Becky! Where are you?"

Two startled faces looked up as Jamie tumbled through the stacks to arrive, gasping, at the table where Myrtle and Becky worked, while Holly followed more sedately.

They had made two detours on the way to the library—to the Inn and to Jamie's tiny cottage—to drop off the dogs and quickly change clothes. Jamie had moaned and groaned at the delay and had, Holly was convinced, grabbed the first things that came to hand. Her choice of teal jeans and a bright orange silk shirt was startling, to say the least. It was annoying, Holly thought, that Jamie looked so spectacular in the outfit.

"We know who did it!" Jamie exclaimed. "It was Henry Sullivan!"

There was a heartbeat of silence and then Myrtle frowned. "How do you come to that conclusion?"

Jamie poured out the story of their expedition, ending with a triumphant, "So you see! It has to be him!"

Holly had been listening with half an ear, her attention caught by the papers spread across the table. Before Myrtle or Becky could respond to Jamie's proclamation, she interrupted, holding up a list. "Are these all the plants you've been checking?"

Jamie looked at her in exasperation. "This is a moment, Holly! We've unmasked a murderer!"

Becky grinned at Jamie's theatrics. "We've just about finished. We've gone through all the *Datura* and *Hyoscyamus* species and listed the ones we know are here." She picked up a separate piece of paper and gave it to Holly, who glanced through the names.

"Three *Datura* species..."

"*Datura metel, Datura inoxia* and *Datura suaveolens*—that we know of." Myrtle sighed. "But no one is growing deadly nightshade or jimson weed, which are the highly toxic ones."

Holly nodded. "*Hyoscyamus albus*?"

"One plant. It's native to southern Europe. Does better with a dry climate. Marie Bronson has apparently been trying to grow it for years." Myrtle shook her head in mild disgust. "I've never understood this need to force a plant to grow where it won't thrive."

"We've gone through everything, Holly. We even checked the Garden Nightshade again, but it doesn't have the right toxins." Becky ran a hand through her hair. "The only plants that have these three toxins are *Datura*, *Atropa* and *Hyoscyamus* and a lot of people seem to grow the ornamental *Daturas*."

"No one stands out," Myrtle agreed.

"But... but... what about Henry Sullivan?" Jamie wailed. "You're just ignoring what I said! He had motive—Amelia cost him a lot of money; opportunity—he was at Sir James's garden on Friday when Amelia was there, and he was at the opening dinner on Friday night; he had means... uh...

hmmm..." She looked at Holly. "What were his means again?"

Holly rolled her eyes. "That's what *I* said when you started shouting he was a murderer. I asked you how he did it, remember?"

Jamie frowned. "Well, maybe he has one of these poisonous *Datura* things in his garden! He's a plant guru after all. And he forages! Maybe he foraged something poisonous! Are you sure you researched everything, Becky? Maybe you missed something. Or maybe he has eye drops and anti-nausea drugs in his medicine cabinet. Whatever. He did it. I know it."

"That may well be," Myrtle's tone was perfunctory, "but the police will require more solid evidence."

Holly stifled her smile. "You keep thinking about it," she advised Jamie, before turning her attention to Becky. "Did you have time to look at the newspapers again? Did you find anything about the slat house fire?"

Jamie thumped down into a chair. "Fine. Ignore me."

"There were a couple of articles about the fire," Becky said, chuckling at Jamie's antics. She picked up her notebook and flipped through it. "Yes, here it is. Inspector Peter Gold was in charge... That was your dad, right Holly?"

Holly nodded. "I don't remember this case at all. Mind you, Dad didn't always talk about work."

"There probably wasn't much to talk about in this particular instance," Becky said. "The fire occurred on the evening of the fifth of May, there was some sort of inflammatory substance discovered—so it was arson—and the fire department couldn't get the blaze under control fast enough, so the whole building was destroyed, and no culprit was ever identified. There were no witnesses—or none that ever came forward. Sir James and Lady Murray were at a dinner and came home to find the place in flames and a small crowd watching. There was a photo. I took a copy."

She passed the photo to Holly, who peered at it. Jamie hopped up to crowd close. "Recognize anyone?"

"It's too dark," Holly said, squinting at the image. "Did you look at it, Myrtle?"

"Yes. I could only recognize Sir James and Clare. They're right in the foreground."

"Oh yes, I see Sir James now," Holly agreed. "He hasn't changed much. Clare looks furious."

"And rightly so," Myrtle snapped. "All that work. Lost!"

"They say arsonists watch the fires they set," Jamie said. "Do you see Henry Sullivan there? Ugh! Everyone's too small!"

"I'll try and enlarge it," Becky offered, taking back the photo. "I did find another article that's interesting." She held out another photocopy.

"Oh!" Jamie exclaimed, snatching the piece of paper out of Becky's hands and scanning it. "It's the Sanders trial! And look! It ended on the third of May! Right before the fire was set! I'm telling you, it's Henry Sullivan! He had to pay out all that money and was furious at Sir James, so he set the slat house on fire to pay him back."

"It's possible," Holly said, after a moment, "but we have no proof, Jamie."

Myrtle looked smug. "Besides, Henry Sullivan had an alibi for the time of the fire."

"What?"

"I thought the same as you," Myrtle sniffed, "but as it happens, he was at the Annual General Meeting of the Rose Society on May fifth."

"The Rose Society?"

Myrtle nodded. "Yes. Henry was the outgoing president.

It's all documented in the minutes. He was at the head table for the entire meeting and could not possibly have set the fire."

Jamie deflated. "Well... he could still be the murderer. Maybe the fire doesn't have anything to do with Amelia's death after all." She perked up a bit. "Maybe Amelia was looking at something else in the archives."

"I can look again," Becky offered, then glanced at her watch. "I'm sorry, but we're going to have to get moving. I need to lock up tonight and François will be here any minute to pick me up for the culinary event. And Rob's coming too. I invited him to sit with us as requested."

"Oh good," Jamie said. "Maybe he'll believe me!"

"Becky, do you mind if I take this plant list with me?" Holly asked.

Becky looked surprised. "That's the list of all the species that have the toxins. Don't you mean you want the other one? The list of plants on the island?"

"No. This is the one. What's it called when you know you know something, but can't quite remember it?"

"Tip of the tongue phenomenon," Becky offered.

"That's what I have," Holly said, staring at the plant names. "There's something on here that's ringing a faint bell. Maybe it will come to me if I keep looking."

"Sure, take the list." Becky's phone chimed. "Oh, that's François."

They exited the archives in a group.

28

The Horticultural Hall was packed by the time Holly arrived. She bumped into her mother and aunt in the doorway and paused to chat for a moment, while Jamie hastily scanned the room and then rushed to join Becky and François.

"I haven't seen you all day, Mama. Do you want to sit with us?" Holly asked.

Maggie smiled. "No, thank you. Laura and I are joining the Fosters and your Gramps tonight. Besides, I can see you already have a full table over there!" She glanced around. "It looks very nice, doesn't it? Who did the decorations, do you know?"

"Had to be the Garden Club," Holly said, admiring the little bowls of bougainvillea and ferns that graced each table. "Oh look, Lucy and Pete came after all." She waved to the couple who were sitting at a table with Bob Schafer.

"I persuaded them," Maggie said. "I know Lucy was very keen originally, and since it looks like her book deal will continue, she might be able to use this."

Holly's eyebrows arched up. "She's heard from the publisher? Open Skies?"

Maggie nodded. "Just today. They've told her to send them the draft as usual. Since she's been writing the books all this time, I can't see them turning her down now." With a laugh, she directed Holly's attention across the room. "Jamie is getting very agitated. You'd better get to your own table, Holly."

Holly threaded her way toward the table Jamie had commandeered, which was set a little aside from everyone else. Pleased with herself, Jamie beamed at Holly as she approached. "Nice and private. We can cross-examine Rob without anyone hearing us."

Becky rolled her eyes. "You'll be lucky. He won't discuss the case; I can guarantee it."

"Bet you he will," Jamie said right away. "We're his consultants! Holly said he said so."

François, sitting beside Becky, grinned at this. "Are you indeed? I thought he specifically said you weren't to interfere in police matters."

"I did." Rob appeared and sat down beside Holly. He raised an eyebrow at an unfazed Jamie.

"It's not interference to share helpful information," she said, raising an eyebrow right back at him. "Informants, remember? Didn't you tell Holly that?"

Before Rob could respond, there was the sound of a microphone being tapped.

"Good evening, ladies and gentlemen."

Myrtle scanned the room with a stern expression and the murmur of conversation died away. As everyone looked her way, the president of the Garden Club launched into speech. To the obvious disappointment of some of the attendees, she managed to skirt the subject of the murder while recapping the events of the week, before introducing the speaker for the evening.

"... Mr. Henry Sullivan, the president of the newly formed Foragers' Club on Hibiscus Island."

Polite applause sounded around the room as Mr. Sullivan made his way to the podium. Jamie leaned forward intently, watching him with narrowed eyes.

Henry Sullivan was a slightly built man in his early to mid-sixties, with thin graying hair and a small wispy mustache adorning his upper lip. He wore jeans and a bright blue t-shirt with the words Foragers, Assemble! printed across the front.

Holly stared at him, wondering if he could really be a murderer. He didn't look like one.

"Tonight, we celebrate the bougainvillea," Mr. Sullivan began, "but in the spirit of foraging, we will also share with you some of the other amazing foods available on this small island we call home. If you look at the tables against the wall over there, you will see we have collected a wide range of edibles for you to try tonight."

Holly, along with everyone else, looked across the room.

"*Mon Dieu!*" François exclaimed. "It looks like we'll be grazing on grass!"

Becky nudged him violently, but Jamie choked with laughter as she stared at the piles of vegetation. "It really does look like a bunch of weeds."

"I think those are just the raw ingredients—for demonstration purposes," Rob said. "They're bringing out plates now."

Becky craned her head, a dubious frown on her face as a parade of dips, biscuits, breads, and other assorted finger foods passed by. "They all look a little strange. And what on earth is that?" She pointed at a bright green liquid in a jug.

"It looks like a smoothie," François said. "A particularly virulent one." He shook his head and muttered, "Becky, don't eat too much!"

As conversations bubbled around the room, Henry Sullivan continued to speak. "We'll bring selections to each table, but before we do, let's talk about bougainvillea!"

Holly sat back to listen, discovering that Henry Sullivan was an interesting and amusing speaker. She learned that bougainvillea flowers were a popular deep-fried snack in Thailand, and that bougainvillea tea, with its anti-bacterial, anti-viral, and anti-inflammatory properties, was used in some places, such as Mexico, as a cold remedy.

"Bougainvillea is also being studied to evaluate its effects on fertility," Mr. Sullivan continued. "Yes, indeed. An aqueous extract of *Bougainvillea spectabilis* has been shown to have anti-fertility potential in mice. It's quite fascinating."

Jamie's mouth dropped open, but before she could speak, Holly kicked her under the table, hissing, "Don't say a word. Not one word!"

"Of course, the color of bougainvillea makes it particularly appealing in salads and in drinks," Mr. Sullivan said. "The dishes being placed before you contain wild spinach, island-grown arugula, dandelion leaves, purslane, and fennel, as well as bougainvillea."

"It's pretty, I guess," Becky said as she poked the leaves gingerly with her fork. "Which one is purslane, Holly?"

Holly pointed. "That one. That's the fennel and that's the wild spinach."

Volunteers circled the room, explaining the various properties of the different foods to the guests, whose reactions to the offerings differed as widely as the foods. When, finally, a fuchsia-colored drink was delivered to the table, everyone eyed it with suspicion.

"What's that?" Rob asked, ever cautious.

Overhearing, one of the volunteers stopped near the inspector. "That," he smiled, "is bougainvillea switzel. It's an old-fashioned drink, also known as shrub vinegar."

François groaned. "Shrub vinegar? *Mon Dieu!*"

"No really, it's fine," the young man said. "It's delicious, I promise."

Becky looked at him skeptically. "What's in it?" she demanded.

"It's made with filtered water, fresh pineapple, lemon, apple cider vinegar and four cups of bougainvillea flowers. That's what gives it the color." He looked around and then whispered, "And there's a little bit of sugar in it too."

"Sugar?" Jamie exclaimed. "I thought you guys didn't approve of the white poison."

The young volunteer looked sheepish. "The purists don't like it, of course, but Mr. Sullivan okayed it for this drink. He said you'd probably all need a little sweetness after taste testing all the food." He grinned. "Mr. Sullivan had some too, even though it makes his arthritis act up."

"Is he good at foraging? I'll bet he knows all the really poisonous plants, doesn't he?" Jamie asked, looking up at him with an innocent expression.

Holly and Becky rolled their eyes at this blatant fishing, but the young volunteer nodded.

"He's very knowledgeable. Makes his own medicines and wines and everything, you know. He even went away and did a course on herbal medicine. It's a fascinating subject."

Rob narrowed his eyes and opened his mouth, but Jamie got in first.

"Medicines?" She sat up, alert. "Like what?"

"Well, he makes a really effective mullein syrup for

coughs," the volunteer said enthusiastically. "I've had that before, but I always add a bit of lemon and honey to mine. It's very good! And he also makes a sort of cordial—a tincture really—for his arthritis. He calls it moonflower wine. It's made from a local plant."

Holly's mouth dropped open. Moonflower? She grabbed her purse and began to rummage through it.

The young man laughed as he continued, "He says he makes it by the light of the full moon, but I'm sure that's just a joke. If you're really interested, the Foragers' Club meets here once a month here and we often discuss herbal remedies. I hope you all enjoy the switzel!"

"Uh huh," François said, still skeptical, as the volunteer moved away to another table. "I really think that—"

"Of course!" Holly interrupted. "I *knew* I knew something! I know what was used to poison Amelia!" She looked up from Becky's plant list triumphantly and turned to Rob, keeping her voice low despite her obvious excitement. "It's *Brugmansia*! Angel's Trumpet is the poison!"

"I'm sorry? What?"

"Yes, what are you talking about?" Jamie hissed, lowering her voice as she leaned towards Holly. "What do you mean a trumpet's the poison? And what's a brugmansia? What's it got to do with moonflowers?"

Rob glared at her. "Stop talking, Jamie." Ignoring her indignant expression, he turned to Holly. "Explain."

"Angel's Trumpet is sometimes called moonflower and it's part of the *Solanum* family," Holly said. She held out the list. "See? Here it is. *Datura suaveolens*. That's the old name. It's known as *Brugmansia* now. It has the alkaloids that were present in Amelia's tox screen."

"How do you know about the tox screen?" Rob exclaimed.

"Henry Sullivan made the poison?" Jamie's eyes lit up. "You see? I told you it was him! He had opportunity, motive, and now we know he had the means too."

Rob drummed his fingers on the table, looking darkly at them all. "I told you," he began but was interrupted by a snort of laughter.

All eyes turned to François.

"Rob, my friend, they are incorrigible! You may as well give in." His eyes twinkled as he looked at his wife. "Why don't we all go back to our house? We can have some real food and you can confess to the inspector exactly how much interfering you have been doing!"

"Great idea! I'll just let Myrtle know! She'll definitely want to be a part of this. And besides she'll know all about the trumpet thing as well. Don't leave without me!" Jamie pushed back her chair and rushed off across the room.

Rob opened his mouth and half stood, then sank down again into his chair. He pinched the bridge of his nose and closed his eyes before turning to Holly. "You say this Angel's Trumpet is poisonous? And that it could be what caused Amelia Cartell's death? And that this is what the moon-flower wine is made from?"

Holly nodded. "Moonflower is another name for Angel's Trumpet, and *Brugmansia* is just like *Datura,* so it has those three plant alkaloids."

Rob stood up. "Excuse me one moment." He made his way across the room to Henry Sullivan, pulled the man aside, and spoke to him for a moment.

Mr. Sullivan looked surprised but nodded, then reached inside his jacket and handed the inspector a small bottle. They spoke some more, then Mr. Sullivan clapped the inspector on the shoulder with a smile and turned back to the guests he had been talking to.

"What's Rob doing?" Jamie hissed in Holly's ear as she returned to the table for her belongings. "Now the murderer knows we suspect him!"

"Mr. Sullivan doesn't seem very concerned," Holly noted. She frowned. "If he is the murderer, don't you think he'd look more guilty?"

François intervened. "Myrtle is at the door sending ferocious looks this way. Can I therefore deduce that she is joining us for dinner?" When Jamie nodded, François stood up and gestured for them to precede him. "*Alors, en avant, mes amies.*"

"Hang on, I never tasted this switzel thing." Jamie picked up the glass.

"Don't!" Holly exclaimed—too late.

Jamie took a huge swallow and froze, her eyes wide. Shuddering in disgust, she put the glass down. "Ugh! It's pure vinegar! Disgusting!"

Holly and Becky dissolved into laughter.

29

Holly, who had never been to François and Becky's house before, was immediately charmed by the little cottage. It was still light when they all piled out of the various vehicles, and Holly exclaimed with delight when Becky opened the gate into the fenced garden surrounding the house.

"Oh, it's gorgeous," she said.

"It's pretty small," Becky said, her tone deprecating. "And I don't know that much about plants. Things grow differently here. I keep having to move them or cut them back because they get too big."

"I love it," Holly exclaimed. "It's like a fairy garden. What are you planting on the pergola over there?"

"I thought roses maybe?" Becky looked at Holly. "Could you come by one day and go through the place with me? Maybe give me some advice?"

"Sure," Holly said, "but honestly, you look like you're managing really well on your own."

"Okay, okay, enough with all the horticultural chitchat," Jamie interrupted. "We have a murder to solve—and

François offered real food. So come on, you two. You can tour the fairy garden another time." She grinned at Becky as she spoke.

Myrtle and Rob had gone inside ahead of them, and as Holly entered the front room, she could hear them both talking in the kitchen.

Inside, Holly looked about in curiosity. Becky's cottage was an old building which retained the original wooden floors and ceiling beams, now lovingly restored. The walls were painted a warm yellow and a small sofa and two armchairs, covered in cheerful floral fabric, faced each other across a small cedar coffee table that sat squarely on top of an oriental rug. A large white bookcase, stuffed with brightly colored paperbacks, leaned against one wall, and on the opposite side of the room, a white wooden sideboard held a collection of black framed photographs strewn among pots of white-flowered African violets.

Rob came through an arched doorway carrying a kitchen chair and placed it beside one of the armchairs, followed by Myrtle with a tray piled high with baked treats. She set it on the coffee table, sat down in one of the armchairs, and pulled out her notebook.

"François is making tea, and I can certainly use a cup after that appalling switzel drink that was served tonight!" Myrtle shuddered in remembrance. "I quite appreciate the merits of living off the land, but I can*not* understand why everything has to taste so peculiar."

"That switzel thing was vile," Jamie agreed, "but I liked the bright green smoothie. I can't remember what was in it, but it wasn't too bad." She plopped herself down on the sofa and leaned forward to inspect the goodies in front of her. "Ooh, shortbread. Yum." Taking two pieces, she settled back.

"Now," Myrtle said, "shall we get started? It's getting late and I have to be up early tomorrow to prepare for the Bougainvillea Banquet in the evening. Jamie told me about the *Brugmansia* and I have to say I agree. Well done for spotting that, Holly. Now—"

"Just a minute," Rob said.

Holly and Becky hastily squeezed in beside Jamie on the sofa as everyone turned an enquiring gaze on the inspector.

"Before anyone says anything," Rob began, "I want to make it quite clear that while I appreciate the expert botanical help provided by members of this group and am willing to discuss some aspects of the case with you tonight, this should not be construed as unmitigated approval of all your activities. The Hibiscus Island police department is more than capable of solving crimes unaided by the general populace. We are trained law enforcement professionals, and we know how to do our jobs!"

"Well of course you do, Rob," Jamie said in a placating tone. "No one doubts the ability of—"

Rob took a deep breath and held up his hand. Jamie stopped speaking. "Community involvement, regardless of what you all seem to think, does not, as I've said before, mean citizens should run around trying to solve a murder!"

There was a moment's silence. Myrtle looked affronted, but Jamie just grinned and leaned forward. "Feel better now that you've got all that off your chest? Can we get on with figuring out the murder? Personally, I still think it's Henry Sullivan, don't you?"

Holly felt Becky shaking with silent laughter beside her. She bit the inside of her own cheek in a desperate attempt not to laugh at Rob's thunderous expression.

Before the inspector could respond, François stuck his head round the doorway. "Kettle just boiled. Who wants tea?

Rob sighed and pinched the bridge of his nose. "Got anything stronger? I think I'm going to need it!"

Holly and Jamie collapsed in giggles as François winked knowingly. "I'll be right back."

Once tea had been dispensed, Myrtle cleared her throat. "Shall we begin? Becky, do you have your research?"

Becky jumped up to retrieve a large manila envelope from her bag, which she placed it on the coffee table, and sat back down. François made himself comfortable in one of the armchairs, watching the proceedings with interest.

"I'll just recap everything we know," Myrtle said. "Amelia Cartell, aka Emily Carter, was murdered on Friday, June twenty-first, by person or persons as yet fully unknown. Her body was discovered at the Hibiscus Inn at twelve-thirty on Saturday June twenty-second by Miss Violet Greenley and Mrs. Carolyn Sullivan. She had been dead for at least twelve hours at that point. Her body was underneath a tree and had been covered in branches of *Bougainvillea spectabilis*— varieties Ruby, California Gold and Bridal Bouquet—effectively hiding it from general sight. It was later determined that Amelia Cartell had been poisoned by a cocktail of tropane alkaloids, to wit, scopolamine, hyoscyamine, and atropine, most likely between the hours of five and seven on Friday evening. She demonstrated symptoms of poisoning at dinner on Friday, with evident slurring of speech, light sensitivity, and unsteadiness of gait by seven thirty."

Myrtle paused to look around the table. "Does anyone have anything to add to this so far?"

They all stared back at her, slightly stunned.

Then the inspector heaved a huge sigh. "Well, I'd still like to know how you learned what poison was in the victim's body, but I suppose that's too much to hope for." He took a sip of the amber liquid in his glass.

François smirked. "If you need a top-up, let me know, Rob."

Myrtle smoothed her notes and continued, "Subsequent investigation uncovered a number of further facts potentially related to her death and possible suspects thereto."

Jamie rolled her eyes and opened her mouth, but Rob beat her to it.

"Myrtle, before you go any further, perhaps we could hasten this along if I tell you the police have already satisfied themselves that Miss Robinson, Mr. Hartford, Mr. Sanders and Sir James Murray are not in any way involved in this crime. They all have confirmed alibis for the time the poison was administered—which has been determined to be about five o'clock on Friday afternoon, according to the latest estimate given by our medical examiner. Which means," he continued, cutting Jamie's exclamation short, "that Amelia Cartell was poisoned at the home of Sir James Murray."

Rob gave Myrtle a conciliatory smile. "I'm sure that, like us, you have determined that Amelia Cartell's death is linked to events that happened on Hibiscus Island eleven years ago."

Myrtle's mouth opened, then closed. She blinked and refocused. "Yes," she agreed, looking at the inspector through narrowed eyes. "We've potentially linked it to Sir James Murray's slat house fire on May fifth of that year."

It was Rob's turn to blink. "The slat house fire?" His brows lowered as he considered. "Why do you think Amelia's death is linked to that?"

Holly studied the inspector. He knew about the fire, but had linked Amelia's death to another event. She frowned.

"Well, it's obvious!" Jamie said. "The slat house fire was

revenge against Sir James for the ruling against the Sullivans in the Sanders libel case."

"It does make sense," Holly agreed, eyeing the inspector closely. "Sir James's final ruling against the Sullivans was on May third; on May fifth, the slat house was burned. The police confirmed arson, but no one was charged with the crime. Bob Schafer told us he overheard Amelia talking about the slat house to Sir James on the night she was murdered. He also told us Amelia said she had a scoop."

"You think the scoop was that she knew who set the fire?"

"Yes! And that person killed her to stop her talking," Jamie said.

Rob leaned back in his chair. "Why didn't Amelia say something about this eleven years ago? She didn't leave Hibiscus Island until May thirteenth. Surely she would have spoken up if she knew who set the fire."

"Oh, that's because she didn't know she knew it until she came back to Hibiscus this year," Jamie explained with an airy wave.

Rob blinked in confusion. "I'm not sure I follow."

"Amelia toured the island," Becky explained quietly. "One of her stops was at the Spanish Cliffs Lookout, where she disappeared for a while."

"The Lookout?" Rob exclaimed. "She was on the Lookout? How do you know that?"

"Lucy told us," Holly said. "You didn't know?"

"No, but it's extra confirmation that—"

"And then she went down the trail to Sea Bright," Jamie interjected. "Henry Sullivan's home!"

"Lucy reported Amelia was quiet and thoughtful all afternoon, and the next day—Friday—she came to the library and went to the archives to look up old newspapers.

She also began to look through her old blog. It's reasonable to assume a memory was triggered, and she was seeking confirmation," Becky concluded.

"That's logical," Rob agreed. He gazed at them speculatively. "But why are you so sure that what she remembered was the slat house fire?"

"Because that's what she was talking about on the night she was murdered!" Jamie said. "What else could it have been?"

"I know. It was Clare Murray's death." Holly raised an eyebrow at Rob. "Right, Inspector?"

"Impossible!" Myrtle exclaimed. "Clare's death was an accident. It was, wasn't it?" She stared at the inspector, her voice trembling.

Rob sighed. "You know I really can't discuss—"

"We know most of it already," Holly said. "If you tell us what *you* know, between us we might be able to fill in the gaps."

Jamie nudged her and flicked her eyes up and down a few times in an unmistakable innuendo. With a scowl at her friend, Holly returned her attention to the inspector. "You can trust us not to tell anyone outside this room, if that's what you're worried about."

"It's not that," Rob said. He looked around, taking in the various expressions of the people gathered.

Holly followed his gaze. Becky sat quietly, waiting; Jamie looked like she was about to explode with anticipation; Myrtle... Holly paused. Myrtle's face was troubled, and for the first time that Holly had ever noticed, she looked her age.

Rob glanced finally at François, who gave a very Gallic shrug of the shoulders.

"This is Hibiscus Island, *mon frère*," the man reminded his brother-in-law. "Things are different here."

There was another pause and then the inspector sighed. "Where's my briefcase?"

"It's in the kitchen. I'll get it for you." Becky left the room, returning quickly with her brother's laptop bag and briefcase.

"There's something in these files..." The inspector's voice trailed away as he took out a sheaf of paper and started flipping through it.

Jamie's eyes were bugging out with excitement as she gave Holly an enthusiastic thumbs up.

"Here it is." Rob held up the piece of paper. "This is a complaint filed with the police by Henry Sullivan on May twelfth."

"A complaint?"

"About what?"

"May twelfth? That was the day Clare Murray died."

Holly's statement came last, and everyone looked at her.

Rob nodded. "It was, but Henry Sullivan's complaint was about Amelia Cartell or Emily Carter as she was then. She had apparently gone to his house for her final paycheck and things... had gotten out of hand, shall we say. There was an altercation, and the police were called to escort her from the property. Mr. Sullivan filed a formal complaint, but since Miss Cartell left the island the following day, the case was shelved."

"So," Holly said reflectively, "Amelia Cartell was at the Sullivans' house on the day Clare Murray fell from the Lookout. Was it at the same time?"

"It's hard to know exactly," Rob said, nodding his approval at her question, "but according to Inspector Gold's reports, Clare was thought to have been on the cliff between two and four that afternoon, judging by Sir James's report of when she left the house. Amelia Cartell was on the Sullivan property at three o'clock, and the police were called at three thirty."

"Amelia saw something that day," Holly said, "and she remembered it on Thursday when she was on the Lookout again all these years later. She remembered something that made her realize Clare Murray was murdered and that she knew who did it."

"Clare's death was ruled an accident," Myrtle repeated stubbornly.

"That's true, and there was no evidence to suggest otherwise at the time," Rob said. "I've been through all the reports. Inspector Gold's notes are thorough. If I hadn't seen the entry on Amelia's blog about her altercation at the Sullivans'—and then heard about Lady Murray's accident on the same day, I wouldn't have thought anything of it. The fact that Amelia was on the Lookout the day before she was murdered—and, as you discovered, came down the path to Sea Bright—well, it does all add up to a connection between Amelia, the Sullivans, and Clare Murray."

Jamie looked annoyed. "We didn't see that blog entry. You had an unfair advantage!"

"Clare could have been pushed off the cliff," Holly said. "It would have looked like an accident, and no one would have known differently! Amelia left the island before Clare's body was found. She may not even have known about it until she came back here."

"Do you know what she was researching in the library?" Jamie asked Rob. "I'll bet you do, don't you?"

The inspector shrugged. "I do. Sorry. Amelia Cartell had a photocopy of an article in her bag."

"So unfair!" Jamie exclaimed. She scowled. "What was it?"

"It had to be about Clare Murray," Holly said, looking at Rob for confirmation. "That's how you knew Amelia's death was linked to the events from eleven years ago."

He nodded. "Amelia copied the report about Clare's death. She'd circled the date and the place that Clare died." He looked at Jamie. "I didn't seriously consider the slat house fire, but I think you're right that Amelia knew something about that as well."

Jamie nodded, pleased. "She knew that Henry Sullivan set the fire as revenge and was going to tell Sir James. That's why she went to his house on Friday. And then she tried to talk to him in the Bougainvillea Exhibit! But Henry had already poisoned her with his moonflower stuff, so she just sounded like she was hallucinating, and Sir James didn't listen!"

"But it wasn't—"

"That can't be right."

Becky and Holly spoke at the same time and then both stopped. Becky smiled and gestured to Holly to go first.

"Henry Sullivan couldn't have set the fire," Holly said. "He had an alibi."

Rob sat up straight. "You're sure of that?"

Holly nodded. "Positive. And," she continued when Jamie opened her mouth, "he had an alibi for Clare's death as well!"

A satisfied expression spread over Rob's face. Without saying another word, he put his papers back in his briefcase and stood up.

"What are you doing?" Jamie exclaimed. "Wait a minute! Don't tell me you know who did it!"

"So do you," Becky said. "Look." She slid an enlarged

photo across the table. "Henry Sullivan wasn't at the fire, but someone else was. Someone who lived at Sea Bright and was at Sir James's house on the day Amelia was killed."

Everyone leaned forward. Becky had circled a face.

Mrs. Carolyn Sullivan.

30

The Bougainvillea Banquet was in full swing that evening when Holly finally saw the inspector arrive. She nudged Jamie and nodded towards him.

"Well, finally!" Jamie huffed. "I'm dying to know what happened!"

"You can't ask him now!" François exclaimed. "Jamie! I'm putting out the desserts and I need help. I need all of your help!" He glared at the three girls.

"We're not going anywhere, honey," Becky soothed her irate husband. "What shall we take out first? The petits fours?"

"Maggie and her team are handling the small things," François said. "I need help with the crème caramels and the cake! *En avant! En avant!*" He rushed away, looking wild-eyed.

"Come on, Jamie. We can find out all the details later." Holly dragged her friend back into the kitchen that adjoined the Anglican Church Hall, which was hosting the banquet as it did every year, and put the inspector, and his possible revelations, out of her mind for the time being.

The previous evening Rob had left for the police station, intending to confirm that the moonflower wine was indeed a possible means of delivering the poison, and to send officers to bring the Sullivans in for questioning.

Myrtle had left almost immediately after, refusing all requests to stay a while. "No," she'd said soberly to Holly, who'd followed her out to her car. "I think I'd like to have an early night. No matter what happens, the Bougainvillea Banquet will still take place and I have a lot to do in the morning." She had looked sad and tired when she left, leaving Holly to trail dispiritedly back into the cottage with the thought that being a detective wasn't all it was cracked up to be.

Inside, however, Jamie had been in high spirits and extolling the merits of the Hibiscus Island Detective Club to an appreciative François, who had opened some wine and poured glasses for them all.

"Although," she had said in annoyance, "I think it's really unfair that the police have access to clues, and we don't!"

Becky had laughed, reminding Jamie, "Rob congratulated you on your sleuthing. I've never seen him so relaxed when discussing a case. Actually, I've never seen him discuss a case ever!"

François's eyes twinkled. "He did say that he still wanted you to confine your interests to more appropriate matters from now on."

Jamie waved an airy hand, almost spilling her wine. "Yeah, yeah. He had to say that to cover himself. Well, I say it was a good job, everyone!" She raised her glass. "A toast! To the Hibiscus Island Detective Club!"

Holly hadn't got home till after midnight and had felt decidedly worse for wear that morning. Luckily, she didn't have to do anything for the Banquet until late afternoon, when the Food Committee had pressed everyone into service.

Holly, Jamie, and Becky had been put in the kitchen, to ferry food back and forth to the serving tables while Matt and Sebastian were set to waiting on the guests.

"I just love the community spirit on this island," Becky said enthusiastically as she trundled trays of crème caramels across the kitchen. "Look at all the different people who are here—families, young couples, retirees… It's just wonderful. Like an old-fashioned potluck supper!"

Holly grinned. "You haven't had a Christmas here yet, have you? Just wait till you see how many events we have to work at then! You may change your mind."

"I don't think so," Becky said in a contented tone. "Here, Holly, take these out, will you?"

On her second delivery, Holly stopped at the table where Lucy, Pete, and Bob Schafer sat. "Are you enjoying the evening?" she asked as she slid the glass dishes of crème caramel onto the white cloth. "Congratulations on the book deal, Lucy!"

Lucy beamed at her. "It's great, isn't it? Pete and I are going to continue with our planned travels this summer and I'll keep up with the blog for now, until we figure out what's happening with it. Your nice police inspector told us we're free to leave the island now." Her expression sobered. "He didn't say he'd made an arrest, but I've heard people saying tonight that he's taken someone in. Poor Ms. Cartell."

There was a joint snort from both Pete and Bob Schafer.

"Awful woman," Bob said with feeling. Turning bright red when everyone looked at him, he quickly changed the subject. "Holly, did you hear I've worked something out with Mr. Mackintosh? He's been very gracious, I must say, and is going to give me cuttings of some of his specimens." His face still flushed, he looked down at the plate in front of him. "Oh my! This looks wonderful!"

Holly grinned. "It tastes good too. Enjoy the meal!" She headed back to the kitchen for another tray.

~

AS THE SPEECHES and presentations began, the three girls, drinks in hand, staggered to a small table at the very back of the hall and collapsed into their chairs.

"My feet!" Holly moaned. "They're killing me!" She slipped her sandals off and wiggled her toes.

Becky gave her a sympathetic look, but Jamie scoffed. "Amateur! You're out of practice, Holls. You need to do a few shifts at the Bean." The sound of applause as yet another flower grower went up to receive an award distracted her. "Hey, what do you suppose they're going to do about the Bougainvillea Trophy? Mr. Sullivan's not here!"

"Myrtle is going to announce that he won it but that, unfortunately, he can't be here to collect it tonight. Although I think the trophy is the last thing on his mind right now."

Holly looked up at the sound of Rob's voice. The inspector lowered himself into the chair beside her and gave her a half smile.

"What happened?" Jamie said at once. "Was the moon-flower wine the poison? Was it really Mrs. Sullivan?"

"Jamie!" Holly frowned at her friend. "Give him a chance to sit down."

Rob shook his head wryly. "I've had everyone asking me questions tonight. The island grapevine has clearly been working at full throttle all day! Oh, thanks, Becky!" He shot his sister a grateful smile as she placed a glass of wine in front of him.

Becky patted his shoulder. "Was it bad?"

"She admitted everything," Rob said. "It was Mr. Sullivan who fell apart. Poor man."

Jamie opened her mouth, then closed it. She fidgeted on her seat, squirming back and forth, before she finally leaned forward. "Rob," she implored, "just tell me—was it the moonflower wine?"

"It was." Rob glanced at Holly. "That was good work finding that out, Holly. We hadn't been able to identify anything with those three compounds." He shook his head in disbelief. "It's quite a lethal concoction—our medical expert was appalled when he found out about it—but Sullivan swears it's safe enough if you know what you're doing. He takes very tiny amounts, less than half a teaspoon and claims it helps his arthritis."

"Why did Mrs. Sullivan have it?" Jamie asked.

"Pure chance, apparently," the inspector replied. "When she was asked to fill in for the Garden Club volunteer, she called her husband to tell him that he should pick her up from Sir James's house after work. Mr. Sullivan asked her to get the medicine because he'd had some twinges of arthritis and wanted to be able to take it."

"So, when Amelia arrived at Sir James's, Mrs. Sullivan had a poison right there. Talk about coincidences. But why did Amelia go to the judge's house in the first place?"

Rob leaned back in his chair. "She went specifically to find Mrs. Sullivan. When Amelia left the library on Friday, she visited the Sullivans' house. The house cleaner told her Mrs. Sullivan had gone to Sir James Murray's home and that Mr. Sullivan would be picking her up from there. Amelia took the bus to Murray's garden, waited until Miss Greenley left, and then entered the courtyard." He took a sip of wine. "Myrtle was correct about the anonymous caller, by the way.

It was one of our senior citizens who saw her and called the police. She just assumed Sergeant Hollis would recognize her voice. She popped in today to make sure we had gotten her message."

"What happened next?" Jamie asked impatiently. "What did Amelia do?"

"Well, according to Mrs. Sullivan, Amelia didn't waste any time. She immediately told her that she knew she'd killed Clare Murray. And then, again according to Mrs. Sullivan, sat and smirked evilly."

"I'm sure," Jamie said, glowering at the thought. "Amelia Cartell was that kind of woman. But what an idiot to tell a murderer that she knew she'd killed someone! With no one else around!"

"Were we right?" Holly asked. "Did Amelia see something the day Clare died?"

"Two things actually. Amelia told Mrs. Sullivan she had seen her at the Lookout last Thursday when she visited with Lucy and Pete. She thought she recognized her, saw her heading down the path, and was curious about where she was going. When Amelia realized the Lookout backed onto the Sullivans' she remembered seeing Mrs. Sullivan coming down the hill on May twelfth all those years ago. She'd already heard about Clare's fall from the Lookout—apparently Lady Murray was mentioned quite a lot at garden tours because of her bougainvillea hybrid."

"White Heart," Holly said.

Rob nodded. "That's the one. Mrs. Sullivan told me Amelia boasted about her research in the library and taunted her—her words—with clippings that proved Mrs. Sullivan had motive and opportunity. And then detailed the exposé she planned to write unless Mrs. Sullivan cared to convince her otherwise."

"Blackmail. Typical," Jamie snorted. "Bet you she'd have written about it anyway."

Rob smiled. "One of those clippings was of the slat house fire. Amelia dropped that piece of evidence at the Murray house and Mrs. Sullivan promptly destroyed it."

"Did she say why she did all this?" Holly asked. "I mean, she seemed like she was friendly with Clare Murray. There were so many photos of them on Amelia's blog and they were always smiling. What happened?"

"It was the Sanders libel case, as we suspected. Henry Sullivan was sued and fined a huge amount of money by Sir James, the presiding judge." Rob shook his head, then took a sip of wine. "Even after all this time, I could hear the absolute vitriol in Carolyn Sullivan's voice when she talked about it. She hated Sir James for his ruling—railed to me that it had caused enormous financial stress, had ruined her life, had destroyed her credibility on the island. She'd been embarrassed at work. And so on and so on."

"She was a banker," Jamie said. "I guess it would be embarrassing for your place of work to know all your financial issues. But to kill for that?" She shook her head.

"Oh, she didn't kill Clare because of the libel case. She burned the slat house down because of that—to 'pay Sir James back' and 'teach him a lesson'." Rob made air quotes with his fingers.

"And then Clare found out she'd done it," Holly guessed.

"Yes. In a way, it was sheer coincidence. Carolyn Sullivan was on the Lookout when Clare arrived up there on the twelfth of May to watch the tropic birds. They chatted and the subject of the slat house fire came up. You remember it had happened a week earlier. Mrs. Sullivan said something —she now claims she doesn't know what it was—and Clare realized she was the arsonist. Clare lost her temper—by all accounts she had a fiery one."

"So everyone keeps saying," Jamie agreed. "So, Mrs. Sullivan pushed her off the cliff?"

"They fought. Carolyn Sullivan says they shoved each other, and Clare tripped and fell over the edge."

"Do you believe her?" Holly asked.

"No. I think she was scared Clare would report her actions to the police, and she deliberately pushed her. There was no remorse in her at all. And remember, Clare's body wasn't found for three days. She never said a word all that time. She could easily have reported an accident. There was no reason to hide it."

"What about Amelia? Did Mrs. Sullivan say how she poisoned her? Oh, and what about that bizarre hiding of the body? Did she do that?" Becky asked.

"The poisoning was easy. She just spiked Amelia's lemonade in the courtyard."

"You've got to be kidding!" Jamie burst out. "Amelia drank a glass of lemonade handed to her by a woman she'd just accused of murder?! What an idiot!"

"Well, she'd hardly expect Mrs. Sullivan to be carrying a lethal poison, would she?" Holly said. "And it was hot that day. And the lemonade was already made."

"It was, as Mrs. Sullivan put it, auspicious," Rob said, a wry smile tugging at his lips.

"Auspicious? She didn't!" Becky shook her head in disbelief.

"She's a disturbed woman," Rob said. "She admitted to hiding the body as well. That was the point at which we had to have Henry Sullivan removed from the room."

"Poor man," Becky said, shaking her head in sympathy.

"Why'd she hide it?" Jamie asked. "The body, I mean?"

"Well, Mrs. Sullivan told us she had expected Amelia to die in her room at the Inn because she had given her 'quite a lot' of the moonflower wine. She was quite disturbed, therefore—her words—to find Amelia not only at the dinner, alive and well, but talking about Clare's slat house fire to all and sundry. When Amelia wandered away from the main tent, Carolyn Sullivan followed her and overheard her conversation with Sir James—who, as we know, dismissed Amelia's ramblings and left quickly. According to Mrs. Sullivan, Amelia then ambled off through the garden, heading towards the slat house. By this time, she was hallucinating and very disoriented and, again according to Mrs. Sullivan, was talking incoherently about 'butchered bougainvillea' and 'that man.'"

"Oh dear," Holly said, with a half laugh. "That was about Gramps's fight with her when she first arrived."

Rob's eyes twinkled. "What fight? Mr. Mack wouldn't hurt a fly!"

"Focus!" Jamie blurted in exasperation. "Finish the story, Rob! Amelia's death. What happened next?"

"Well, everything happened quickly after that. Amelia suddenly collapsed down by the slat house, Mrs. Sullivan realized she was dead, pondered leaving her where she was in the hopes that people would think she'd collapsed of natural causes and then—and here's where it gets really bizarre—she suddenly remembered the Bougainvillea Trophy."

Holly, Jamie, and Becky gaped at him.

"The Trophy?" Jamie said weakly.

"Mr. Sullivan had entered the competition. Carolyn Sullivan told me, quite logically and calmly, that if Amelia's body had been discovered before the judging, then the competition might have been cancelled and Henry would have lost his chance of winning the trophy and these were the best bougainvillea specimens he'd ever grown. And she wasn't having all her time and effort wasted. That was when Mr. Sullivan collapsed completely—when she spoke of why she hid the body."

"She must be mad!" Jamie was incredulous. "She hid a body so that her husband wouldn't lose out on a *flower competition*?"

"She told us it was hard work dragging Amelia under the tree, that she'd pricked her hands multiple times carrying bougainvillea branches to hide the body, and then she went into a tirade about Violet Greenley," Rob said. He shook his head, remembering. "It wasn't pleasant."

"What was her issue with Miss Greenley?" Becky asked curiously.

"She spotted the shoe," Holly answered. "If she hadn't seen that, it might have taken days before the body was discovered. Mrs. Sullivan must have been furious. No wonder she looked like she was in shock when I got down there."

"What's going to happen to Carolyn Sullivan now?" Becky asked.

"She'll be charged with murder, but I expect a psychiatric evaluation will be ordered as well." Rob sighed and stretched. "We've done our part; it's up to the courts now."

"*Our* part?" Jamie looked pleased.

"I meant the police," Rob said with a grin, "but I must admit your group was helpful." He held up a restraining hand as Jamie's eyes lit up. "In the future, however, I'd still prefer that you limit your involvement in my cases!"

"Ladies and gentlemen." Myrtle's voice interrupted them before an indignant Jamie could express herself. "Tonight is a very special night in the history of the Bougainvillea Festival. Many of you remember former Garden Club member and our dear friend, Lady Clare Murray—and many of us still treasure her contribution to the bougainvillea world, the White Heart hybrid she developed right here on Hibiscus Island.

"This year we have been privileged to once again be able to tour the Murray gardens after a ten-year hiatus, to see Clare's magnificent Japanese wisteria and to view the spectacular plantings Clare took such delight in.

"Sir James has impressed us this year, not only with an informative lecture about the history of the bougainvillea, but also by sharing his techniques for hybridizing the plant that we celebrate this week. Tonight, Sir James has another presentation for us—a tribute to Clare."

There was a round of applause and Sir James Murray stepped up to the podium, holding a covered pot. He cleared his throat.

"In honor of my wife, Clare Murray, I'd like to present—and share with the entire island community—Hibiscus Island's newest bougainvillea hybrid... Clare's Heart!"

The room erupted in cheering and applause as he carefully removed the cover and held up the gorgeous deep pink, white-centered bougainvillea.

Jamie whooped and shouted beside a beaming Becky, and Myrtle was seen to carefully dab the corners of her eyes before joining in the congratulations.

"Well, Miss Gold," Rob said, smiling at Holly, "now that the Bougainvillea Festival is officially over, and the Hibiscus Island Detective Club has, I trust, retired, I seem to recall you promised you'd show me the elusive Sunset Cove."

"Um, no," Holly said. "You were the one who said that maybe I'd take you there! I don't recall agreeing to it."

"And anyway, what do you mean—retiring?" Jamie

spluttered. "The Hibiscus Island Detective Club is here to stay! Right, guys?" She looked at Holly and Becky in appeal.

"Absolutely!" Holly agreed immediately.

"You bet your bougainvillea," Becky said, eyes dancing.

Jamie beamed and linked arms with her friends. "Come on then, let's go fill Myrtle in."

As they sauntered away, Holly glanced back at the inspector, who grinned wryly and raised his glass in a silent toast.

Holly smiled. Life looked like it was going to get a whole lot more interesting on Hibiscus Island!

Remains Among the Roses
Book 2 of the *Hibiscus Island Mystery* series

Roses are red, a pirate is dead... Batten down the hatches! There's murder on Hibiscus Island!

Every year in September, the inhabitants of Hibiscus Island enthusiastically celebrate their cultural connections to the Golden Age of Piracy.

But tales of pirates and privateers, Spanish galleons and smugglers' tunnels, and long-lost treasure can't compete with the mystery of a very modern murder!

When the body of a buccaneer is discovered in the garden she is designing, horticulturist Holly Gold has to abandon the roses and lookout for clues!

On an island awash in a sea of speculation and suspicion, it's all hands on deck as Holly and her crime-solving crew set course in search of a killer.

Dead men tell no tales... or do they?

Release Date: September 2022

ACKNOWLEDGMENTS

This book would never have been written without the support of family and friends. Thank you for reading and critiquing, helping me brainstorm, and giving feedback— but most of all for encouraging me to keep going!

And to my amazing editor, Lida, my *heartfelt* thanks for the proofing, correcting, and polishing! You made my book so much better.

ABOUT THE AUTHOR

Mysteries are Lucy Norman's favorite genre and after a lifetime of reading them she now pens her own cozies from a small tropical island somewhere in the Atlantic.

Lucy has a degree in horticulture, collects old children's books, occasionally quilts, and shares her home with an adorable cavapoo.

Buried in Bougainvillea is her first published book, but Hibiscus Island will definitely be the scene of more murders, mysteries, and puzzles in the future!

Visit lucynorman.net to learn more

CPSIA information can be obtained
at www.ICGtesting.com
Printed in the USA
LVHW100506060723
751539LV00002B/270